CITY MOUSE

a novel

STACEY LENDER

KAYLIE JONES BOOKS

Published by Akashic Books
©2017 Stacey Lender

ISBN: 978-1-61775-525-5
Library of Congress Control Number: 2016954160
First printing

Kaylie Jones Books
www.kayliejonesbooks.com

Akashic Books
Brooklyn, New York
Twitter: @AkashicBooks
Facebook: AkashicBooks
E-mail: info@akashicbooks.com
Website: www.akashicbooks.com

CHAPTER ONE

IT WAS THE BATHROOM THAT FINALLY STARTED US house hunting on the weekends up in Westchester. Sharon and Dave had just moved to Scarsdale from the city and I swear during brunch they slipped Aaron some suburban Kool-Aid with their day-old bagels. While the kids played on a giant plastic gym set in their cavernous empty living room, they proudly gave us a tour of their five-bedroom Colonial, closet by closet. Aaron seemed bored, as usual, but when we entered the en suite master bathroom, complete with double sinks and a rainfall shower, I heard him gasp. "A separate little room for the toilet!" he said, eyes glowing wide with bathroom envy.

"You know," Sharon said, "our builder is working on plans for the house next door."

"We're not quite ready," I replied.

"But we can take the number, just in case," Aaron said.

I shot him a look. *Take the number? Are you kidding?*

Sharon pounced on the opening like an eager puppy. "You guys would just love it here! It's such a great community."

I glanced at my watch. It had taken her less than an hour to get to the "C" word, which meant I had won the over-under bet that Aaron and I had started making on our visits to our recently relocated friends. As if following some ecumenical suburban script, right after the house tour came the crowing about the community. The state-ranked public pre-K their twins were attending (with only eighteen kids per class!), the annual Quaker Ridge neighborhood picnic (with pony rides!), and, the icing, a special pilot composting program. Sharon gestured excitedly to a little green plastic bin on the counter next to the sink. "It reduces our trash output by nearly a third!"

"Impressive," I said. *Excited by the garbage.* In less than two months and twenty miles out of the city, was it possible she was actually turned on by her own trash?

Nearly all of our married friends had embarked on the Great Migration with their toddlers in tow, over rivers and up highways to Westchester, Long Island, Connecticut, and New Jersey, to Short Hills and Chappaqua, Westport, Manhasset, Rye Brook, Milburn, Stamford, and Montclair. Usually it was the birth of their second child that initiated their quests for great rooms and garages and gargantuan cedar jungle gyms. Led by a bevy of pied piper brokers, they seemed to find everything on their wish lists in abundance, in the hamlets to the north and east and west of Manhattan, all within an hour's commute.

We were still happy living in the city, although I knew we'd be a whole lot happier once we finally moved out of our one-bedroom rental. We had been looking for a bigger apartment for nearly two years, ever since the day our daughter Phoebe moved from sleeping in a bassinet to a crib and we put up a temporary wall to create a sleeping alcove for her in our bedroom. Despite the thin slab of plywood privacy, she was still less than ten feet away, and our new routine of half-clothed, quiet quickie sex began—*Shhhhh, don't wake the baby . . . Yes, don't stop, right there, I'm . . . SHHHH! DON'T WAKE THE BABY!*—an act that may have technically qualified as sex, but barely registered as satisfying.

Our search started out with a keen sense of urgency, but our timing couldn't have been worse: right at the peak of Manhattan's real estate market. We thought we had saved enough for a down payment on a comfortable two-bedroom in our Upper West Side neighborhood, one with hardwood floors, an eat-in kitchen, and maybe an extra little room for a den or office. But we quickly discovered that apartments with those "high end" amenities were selling for two *million* dollars. For a two-bedroom apartment! No matter how we did the math, we didn't have even close to that kind of money. Brokers urged us to look in emerging Manhattan neighborhoods where the prices were slightly more reasonable, like Harlem or Hell's Kitchen. But we didn't want to settle. We loved the Upper West Side and figured at some point the real estate frenzy would die down. So we agreed to make do in our small space and wait for the apartment cupid to strike, never expecting to still be looking two frustrating years later while our firstborn slumbered behind the makeshift wall. And now we had baby number two back there, to boot.

Sharon freshened up our coffees while Dave had Aaron mesmerized with a demonstration of how smoothly their custom kitchen drawers glided to an automatic close. Maybe Aaron was blinded by all of that stainless: the cabinets were stainless, the dishwasher was stainless, the fridge was stainless. Even the backsplash was crafted of hundreds of silver rectangles, lined up like a wall of antiseptic armor. I thought kitchens were supposed to be warm and inviting; this one made me feel like I was in a haute designer morgue.

I couldn't wait to leave.

"I think I hear Madison," I said. I had left her in the foyer when we arrived, still snug in her car seat, not wanting to wake her from her midmorning nap.

As I walked over, Madison's eyes fluttered open and she smiled her usual gummy grin. "Morning, Maddie," I whispered, and kissed her forehead. Everyone said she looked just like Aaron, with his signature cheek dimples and, so far, his hazel blue eyes too. I wondered if they would stay. Phoebe's eyes had also started out that bluish-green hue but by her first birthday had turned almost as dark brown as mine.

"Madison's just adorable," Sharon said as I walked back into the kitchen. Through the bay window, I could see Dave was now showing Aaron around the yard out back. "How old is she now, four months?"

"Just turned five," I answered as I held Madison in one arm and with the other ran tap water into a bottle prefilled with powdered formula.

"I miss that age."

"Are you guys still thinking about a third?"

She glanced outside. "Well, actually . . ." she said, and I immediately knew.

"Are you?"

"Ten weeks. But don't tell Dave I told you, we're not announcing it until we get past twelve. To be safe."

"That's great news, I'm so happy for you!" I said.

And I was; she had been trying for a while to get pregnant again. I gave her a mini–group hug with Madison. "How are you feeling?"

"Pretty good, a little nauseous. Thank god it's only one this time. I'm really hoping for a girl. Alexis is such an angel compared to Henry, the little terror. You're so lucky to have two girls."

"Yeah, until they're thirteen and fifteen—then we're screwed," I said. Just as I was about to wonder out loud how their au pair was doing watching three kids under the age of four in the living room, I heard a wail. "Will you hold her for a sec? I need to grab a diaper and check on Phoebe."

Two hours later we walked out through their pristine garage where a huge Elfa shelving unit housed hundreds of rolls of toilet paper, paper towels, paper plates, plastic utensils, and giant containers of ketchup, mustard, and Tide HE.

"You guys certainly have room for it all," Aaron said, eyeing the shrine to Costco and, next to it, Dave's racing bike dangling from a hanging rack.

I strapped the girls into their car seats and hugged Sharon goodbye. "Thanks so much for having us," I said. *Feel good,* I mouthed.

Then came the hard-sell close.

"Really, Aaron, call our builder about the house next door," Sharon said, slipping him a piece of paper. "It's best to reach him on his cell."

Please, please, move where we moved, I almost heard her thinking. *We're desperate for confirmation we made the right choice.*

"And let's have dinner in the city soon," she added, though I doubted those plans would ever make it from the driveway to her calendar.

On the ride home, Aaron couldn't stop talking about the house. "And did you see Dave's study, with the retractable TV?"

"Yes, I saw the study," I sighed, staring out the window at the blur of trees lining the Hutchinson River Parkway. "Don't you think they seemed different somehow? It's like they moved and *poof*—Sharon's a housewife channeling 1950. Can you believe she quit her job?"

"She always said how much she hated being an analyst."

"But she just passed her Series 7 tests! All those months of studying seem like such a waste now. I guess with the commute and a third it would be too complicated."

"A third?" Aaron glanced at me, then back at the road.

"Yep—she's pregnant. But don't tell Dave I told you—they're keeping it on the QT for a couple more weeks."

"Three kids. Wow." He squinted and I could see his lips turn into a frown under his weekend stubble. "Well, their house is certainly big enough. It's not like they're living on top of each other in a one-bedroom apartment." He was well past the stage of hiding his displeasure about the glacial pace of our apartment search, but I wasn't in the mood to engage in yet another argument about it.

"We're seeing that new listing tomorrow; remember the one I told you about on 92nd Street? And another one a little farther north," I said. "But maybe we should reconsider the idea of a bigger rental. It would give us another bedroom, and more time to find a place we really love." *And to make sure we're not overextending ourselves in case your company doesn't make it through the end of the year,* I thought, and then wished I hadn't. Aaron didn't need any negative work karma, especially not now.

"I've told you a thousand times—we are *not* moving to another rental. We've been throwing away our money for way too long as it is. I want to buy. It's time."

"Renting again isn't my first choice either. I'm just saying it might make sense for right now, until the market calms down a little. Maybe we could find a six-month lease," I tried. He didn't look the least bit convinced.

It was silent in the backseat and I turned around to find both Phoebe and Madison dozing in a tandem afternoon nap. Riding in the car always put them out, and for a second I thought about waking them up; we finally had them on a sleep schedule that got them down and kept them down most nights, and a late-day nap had the potential to erase many agonizing weeks of sleep training. But I was thankful for the quiet and took the opportunity to turn off the *Frozen* soundtrack and switch to the classic rock station for a rare moment of audio relief.

"It's crazy the way we're living," Aaron continued. "And we don't have to, Jess. Wouldn't it be great to have a backyard for Phoebe and Madison to run around in?"

"We have Central Park," I said. "Our yard is acres bigger than that patch of green behind Sharon and Dave's house."

"Central Park isn't *ours.*" I felt the speech about to come. "I can't help it, I want more space," he said, his voice sounding stronger than usual. "I want a study. I want a place to eat that's not in our living room. We've been looking at all these apartments and haven't found anything that even comes close to what we want. I've been thinking about it a lot, and I really feel like we should buy a house."

A house?! My brain actually froze for a second. After I was able to process that, yes, the person sitting next to me was still my husband, and yes, he had just said he thought we should buy a house, I found myself responding the way I usually did when I heard something I didn't want to hear—I rejected it. "You don't want a house," I said quickly. "A city boy like you? Maybe breathing in all that fresh air today over-oxygenated your brain? Don't panic, though. Once we get back into the pollution, I'm sure you'll be right back to your normal self."

"I'm not kidding, Jess. We have to think about what's best for our future, for Phoebe and Madison's future. Don't you want the girls to grow up with their own bedrooms?"

Those words were straight out of Sharon's mouth, not Aaron's. *If Mom says no, go ask Dad.* Pregnant or not, I was pissed at her. She had no right to be working Aaron behind my back.

"Right now we just need to focus on getting them out of *our* bedroom," I responded evenly, trying to stay calm. "And what I really think is best for Phoebe and Madison is for them to actually *see* us. I'd much rather live in a smaller apartment in the city than have both of us commute for two hours every day. I barely get to spend enough time with them during the week as it is. And you always say how you love being able to jump in a cab and be home in ten minutes to kiss them good night. You'd never get to do that if we lived in the suburbs. You'd never even see the girls."

But my commute touché didn't seem to dissuade him.

"Think about it—if we had a house, there'd be room for you to have an office. Maybe you could finally convince your boss to let you work from home one day a week."

Aaron knew that since Madison was born I had been fantasizing about working Fridays from home. I didn't want to stay home full-time—not that I could if I wanted to. With Aaron working at yet another start-up, my salary was a necessity. But the truth was, unlike many of my friends who took the opportunity after giving birth to quit jobs they loathed, I actually liked mine. I liked waking up in the morning and putting on clothes that were *Dry Clean Only*. I liked having business cards with the words *Account Director* typed neatly under my maiden name. But now with two children, two babies still, really, I felt like that one extra day at home would tilt the week ever so slightly into a better balance. The Broadway theater clients our agency serviced didn't run on a regular nine-to-five schedule anyway; I could easily jump on a marketing conference call during nap time and approve ad copy on my phone while at playdates or on visits to the Central Park Zoo. A bunch of working moms I knew had Fridays off, including my best friend Liza, but she was one of Kate Spade's top handbag designers and probably could have negotiated working Monday through Friday from home if she felt like it. She had been helping me write a proposal to present to my boss, but I had been too nervous to ask, too afraid of hearing no.

"Plus," Aaron said, taking my silence as an opportunity to push it, "we could have a whole house for the same money as an apartment, maybe even less. Dave said the house next door to his is slated to break ground the end of next month and will be ready by the summer."

I couldn't believe their slick sales job had worked so effectively on him. "There is *no way* we are moving next door to Sharon and Dave!" I exclaimed, feeling my face get hot. "I know he's one of your best friends and I like Sharon and all—but take a second to think about what it would be like to live next door to them, to see them every single day *for the rest of our lives*. Walking down the driveway to get the paper and having to make small talk when you're barely awake: *Morning, Sharon. Morning, Dave*—over and over for the next forty years like *Groundhog Day*, only worse, we'd actually be living it, for real."

Aaron laughed, and I felt a little relieved. "Okay, okay. You're right. So maybe not the house next door. But you've got to admit, we could get so much more for our money outside the city."

We could get more of nearly everything outside the city. More rooms, more shelf space, more outdoor space, more personal space, more light, more heat, more water, more air—there was no disputing there was more of all of it across Manhattan's moat. But I didn't want any of it. I had been raised on a suburban street much like Sharon and Dave's, twenty minutes north of them in Mount Kisco. I had grown up with the space and the dog and the bike and the aching desire to get my learner's permit on my sixteenth birthday. When my parents called me sophomore year of college and broke the news that they had boxed up my high school mementos and were moving to a tidy little condo a block from the beach in Miami, another person might have mourned the end of an era. But I felt zero regret about severing my suburban ties for good. In my mind's eye, I had always envisioned my future in Manhattan. And until now, I'd thought that Aaron felt the same way.

He loved to wax poetic about his city upbringing in tree-lined Forest Hills, Queens, nourished on bodega-bought groceries and NYC drinking water straight from the tap; how lucky he was to be able to walk to PS 352 around the corner and play in epic after-school street hockey and stoopball games with his best friends until dusk; how close he was to his older brother because they shared the second bedroom. Even after high school, he chose urban: Penn in downtown Philly for college and then Columbia for business school.

Deep down I didn't think Aaron really wanted to move out to the suburbs. But I knew it was getting harder and harder for him, visiting his buddies living out on private-equity easy street. Dave's gigantic house had probably cost a good two million dollars, if not more. It was sparkling and luxe and vastly appealing in its own way. Even I had left there wishing we had that much room to store toilet paper.

Yet beneath their shiny countertops I knew they had to have new-home headaches not out for display—septic system backups and sodium borate termite treatments and pine trees dripping stubborn sticky sap on their new backyard fences. There had to be some ambivalence, maybe even some doubt, perhaps some feelings they might never admit—that they were strangely happy and safe and comfortable in their big new house with the people around them all looking and earning and thinking a lot like they did.

As we crossed under the George Washington Bridge and started down the Henry Hudson Parkway, I caught sight of the Gothic grandeur of Riverside Church rising above the gulf of buildings surrounding it, my personal landmark that we were almost home. Even after twelve years, it always surprised me how excited I was driving back into Manhattan; I felt a pulse of promise that anything could happen. And that it would.

It's our turn now to get lucky, I thought. Time for the broker gods to cast their smiles upon us and reveal a gem amid the strass, an apartment for us to love and to hold, to close on and inhabit by the end of the year, and put Aaron's nascent house lust to bed forever.

We took the 96th Street exit and drove around the ramp to Riverside Drive. "They had two sinks in their bathroom," Aaron said wistfully. "I love you, Jess, but can't I just have my own sink?"

CHAPTER TWO

THE NEXT MORNING I LEFT AARON WATCHING Nick Jr. with Phoebe while I ran the two quick blocks to Central Park, pushing the jogging stroller with Madison bundled inside. The late-November air was chilly, and I zipped my fleece up all the way, while following the running path down around the lake. The ancient oaks and maples were soaked in fall, a vibrant backdrop of reds and oranges and golds I knew would soon fade into winter's quiet gray. Rounding the corner at 72nd Street, we passed a pod of Italian tourists staring up and snapping photos, and made it to the fountain just as our 9:15 Strollercize class was starting.

I found an empty spot in the circle next to Liza and her six-month-old, Jack, wrapped like a burrito with his little round face poking out of his down stroller sack. Wanda, the trainer, nodded in my direction and continued with the warm-up. "Now reach your arms back and zipper that black dress. Come on now, get back there. Reach!"

I stretched my arms up and then down my back as far as I could, grateful to be under the sky's ceiling instead of stuck in a gym.

In between stretches Wanda reminded us the new

winter schedule would be starting soon. "And don't forget, Get Your Sex Life Back Week starts today."

"Ha! What sex life?" Liza joked. Everyone giggled.

"*Exactly.* Today we'll be finding those Kegel muscles
to help strengthen our pelvic floors. And tonight your
homework is to put those babies to bed, turn off the TV,
and surprise your partner with oral sex."

"Not in front of the children!" one of the moms cried,
putting her hands over her baby's ears, pretending to be
aghast.

"You had to pick the one week my husband's in LA?"
another mom moaned.

Wanda just smiled. As the founder of Strollercize, she
was on a personal mission to empower every new mom
to not only get her pre-baby body back, but to wake up
each day feeling confident and capable no matter how
little sleep we might have had, or more likely *not* had, the
night before. She wanted our resolve to be as strong as
our triceps, and I tried the best I could to follow Wanda's
recipes for a fit and happy mom life, even if sometimes
her methods seemed a little bizarre to me.

"Ever heard of phone sex, Sarah? Straighten out that
elbow and *then* stretch it over . . . That's it. Better. This
is your week to take control and rediscover the power of
pleasure—*every night for one week*. Sex is like exercise:
the more you do it, the better you'll feel. Plus, you'll burn
extra calories. You can thank me later."

"But I read somewhere if you give a blow job and you
swallow it's like fifty calories," Sarah said.

"Who swallows?" Liza asked.

I do, I thought. *I hope it's not fifty calories.*

"The average ejaculation has only about five calories,

not fifty," Wanda corrected. "And we'll do an extra set of push-ups today to burn those. Now, hands on your hips and lace up that corset. Tighten up those stomachs and pull it all in."

I tried to remember the last time Aaron and I had sex every night for a whole week. Back when we were trying to get pregnant, probably. Or our last oral tryst: *mutual* oral tryst. Going down on me had never been his favorite foreplay, and it usually required me giving his head a not-so-subtle nudge southward. But could it be that he hadn't been down there since *before* Madison was born? Since before I was even pregnant with her? God, I hoped I still had mommy amnesia, because if I was remembering correctly, that would be over a year ago. Not good. Maybe we could use a designated Get Your Sex Life Back Week; it would be hard to argue about houses or apartments or anything else with our mouths preoccupied. I felt myself blush even thinking about it.

"Let's roll!" Wanda shouted, and I fell in behind Liza, down the path past the boathouse. Liza always ran faster than I did, her blond ponytail bobbing with each long stride. She didn't even need Strollercize; she'd barely gained twenty pounds during her second pregnancy, while I had once again gained a whopping forty. But since rooming together freshman year at Northwestern, we had tried nearly every food and fitness craze, more for laughs than anything else—from the Cookie Diet to Pilates reformer classes, circuit training, spinning, juice cleanses— and while most of them worked to make her already slender body even more slender, for me, it all depended on how much wine and late-night Ben & Jerry's I deemed essential to go along with it.

After college, Liza and I both moved to Manhattan, continuing to room together, and, give or take a year, followed along parallel marriage and baby tracks. A month after I had Phoebe, Liza had Thomas, and when I read about Strollercize on one of those mommy blogs, I convinced Liza to take a break from her SoulCycle addiction to try it with me. Beyond the kitsch factor, the workouts actually turned out to be a great mix of strength training and sweating—bonus, without needing a sitter—and also gave Liza and me the chance to catch up in person several mornings a week.

We made a left up the Great Hill—it was a gradual climb and the hardest part of the route. I picked up my pace so I could swing in beside Liza and report the latest.

"Yesterday we went to visit Aaron's friend from business school who just bought a huge house up in Scarsdale, and now Aaron can't stop talking about how much he wants one," I panted, nearly out of breath as we neared the top of the hill.

"A house? What happened to the apartment on 68th Street?"

Wanda yelled, "Walk it in high heels over to the benches, ladies!" I stood up on my toes and twisted my hips, pretending to be wearing a pair of sexy four-inch heels.

"The building didn't have an elevator, and we couldn't get past the thought of hauling a stroller up a three-floor walkup every day," I replied. "The market's still so crazy, we can't compete for any of the places we even remotely like. I'm starting to lose hope."

In addition to Liza's successful career, her husband

Richard had just made partner at a big law firm. They lived in a 2,500-square-foot, three-bedroom co-op on East 73rd Street. They were staying.

"Have you thought about Brooklyn? Someone from my office just moved to Williamsburg with her family and she's been raving about it," Liza said.

"Legs wide, feet apart, and imagine you're squeezing a credit card in between your butt cheeks," Wanda instructed. "Bend your knees, come up, and squeeze."

"Aaron's dad grew up in Brooklyn in a tenement with three brothers, two sisters, and a great uncle from Hungary," I said, squeezing as tight as I could, trying to feel where my Kegel muscles might be buried. "Aaron can't even think about moving there; he considers it a huge step backward."

"But Brooklyn's not like that anymore, it's really nice. Parts of it anyway. You can get some good deals on whole brownstones, if you're willing to renovate."

"That might be, but Aaron won't even discuss it." I sighed. "The way things are going, we might as well move to Westchester." It was the first time I had said those words out loud and I felt a knot in my stomach that wasn't from the exercising.

"Give me a break! You're not moving to Westchester. Something will come up."

The final leg of the route took us back down in front of the fountain where we had started. We parked and locked the hand brakes on our strollers at the top of the stairs, and while Liza's baby fussed, Madison sucked contentedly on her pacifier, wrapped in her tan sheepskin Bundleme. I bent down and kissed her forehead—she was born a total Strollercize pro. We left the line of babies under Wanda's watch, ran down the thirty or so steps, and waited at the bottom for her signal.

"Ready, set . . . sprint! C'mon, Jessica, pick up those knees!" she yelled. I tried to go faster but my leg muscles were completely fatigued. I tripped and missed a step, catching myself before wiping out, but finally made it up to the top. Wanda directed us back down for another round, and when we got to the top again we found her shooing off the tourists who were snapping pictures of our babies in their stroller lineup.

As we packed up to leave, some of the moms worried out loud about where the photos might end up. I nodded along, but secretly liked the idea of a picture of little Madison in a grand leather photo album somewhere in Perugia, pasted on a page next to the glorious Central Park trees and the Delacorte Theater and the lake and the taxis and the Empire State Building—a part of me included as a New York attraction, right in the middle of it all.

That night, after we put the kids to bed, I was excited to start Wanda's oral homework but Aaron had an emergency two-hour conference call with his West Coast development team and then conked out on the couch in front of the ten o'clock news. Not an auspicious kickoff to our nookie every night for a week.

I spilled out the wine into the sink, put the leftover containers of tikka masala and rice in the fridge, and tied up the garbage bag to take out in the morning. I picked up a Let's Rock! Elmo off the floor and threw it into one of the giant plastic toy bins that had overtaken our living room, bursting with board books and half-dressed baby dolls, a set of wooden instruments and dozens of assorted blocks in bright primary colors. But I had forgotten that this particular toy didn't have an on/off switch—no doubt created by a sadist toy maker without any kids—and Elmo started shouting, *"Elmo wants to play with you!"* over and over, flashing and crashing his electronic drum and cymbal. The racket didn't appear to disrupt Aaron's hard slumber and I prayed it wouldn't wake Phoebe and Madison sleeping just behind the door in the other room.

In addition to the toys, piles had sprouted on our floor like mushrooms, half-read newspapers and size three diapers and empty water bottles going out for recycling. Our few shelves held some old hardcover books and a framed photo from our honeymoon, now almost seven years ago; our tan, pre-kid selves, smiling on the beach in Grand Cayman after snorkeling with the stingrays, an outing I had been nervous to take, but Aaron had assured me would be worth it. And he was right—peering through our masks underneath the turquoise water felt exhilarating and scary as a swarm of smooth, flat, prehistoric-looking sea kites whizzed by us, eating the bait right out of our hands. That day suddenly felt like seven million years ago. Now we fed mashed-up carrots and bananas to our children in a giant plastic high chair propped next to my parents' old dining table shoved in a corner. And near our front door stood not one, but two enormous strollers, my one-seater for running and a double-wide, both too big to ever try to fold.

I stared at Aaron, his head propped awkwardly on a throw pillow. My husband, lying there, genuinely exhausted. I hated how tired he'd been lately, how these conference calls had become our nightly norm. Tonight he found out that the new triggered e-mail platform wasn't going to launch on time, and now he was going to have to hit the road this week to smooth things over with investors in San Francisco and Austin. Again.

ZebraMail wasn't supposed to be fraught with the same frustrations as his previous start-up ventures. This time, he was on the management team of a company with a big-name advisory board and the real possibility of a public-sell exit, if all went according to the business plan. But three years and three rounds of financing later, the e-mail marketing software space was flooded with clones, and we were both beginning to wonder if all of his hours of sweat equity and taking only a small cash salary had been worth it. Not that we ever spoke those words aloud. It was way too depressing to think that all the stock options and promises on paper we thought would be financing our future now might not be worth anything at all.

I want to live better. For Phoebe's and Madison's futures. For our *future.* I didn't know where our future would take us, but I knew I didn't want it to be in these jam-packed six hundred square feet.

I wanted to make a home for our family, a home with baked lasagna and recessed lighting and walls painted a color other than Linen White. To pick out fabric for a couch not made in Sweden and to buy a dining room table with upholstered chairs. To host my first dinner party. In less than three months I'd be thirty-four; it was about time we finally took our wedding china out of storage. I didn't want the staid suburban life our friends had begun falling into, but I had to admit, I was starting to get jealous that they had at least decided, that they had started building their kitchens and their great rooms and their lives together as a family, while we were stuck circling, waiting for our runway. Circling for so long now Aaron wanted us to land in a house.

Maybe some primal male urge to provide shelter had convinced him that we would be happier in the 'burbs, far from the city's cramped quarters. But if my urban husband ever came face-to-face with the actual lawn he'd have to mow and the leaky roof he'd have to worry about fixing, I bet he'd truly appreciate our life in Manhattan with a doorman at our service to take in the groceries and the dry cleaning. Maybe a quick trip up to Westchester to look at a few houses in our price range—not nearly at the swank level of Scarsdale—might actually work in my favor. With luck, it would be enough to remind him that an almost-perfect two-bedroom a couple of extra blocks from the subway would be the right move for us after all.

I pushed aside the four-foot stuffed tiger Aaron's cousin had sent us as a baby gift and fought some other minor obstacles for access to my laptop, which rested on our mostly obscured antique wooden desk. Fingers fluent in my search routine, I quickly typed *www.nytimes.com*, clicked on *Real Estate* and then *New York*. But instead of heading next to my usual Manhattan, I took a quick detour over to *Tri-State* and scrolled down to the very bottom of the counties to find Westchester. The towns sprung up in a long alphabetical list: *Ardsley, Armonk, Bedford, Briarcliff*. I highlighted a few that were closest to the city—*Pelham, Larchmont, Mamaroneck*—and in a nanosecond, thirty-four houses appeared on my screen, each in a neat little rectangle.

I scanned through and easily discarded the top and bottom ends. Then one caught my eye: a white brick house on—could that be right?—a quarter of an acre. Almost less land than our apartment was sitting on. *But,* I thought, *it still counts as a house.* I typed Aaron's e-mail address and the subject line, *Road trip next weekend?* and paused, unsure if I should go through with this. But then I imagined the pleased look on Aaron's face as he checked his messages the next morning and finally pressed send, feeling better and worse at the same time.

I slid in behind Aaron on the couch, curled myself into his side, and he molded his warm sleeping body to mine.

"Love you," I whispered.

"Love you too, Jessy-bear," he said; he was the only person who ever called me by a nickname, one that had stuck from the first week we'd met.

I gently led him into bed. He pulled me close under the covers and we drifted off to the seraphic sound of our babies' breathing and the lingering smell of curry.

CHAPTER THREE

WHO KNEW HOUSE HUNTING COULD BE an aphrodisiac? Mamaroneck, Purchase, New Rochelle, Harrison—the more towns and houses we visited, the more energized Aaron's libido became. Morning sex in the shower and then again at night on the kitchen floor. Fooling around like teenagers straining the springs of our tired old couch. One Sunday afternoon, with the kids pacified in front of the TV, we sneaked off and did it in our actual bed, justifying that the extra half hour of *Little Einsteins* might help boost their IQs anyway.

The fact that we couldn't get very much house for our budget in Westchester didn't dissuade Aaron. Not even a little. Every flaw I casually pointed out to create fissures in his suburban fantasy (*Renovating that bathroom would really cost us . . . Does that staircase look dangerous to you?*) only drove him to want to see more. And to take off our clothes more.

The houses weren't as bad as I thought they would be. Or maybe all of the listings we toured over those blissful December weekends just looked good through my sated eyes. Standing out back, in the freezing cold on those postage stamp–sized patios with Aaron's arm tight around my shoulder, hearing his voice full of hope and possibility, I was actually starting to be able to imagine the cracked rocks replaced with sod and swing sets. The attic converted to a guest bedroom. *The space we need to grow.* Our outings hadn't yet produced a home that hit everything on Aaron's new lengthy list of house requirements, and for once I was happy he was so hard to please. I secretly hoped we'd never find a house, I just wanted to continue looking to keep the sex streak going.

When one of Aaron's colleagues suggested we might have more luck across the Hudson River in Rockland County where there was more land and a new express train, I convinced Aaron we should leave Rockland in the "maybe" pile for now, along with the listings and school-rankings research he'd compiled from towns in Bergen and Essex counties in New Jersey. I didn't want to dampen his enthusiasm, but he agreed that a river crossing was too much chaos to deal with in the holiday traffic. Besides, I needed something hot to look forward to on those cold nights come January.

The Tuesday before Christmas, my phone rang at work. It was Liza.

"Hi, Jess. Can't talk but I found you an apartment. It's absolutely to die for—and it's on the Upper West Side! Write down this number."

I hadn't told Liza about the house hunting; it was the first secret I had kept from her in our seventeen-year friendship. I wasn't sure whether I was afraid she'd be disappointed in me that I'd caved to Aaron's suburban wishes or if I didn't want to fully admit to her or even myself that Aaron's revved-up desire was making me happier than I'd been in a long time and I didn't want to risk saying or doing anything to make it stop.

"Liza, I—"

"Sorry, someone just came into my office, gotta run. The broker is literally sitting at his desk right now waiting for your call. Keep me posted!" she chimed, then hung up.

I stared at the number. Liza's list of contacts and favors ran deep and wide—who knew what she might have traded on my behalf. Plus, she didn't use the words *to die for* very often.

At lunchtime I jumped into a taxi and a small marble of guilt start to form in my stomach. I met the broker in the art deco lobby and as he pressed the *PH* button, I literally felt a shiver. I had never been to a penthouse apartment before, let alone looked at one to buy. As the elevator opened onto a freshly painted landing, I reminded myself that I had been in this situation many times before—arriving into a tasteful hallway, only to find cracks in the plaster and a living room with windows facing a brick wall. He slid the key into the lock of *PH-A* and we walked inside.

What I saw was better than *to die for*—it was incredible. The apartment's soaring ceilings, nearly twenty feet high, made the open living space feel almost like a loft. Sun streamed in through the floor-to-ceiling windows, revealing an unobstructed view of the Hudson River. *A river view.* I felt like I was floating on top of the city.

"The sponsor put in all new appliances," he said, walking around the island of the open kitchen with tall built-in cabinets lining the entire wall behind him. He gestured to a large empty space in front of the windows and said, as if reading my mind, "And a dining room table placed here could fit at least twelve."

My left brain told me to stop, to not act like I wanted it too badly, to erase the imaginary scene unfolding at the table where I saw myself tapping a glass to toast our new apartment. To appear only slightly interested, to start with neutral body language, guarded and cool. But I couldn't help myself; I knew in my bones this was it. "This is totally amazing," I blurted.

"Wait until you see the terrace," he said.

I floated behind him out the terrace doors, buoyed by joy. After more than two long years, I couldn't believe my luck. I had finally found the apartment we had been waiting for. The one that had been waiting for us.

The view was pinpoint clear for miles all the way up to the George Washington Bridge. From our perch, the muted sounds of the city seemed far, far below, like the fluid hum of blood. I spied a number of rooftop gardens on neighboring buildings below us, dormant, waiting for the spring, sprinkled with potted winter pines and outdoor tables and chairs of weathered wood. The secret nests of those who lived above the others, suspended high over Manhattan. *This could be ours*, I thought. *Our terrace, our view, our table, our life.*

Inside, there was a separate wing with two oversize bedrooms plus an extra little den. I opened a closet to a holy vision: a full-size washer and dryer! "I have to call my husband," I said, digging through my pocketbook for my phone.

"Hurry and jump in a cab," I told Aaron. "It's a surprise. A good one, don't worry. Yes, right now. See you in a few."

While I waited, I walked around the apartment again, fingertips grazing the walls as if they were already mine.

* * *

"And here's where we could set up our office," I said, showing Aaron a windowed alcove in the den.

"Did I mention it's zoned for PS 9, one of the best public elementary schools in the city?" the broker added. I knew Aaron would be as thrilled as I was at the bonus of not having to worry about costly private school tuition.

During the walk-through Aaron was mostly silent, inspecting the places where the walls met the moldings. Such a natural negotiator, so calm and aloof. He was wearing one of my favorite ties too, the light blue one with a darker blue stripe that matched his eyes. He must have had a pitch meeting that day to be wearing a tie.

The broker looked at his watch. "I have another showing downtown at two o'clock. This apartment goes on the market first thing tomorrow. If you want it, it's yours for the asking price and we can draw up the papers."

"We'll call you by five," I said, taking one last mental picture as we headed out the door.

Aaron and I walked up 85th Street toward West End. I held tightly onto his arm, feeling chilly and excited. "Can you believe it? A penthouse apartment! That we can afford! Brand new, with everything we've wanted—a washer and a dryer and a ton of storage space. Zoned for PS 9, no less. And can you get over the view? It's like a dream up there."

"Yeah," Aaron muttered, "*your* dream."

"What?" I looked up at him, confused.

He dropped my arm. "What the fuck was that, Jessica?"

I was stunned. "What was that? *That* was the fabulous apartment we've been waiting for. That's what the fuck *that* was." I couldn't believe he was even questioning me.

He peered down at the sidewalk and then back at me with anger in his eyes. "I can't believe you dragged me up here and wasted my time with that place. I thought we were done with this—done with looking at goddamned apartments. Tell me—have you been running around looking at apartments behind my back?"

"The broker called *me*—out of the blue," I lied. "And thank god! Do you know how lucky we would be to get that apartment? To live in a penthouse right here in the city instead of some crappy Colonial up in Tarrytown?"

"You're not getting it, Jessica. I do not want to live here. I don't know how many times I have to say it for it to sink into your head. Ready? I'll say it again to make sure you hear me!" He was shouting now. "I do not want to live here! Got it?"

I had never heard him so acidic, so mean.

"What is wrong with you?" I said, feeling the mad hot tears starting to roll down my cheeks. "We've looked at a hundred apartments and now at least twenty houses. Nothing's ever good enough for you! Today I found the perfect apartment! I found a chance for us right now to move to a bigger space—an incredible space—and still keep our life here. And instead of thanking me for finally finding it, you're screaming at me like I'm a child!"

"You're so fucking selfish you can't even see it," he responded. "It's not a chance for us—it's a chance for *you*. It's what *you* want—not me! Haven't you even stopped for a second to think about what might be best for the other people you happen to live with? Like your children? Your husband? It was *never* our deal to stay in the city forever. You said you were ready and I thought we were on the same page. But obviously we're not. Far from it." He turned and started to walk away.

"I can't believe you're walking away from me!" I screamed. I noticed two people turn to stare, and then look away quickly. *Oh my god,* I thought, we *are that couple, fighting on the street in public.* "I am trying so hard, Aaron, so hard. I am the one trying to solve this and you're not helping one bit. And now you're walking away. I don't know what else to do anymore!"

And with that, I started to really cry. I put my hands over my face, feeling my chest heave with each wail. *This is not really happening to me, this is not happening.* All I wanted was for Aaron to come back, for him to put his arms around me and tell me we would work it out, that it would all be okay.

But he didn't. He didn't say one word. He just quickened his pace until he disappeared up the street.

The rest of the day the air around me felt heavy, like gravy. Tucked behind my office door, I stared at the ad comps and window cards that needed my approval but couldn't find the energy to review all the tiny details. The fight played over and over in my head—his angry eyes, his scathing, hurtful words—*I do not want to live here. You're so fucking selfish* . . . The back of his coat as he walked away. Every time my cell phone vibrated I expected his number to flash up—and every time it wasn't him I sank a little deeper into my chair.

I rode the long afternoon hours at first fuming that he hadn't called to apologize and then slowly settling into a corner of stubborn resentment. Finally I thought, *This is ridiculous. I should pick up the phone and call him.*

We're adults—we're married—we're not in high school!
But my indignant side prevented me from dialing. *You
weren't the one who walked away,* it said. *Don't you dare
be the one to call him first.*

But what if our fight was the start of something deeper,
the first crack that starts our fall? *Maybe now I've blown
it; I played this house thing completely wrong, and for
what? So I can live my life alone in a box on this island
that couldn't care less whether or not I'm even here?*

At five o'clock I started to think about heading home,
looking forward to hearing Phoebe's excited "Mommy's
here!" and Madison's unconditional slobbery baby kisses
on my cheek. Just then, a calendar reminder popped up
on my computer screen—*Office Holiday Party, 6-9 p.m.*

Ugh. It had totally slipped my mind. I couldn't think
of anything I was less in the mood for than summoning
an hour's worth of feigned holiday cheer, but end-of-year
bonuses were due to be distributed and a little extra face
time could be essential to move up on my boss Sybil's
nice-or-naughty list. I knew I had to at least do a drive-by.

I called to ask our nanny if she could stay a little late,
and before heading out, I decided to break the acrimo-
nious silence and quickly sent Aaron a short e-mail: *Plse
be home by seven. Forgot I have my office holiday party
tonite.* My fingers automatically typed my usual *Love, J,*
but then I erased it before pressing send.

Sybil, our agency's cofounder and president, had cut
spouses and significant others out of the holiday party
mix a couple of years before. "Budget," she'd explained,
but she spared no expense on the party itself, taking over
the rooftop at the Gansevoort Hotel. Yet even with the
top-shelf booze and tuna tartare it was usually a bore.

The guys from accounting huddled in their usual spot next to the bar and the creatives took turns outside for a smoke in the cold while Sybil and her minions bobbed and weaved like honey bees among the heaviest-hitting clients.

When I arrived, the room was sparsely populated with some of the more junior account managers sitting on the low, white modern couches, votives glowing on the tables. I ordered a glass of white wine and checked my phone—still nothing from Aaron.

I felt a tap on my shoulder and turned to find my assistant Megan. "Hi, Jessica!" she chirped. She was always so irritatingly upbeat. "I didn't see you leave the office. Have you met Lindsay?" she asked as a slim blonde joined us. "She started last week, in publicity. Lindsay, this is my boss, Jessica. Jessica, Lindsay."

As I pretended to be interested in Lindsay and her midtwenties existence, living in the West Village with three roommates, and she pretended to care about mine—yes, I've really been at the agency eight years; two girls, two and a half and six months old; the Upper West Side—it was obvious how little we had to talk about. Less than ten years and five stops on the express train separated us, but at that moment I felt strata apart. Not too long ago I'd been her, with a ten o'clock dinner reservation and the address of a late-night after-party scribbled on a piece of paper in my back pocket, wrapped around a credit card and a couple of twenties. *Thank god now I'm not*, I thought. I had hated the New York singles scene, hanging out in crowded bars and scoping out guys who most of the time ended up being bridge-and-tunnel from New Jersey and Long Island. Struggling to stay awake and out until two, three, four o'clock in the morning, and then scraping enough cash together for a cab ride home, usually alone. All I wished for now at two a.m. was to be fast asleep, at home in my bed. With my husband.

"Do you have a picture of your kids?" Lindsay asked politely.

"Sure," I said, pulling up a recent shot on my phone and feeling a twinge of sadness that there was still no message from Aaron.

Lindsay smiled at the picture of Phoebe hugging Madison. "They're adorable. You're so lucky."

I am lucky, I thought. I am so lucky to have two beautiful, healthy children. And I am so lucky to have Aaron. *So what am I doing?* Why am I jeopardizing my relationships with the most important people to me over a stupid apartment, over some glamorous life in Manhattan that's not even close to the one we're actually living? It *is* time. It's time for me to be a good wife and a good mother and do what's right for all of us, not only me. What matters is that we're together, living in a place where we all have room to grow. *It's not me giving up if we move to the suburbs*, I realized. It's me moving forward, together with my family.

"Will you excuse me a second?" I said, and turned to scan the room for Sybil so I could say my hellos and get the hell out of there.

As I edged my way toward the bar on a last once-around, I felt my phone vibrate. It was a text from Aaron: *I'm home.*

It was only two words, but they were the two most important ones.

C HAPTER FOUR

My favorite part of the Village of Suffern was that it didn't have a Starbucks. The Starbucks was a mile up the road, technically in Airmont, not Suffern, relegated to the strip mall alongside Walgreens and Applebee's and Provident Savings Bank. On the days I commuted to the city for work, I smiled driving past the Starbucks and stopped downtown instead at the Muddy Cup, a well-worn coffee shop with big wooden tables and paintings by local artists hanging on the walls, a place where they served organic coffee in ceramic mugs with mismatched plates and had fresh muffins loaded with raisins and pecans. At the self-serve counter I filled my new silver travel mug with a dark breakfast brew that stayed hot nearly all the way to Penn Station.

I loved the quiet village on those early June mornings before most of the shops were open. The stores weren't fancy; there was no place to buy Stuart Weitzman pumps or a Ralph Lauren throw. There was a thrift shop, a uni-sex haircut salon, and a family-owned furniture store; a decent Chinese restaurant, a veterinarian's office, and the Ticket Stop for bus and train and lottery tickets. Framed by the backdrop of Rockland County's rolling Ramapo Mountains, Suffern felt like the edge of suburbia that hadn't given in to change just yet.

It all happened so fast—like getting married, buying a house felt like a giant leap of faith. After all the almost-maybes, we found it: a beautiful, brand-new Victorian-style house perched on a hill with a huge wraparound porch and scalloped shingles painted a perfect shade of dreamy gray. *Welcome to the Montebello Pines.* On 2.3 acres, with a bonus—a heated driveway; and the closets, oh my god the closets! Pristine closets with more space than we could ever fill.

A tour, a handshake, and then a contract. Passing inspection without a hitch. Learning about the forced-air furnace and the sprinkler system with rain-sensor controls. *Congratulations! Your mortgage is approved.* Signing the papers felt so adult—by law, we were bound, indebted to the bank for the next thirty years.

Thirty years.

I initialed *JA* again next to Aaron's scribbled promises, when an unexpected exhale escaped from my lips. Aaron placed his hand on mine. *It's all good,* he smiled, and I could feel his reassurance start to seep into my skin. For months I had convinced myself I was ready but now it was real, we were actually doing it, we were moving out of the city and into a house in a town where we didn't know anyone—a town named Suffern, no less—blazing a new trail like a pair of white-collar pioneers.

But we are doing it differently, I reminded myself. We're not saying goodbye to Manhattan—*hello,* we'll be there almost every day for work. We'll meet Liza and Richard for lunches and dinners, once a week at least. And on any Sunday morning we can jump in the car and in less than an hour be the first in line for the new exhibit at the Children's Museum, with a stop at Levain for our favorite cookie snack on the way home. To *our* home, together. I loved saying those words, *our home*. Even if the bank owned most of it.

The move itself had been surprisingly simple. Leasing a second car, an Outback wagon, I conceded, as it did make more sense to have enough room for the groceries, plus it had better gas mileage than one of those huge SUVs. Registering for preschool. On my computer I had searched *Suffern preschools* and in a second found Suffern Montessori, Laurel Meadow, the Goddard School—plenty of choices, all within a ten-minute drive, and all with a space available for the fall—not like cutthroat Manhattan. It had even been easy to find a new nanny—by kismet, it turned out an account rep in my office had a cousin in nearby Spring Valley going to school at night for her teaching degree who was looking for a live-out position. And a few interviews later, we had Noreen, an energetic young woman with fiery red hair pulled back in a braid, whom Phoebe and Madison took to right away.

Taking a week off from work for the move had given me just enough time to fill the fridge with food and give Noreen the rundown before jumping on the train to navigate my daily trek back into Manhattan. I hoped Aaron and I might be able to commute in together, but it turned out he needed to leave an hour earlier to get to his office on time. Most mornings he was able to catch a ride to the station to make the 6:28 train with a finance portfolio manager he met who lived around the corner. My train didn't leave until 8:19, which provided me time to give Phoebe and Madison their breakfast before driving to the station. If Aaron knew he needed to work late, he took the car and drove in and Noreen dropped me off and picked me up at the station, with Phoebe teaching Madison how to blow kisses from the backseat. We were only a few weeks into our new routine, but so far, it was working.

After I got through my initial panic of leaving the kids with a brand-new nanny and traveling so many miles to work, in my commute I discovered a new secret joy: one free, uninterrupted hour of Me Time—each way! I found the exact spot to stand on the platform to score an empty window seat in the right car for my transfer at Secaucus, and quickly learned the unspoken protocol of my new silent travel partners: brief, polite eye contact with an accompanying nod. Never a word to uphold the sacred safe zone of commuter anonymity. Then I'd put on my headphones and press play to start my marvelous solo hour. First, text Noreen to make sure drop-off went okay and zip through my e-mails. Then I had time to read whatever I pleased: the *New York Times* or Media Ink in the *Post*, catch up on back issues of *Travel + Leisure* and *Elle Decor*. Time to make lists of things I needed for the house: bath towels, bulletin board, a comfy upholstered chair for our bedroom. Window coverings and more of those kid-sized hangers. Or sometimes I'd sit and look out the window, listening to the hum of the train running fast through the fields and let my eyes fall into sweet stolen minutes of much-needed sleep.

And on the days I managed to stay awake, I'd take frequent sips of my still-warm coffee, sit back in my seat, and smile, ready for our first summer in our backyard, catching fireflies.

On Saturday morning I was unpacking the box labeled

KITCHEN MISCELLANEOUS when the doorbell rang. I opened the door to a woman about my age, maybe a little younger, holding a round red tin with waxed paper peeking out the sides.

"Hi, I'm Alyson." She smiled through lips shimmering with a peachy gloss. I noticed greenish eyeliner rimming her deep-set green eyes, and her cheeks had a hint of blush. Ten a.m. on a weekend seemed kind of early to me for makeup, but maybe she was selling something or on her way to a luncheon, because she was all put together in a turquoise tunic belted over white capris and wearing silver sandals with a small wedge heel.

"We live next door in the Tudor. And we made these this morning for you—chocolate chip," she said, handing me the tin.

"Thank you so much, that was so nice of you!" I replied. I could feel the warmth of the cookies from inside the box. "I'm Jessica. Jessica Almasi. It is *so* nice to meet you!"

Aaron and I had been wondering who lived in the big house at the end of the long, winding driveway next to ours. We could make out a sliver of backyard through the trees and had seen their black Lexus SUV coming in and out a few times, but hadn't yet spotted anyone. We kidded around that they were mafia. FBI. A family on the run from the law in Uruguay.

A little girl who looked about Phoebe's age peeked out from behind Alyson's leg, a leg so skinny it was practically the circumference of my arm. "And this is Emmy. Emmy, this isn't like you, come out and say hi."

I crouched to eye level with Emmy. Her hair was up in pigtails separated by a very straight part. "I have someone inside you might want to meet. Do you want to come in?"

Alyson answered, "Sure, but just for a minute."

As we walked inside I cringed at the sight of our undone house—half-opened boxes with brown paper and bubble wrap strewn about the floor, frames leaning against bare walls, single bulbs hanging from the ceiling where light fixtures would eventually be. And, I realized, I hadn't yet showered.

"Sorry about the mess," I mumbled, tucking my hair behind my ear and grabbing Phoebe's pajamas off the floor. We were far from company ready.

"We were so curious who was going to move in," Alyson said, eyeing the kitchen. Her nose had that molded pinch and slope, groomed smooth like an Olympic ski jump. "And what it was going to look like inside. I like these floors. Very homey."

"Thank you," I said, wondering for a second if *homey* was a compliment or not. It had to be—the wide planks of reclaimed eastern white pine were one of my favorite details of the house, one of many touches the builder had added to give the new construction the feel of an original Victorian, with antique-looking cabinet handles and wide crown moldings in the dining room and even a refurbished claw-foot tub in our master bath. Standing in our sun-filled kitchen, sometimes I swore I could feel an actual connection to the people before me who might have once stood on the same pieces of timber.

"We still have a ton of work to do—wallpaper the bathrooms, hang up all the lights." *If I can ever find time to go shopping for lights.* "And eventually fill in with some furniture. Moving from our apartment, we had next to nothing. Basically a couch and a bed and a couple of end tables."

"Where did you move from?"

"Manhattan. The Upper West Side?" I asked, as if she might not know it. *Duh*. "How about you? Have you lived here long?"

"I'm actually from here," she said. "I grew up a few miles up the road, off Airmont, across 59. And my husband Jeff is from New City. We moved back from Weehawken after we got married and have been in the house six, almost seven years now. True Rockland County-ites, back to the nest, I guess."

"I'm originally from Westchester. Mount Kisco." I hadn't introduced myself like that in ages, but it actually felt good for a change to be able to leverage my suburban DNA.

I looked down at Emmy who was still attached to Alyson's leg. "How old are you, sweetie?"

"She turned three the end of May," Alyson said.

"My daughter Phoebe turned three the end of May too! Which day?"

"The twenty-sixth."

"The twentieth! I have another daughter, Madison—she's one. Finishing her morning nap upstairs right now." It still felt funny to hear myself say *upstairs*. "She'll probably be up any minute."

We entered the den where Phoebe was vegging out on a blanket on the floor in front of *Mickey Mouse Clubhouse*. "And here's Phoebe," I announced. "Phoebe, look—this is Emmy. She lives next door and guess what—she just turned three also!"

Before I could warn little Emmy to take it slow, she ran right up and thrust her wrist in front of Phoebe's nose. "Look at my new bracelet," Emmy declared. Phoebe glanced at the colored beads and then went right back to watching TV.

"Okay, time to turn it off," I said, grabbing the re-mote. *Please, please, please don't be shy, just this once*, I said with my eyes to Phoebe. *This one's important—she's your new next-door neighbor.*

"Sorry, it takes her a little bit to warm up," I ex-plained.

"Please, it's fine," Alyson said. "Not a big deal."

I was relieved to hear her say that. And Emmy didn't seem fazed at all by Phoebe's brush-off, making herself right at home digging through the bin of Littlest Pet Shop figures while Phoebe stared at her warily, anchored to her spot on the floor. I hovered, ready to intercede, and tried sending her one of the positive mental messages I'd recently read about in an article discussing how to help shy kids feel more confident. If you think it, they will feel it, the article had advised. *Phoebe, you are strong.*

"Go ahead, Phoebe, show her your new vet house," I pushed. Although I knew my words wouldn't do much to convince her and she would only engage with Emmy if and when she was ready. I took a deep breath and thought, *Phoebe, you are brave.* She didn't move an inch. *For god's sake, Phoebe, play a little!*

I wished I had known they were coming. I would have set up the kitchen table with some crayons and pa-per and snacks laid out on a cute little tray. I would have definitely prepped Phoebe about making-new-friends manners. I would have at least showered. Too late for that now. Next time I'd have to be ready for the unan-nounced drive-by, no longer with the luxury of a door-man buffer. I wished my doorman was still around to help me break down all of these boxes too.

"I was trying to get a few more things unpacked while my husband Aaron's at the gym. It feels like we'll be swimming in cardboard forever."

"Which gym?" Alyson asked.

"Planet Fitness."

"Me too. There's an amazing spin class on Tuesday mornings at nine if you ever want to go together."

That must be how she stayed so thin. I had never tried spinning but it seemed like torture, going round and round for miles and never actually getting anywhere.

"I wish I could, but I work on Tuesdays. Mondays through Thursdays in the city. But starting next week, I'll be working from home on Fridays!" I said excitedly. "I finally convinced my boss. It took me awhile to get her to agree and I'm really looking forward to it." Why on earth was I talking so fast, spilling these inane details she probably couldn't care less about? I told myself to slow it down.

Alyson asked, "What do you do?"

"I work at an agency that does advertising for Broadway shows, Becker Glancy."

"That sounds like fun," she said, glancing out back through the curtainless window. *Curtains, I have to remember to put curtains on the list.*

"It can be. But I'm just getting used to the commute. Our office is in Midtown so the train's not too bad so far, but with the kids and the move and hiring a new nanny and everything, it's been a little overwhelming." Yet again, sharing way too much. What was wrong with me?

Alyson didn't offer up whether or not she worked, and next came that slightly uncomfortable mommy moment of whether or not to ask. I let it sit another second and then decided to go with the generic, "Are you working?"

"Not right now. I used to be a sales rep for Pfizer, but when Emmy was born I decided to stay home for a little while. Now a little while's turned into three-plus years."

"Oh," I said. It was hard to tell from her answer whether she was happy being home or not. Navigating the working/not-working mom divide was always tricky, especially with new friends, and I certainly didn't want to risk offending my new next-door neighbor by saying the wrong thing.

I suddenly realized that not only had we hit a too-long uncomfortable silence, I was also being the world's worst hostess. "Would you like to sit down?" I asked, gesturing to the ottoman doubling as a makeshift couch. "And I am so sorry, I haven't even asked, would you'd like something to drink?" I leaped over to the kitchen, opened the refrigerator, and rattled off, "Water, coffee, Pellegrino? Milk, orange juice, apple juice for Emmy?"

"That's okay, I'm fine. We just wanted to stop by and say hello."

I looked over and saw Phoebe had finally started sorting through the toy bin next to Emmy. "Look at that, they're playing so nicely!" I exclaimed. *Thank god*, I thought.

I brought Alyson a glass of water anyway. "Thank you," she said, taking an obligatory sip.

"Where's Emmy in school?"

"A preschool called Laurel Meadow."

"That's where I signed up Phoebe!"

For the first time since she'd arrived, Alyson's eyes lit up. "You are going to totally love it! The new director's terrific. And this summer they're renovating the art room."

With her free hand, she then took an iPhone out of her back pocket, skimmed the message on the screen, thumbed a response, and slid it back in her pocket in a move so fast I wondered if I had actually just seen her do it. I thought it was kind of rude to be checking her phone while we were in the middle of a conversation, but then she said, "Emmy—two more minutes and then we have to go meet Daddy." A text from her husband, of course. "Maybe you could join our Laurel carpool."

"Sure, if I could ever figure out where I'm going," I said, not wanting to remind her it would be our nanny picking up and dropping off most days. "Driving around I feel like I'm always getting lost. Especially at night." Suffern, it turned out, had very few streetlights and more than a few deer coming down from the mountains in search of food. Not a great nighttime driving combination.

"I'd be happy to show you around. And let me know if you need anything else—pediatrician, dermatologist, the best spots to eat. I can make you a list, if you want—I know all there is to know about Suffern."

"Thank you so much," I gushed. "I would really, really appreciate that."

Alyson looked at her watch. "Time's up, Emmy." The girl obediently stood up and took Alyson's hand. "If you happen to be free next Friday, Jeff and I are having some friends over for a Fourth of July barbecue. You can bring the kids, bring your bathing suits. Write down your e-mail and I'll forward you the Evite."

Next-door neighbors not only with a daughter the same exact age as Phoebe, but a pool! "I'll double check with Aaron but I'm sure we'll be able to come," I said, a little too eagerly, scribbling my e-mail on a ripped-off corner of red construction paper, the only scrap of paper I could find.

I led them to the front door and called back, "Phoebe, come say goodbye to Emmy," but she didn't. "Next time," I apologized. "And thanks again for the cookies, that was so nice. And for the invite. To the party."

"See you next Friday if not before."

I watched as Alyson walked down the driveway holding hands with her daughter. *Why, why, why,* every time she asked me a question, did I babble on like such an idiot? And how many times could I possibly repeat the word *nice*? That's so *nice* of you; you are so *nice*, over and over, like meeting a new friend in the second grade. She was probably walking home regretting she even invited us to their party. I guess it was the hospitable thing to do; we'd see a bunch of cars and wonder what was going on. But still. Next time I'd have to be more prepared for when people dropped by. And I had to remember to bring a terrific hostess gift, maybe pick up some chocolate from Jacques Torres in the city or that sun tea kit I'd read about in *Real Simple*. And definitely something for Emmy.

Most important, Phoebe had met someone in her school, a friendly face to help her feel comfortable on the first day. Maybe even a friend. And she had all summer to work on warming up.

CHAPTER FIVE

"MARGARITAS, GIRLS?" ALYSON ASKED, holding a tray filled with icy drinks in translucent neon-orange plastic cups.

"Hand me one of those bad boys," Alyson's friend Tami said, taking a break from unloading towels out of her striped beach bag to grab one. She had introduced herself as Alyson's BFF from way back in elementary school, a "townie" still "slumming it" in Suffern. She took off her hat, one of those cowboy beach hats woven of straw, practically the same shade as the streaks of blond in her long wavy hair. She placed her oversized tortoise sunglasses on her head and took a long, slow sip out of the straw, like she was drinking a milkshake. "Mmmmm, yummy. Love your suit, Aly—is it new?"

We were the only two families so far; Alyson had e-mailed us to come by early so Aaron could meet Jeff and she could show us around before the others arrived. The day was bright and cloudless and toasty already, and the local forecast predicted that we'd hit a humid eighty-six degrees by midafternoon.

I licked the salt from around the rim of my drink and tried a taste—it was super strong and tart, with a hint of fresh lime juice cutting through the tequila. Icy and

delicious. I wondered how much of it I could drink before it wouldn't be safe to watch the kids in the pool. But
Aaron seemed to have everything under control without
my help, spotting Phoebe jumping off the shallow end
steps while twirling Madison around in the floaty-ring. It
felt good to be off duty for at least a little while, relaxing
next to a pool with a grown-up drink in my hand on
a hot afternoon, just like vacation but sans the hassles
of airplanes and rental cars and struggling to set up a
Pack 'n Play. A thirty-second walk next door had been
all it took to enter a backyard paradise straight out of a
landscaping magazine, and so far, our first barbeque to
get to know the neighbors was off to a good start. Aaron
looked up at me and smiled—I toasted him, holding up
my drink in the air.

Tami yelled over to her four-year-old twins rummag-
ing through a giant container overflowing with noodles
and kick boards and super-soaker water guns: "Get over
here *now,* Aidan, and put your swim shirt on. Brianna,
you too." Her voice was low and scratchy, almost like a
man's, incongruous with her delicate features. "They never
fucking listen to me. Chris!" she barked to her husband
who was still up on the top level of the deck near the driveway. "I need you to go to the car. I forgot to grab the twins'
water wings. Before they jump in the pool?" He dutifully
headed back out to the driveway and she sat back in her
lounge chair, looking almost, but not quite, satisfied.

Whoa—that was some way to speak to her husband.
And quite a mouth. But maybe she'd had one of those
frustrating-kid mornings. As if she heard me thinking, she
said to Alyson, "Did I tell you I'm giving up cursing this
summer?"

"Yeah, right, good luck with that one," Alyson said. "Remember last summer, when you 'gave up' sugar? For like a day?"

"Well, that was different. I was pregnant. My body *needed* sugar. But I'm serious about the cursing thing. We had to do something after that episode in Shop Rite."

"Tell Jessica."

"So I was in the supermarket a few weeks ago with the twins arguing whose turn it was to sit in the cart and who got to hold the list. I sent Brianna down to the end of the aisle to get the Quaker Oatmeal Squares and of course she picks the one from the bottom of the pile. As I see the whole pyramid of boxes start to come down all over the place, all of a sudden I hear her start screaming at the top of her lungs: *SH-IT! SH-IT!* It felt like everyone in the whole freaking store ran over to see, thirty boxes of cereal on the floor and a little girl screaming the s-word."

I giggled and took another sip of my margarita. "What did you do?"

"I swooped her up and did a beeline over to the frozen foods to finish up and get the hell out of there. On the drive home it hit me how many times they probably hear curse words in a day—at least ten probably, between Chris and me. Maybe more. She didn't pick it up watching PBS Kids."

I imagined those silhouettes on *The Electric Company* teaching how to sound out the words: *SH—IT. SHIT!*

"It's not such a big deal," Alyson said, kicking off her flip-flops and putting her feet up on an ottoman. "Just tell her it's a bad word and not to say it anymore."

"You know how impossible the twins are, Aly. Especially Brianna. The minute I tell her not to say something it'll be the only word out of her mouth. And then there's Aidan's tantrums. So I didn't even get to tell you: yesterday I finally got Chris to go with me to that parenting consultant, the one I told you our pediatrician recommended?"

"You mean the psychologist?"

"*Shhh*! Ix-nay on the ychologist-psay. To get Chris to go I told him it was a 'parenting consultant.' I wasn't even going to bring him but he kept giving me so much crap about the kids' behavior. He's not the one there every morning trying to get out of the house when Brianna can't find her shoe and Aidan's missing his Nintendo DS and I'm yelling, *We're late!* and then Aidan starts crying and Brianna joins in and before I know it I've got two kids screaming and flailing on the floor. Any semblance of control we used to have has gone totally out the window. Ever since Connor came along."

"I don't know how you do it with three," I said, looking down at the chubby infant sucking hard on a pacifier in a car seat at her feet. "I can barely keep it together with two. How old is he?"

"Four months, little Connor. Our unplanned bundle of joy. Couldn't you just eat him up though?" she said, tickling the bottom of his feet.

"I didn't know that babies could suffer from the unfortunate condition of diaper-muffin top. Guess the acorn doesn't fall very far from the tree," Alyson quipped.

"Fat and happy, that's how we roll," Tami responded without missing a beat, and then added, "And fuck you, I only have another five or so pounds to go." She was wearing a loose, caftan-style cover-up but didn't look at all overweight to me.

"So anyway," Tami continued, sitting back in her

lounge chair, "we went to see this woman, this *consultant,* who was very nice, by the way, if you ever need any help, and she told us in order to get rid of the tantrums we had to start a weekly sticker chart. Things we can do better to help make our family run more smoothly. And I mean *all* of us had to make one, even me and Chris! I've always been anti–all that crap but at this point I'm willing to try almost anything. So she said to start with some relatively easy ones for the kids, like *Wash your hands after you go to the bathroom* and *Say please*—things they should be able to get a sticker for without too many reminders—and then each week add a harder one they'd have to work on, like *No crying in the morning before we leave the house.* And if one of them throws a fit about the shoes or whatever, they lose a sticker. At the end of the week, if they get most of their stickers they get a little prize. So last night we sat down and made the charts and I put *No yelling* and *No cursing* on mine.

"What about Chris?" Alyson asked skeptically.

"I wanted him to put *No more rhetorical comments about the house being messy,* but he went with some bullshit one like *Spend time with Aidan playing Wii baseball.*"

"I think you just lost a sticker, Tam," Alyson said.

Chris came down the grand stone staircase, water wings in hand. "Thanks, babe," Tami said, bouncing up to take the wings and giving him a peck on the cheek in return. "Chris, this is Jessica, she just moved in next door to Aly and Jeff. You know, the new house over there. The Victorian."

I liked how she said it, Vic*tor*ian. It sounded so luxurious, like an English manor. "Nice to meet you," I said, and stood up to shake Chris's hand. He was big, over six feet tall, with a shaved head and broad shoulder muscles visible through his Mets T-shirt. "Wow, a Mets fan, like my husband Aaron. All I keep seeing around here is Yankees."

"Yeah, well, you're deep in pinstripe territory, better get used to it. I grew up Mets/Jets out in Commack. Not an easy life rooting for those teams up here."

"Aaron grew up in Queens and has been a Mets fan forever."

"I'm sorry to hear that," Chris said jokingly, and offered a "Hey" across the pool to Aaron. Aaron waded over to say hello.

"Chris is a Mets fan," I told him. *Of course he is*, I chided myself—why else would he be wearing that shirt?

"Yet another woeful season, ten games under .500," Aaron said.

"Until they pony up some money for relief pitching, it's gonna be tough to win. Like a déjà vu nightmare from last year," Chris said.

"So sad, but so true."

"If you ever want to go to a game sometime, I've got a share of some sweet season tickets, seven rows behind the dugout."

"Sounds great," Aaron said.

So far we were hitting the jackpot: one friend with a pool, another with Mets season tickets.

Aidan and Brianna got situated with their sunscreen and goggles and water wings, and a few minutes later the three husbands were in the pool with all the kids. It couldn't have been a more perfect setup—the men taking care of the children for once and the women lounging with their feet up in the shade of a big canvas umbrella like at a fancy resort. What a relief to not be battling it out with the crowds in the city for a tiny piece of grass on the Great Lawn. A level acre of bright green sod and rows of leafy young trees surrounded their yard's perimeter, with bunches of flowering shrubs, azaleas, and hydrangeas artfully completing the verdant tableau. I sighed, picturing our fledgling yard with its mounds of dirt and tufts of early grass trying to grow. I knew it had potential, but Aaron and I didn't have the slightest idea what to do with seeds and a bag of dirt even if the bag said *Miracle-Gro* on it. I wished we already had a finished masterpiece like Alyson and Jeff had. If our backyard was going to look anything remotely like theirs, we'd have to hire a small army of landscapers.

"Who's coming over today?" Tami asked. "Carolann, Ivy, who else?"

"Ivy can't come until later," Alyson said. "And Carolann's away on vacation this week. At her mother-in-law's on Long Beach Island. Beach Haven, I think."

"A week with her mother-in-law? That's not a vacation. That's an *oblig*cation."

"An *obligcation*, I love that!" I said. I had to remember to tell that one to Liza.

Tami was definitely funny. A little rough around the edges, but easy to talk to. Especially easy, as she was doing most of the talking. I shouldn't have spent so much time worrying about meeting new friends, moving to a town where we didn't know a soul—the new kid, now in my midthirties. *Hi, what's your name? Want to come over after school and play?* Though that's the way it usually happened, chatting while watching the kids at a playdate after school. But I knew that just because your kids played well together didn't mean necessarily clicking with the mom. Meeting new mommy friends was like a blind date: either you felt it or you didn't in the first five minutes, and so far, I was thankful to be feeling it—and I was also feeling buzzed already after half a drink.

"Another margarita?" Alyson asked, filling my glass before I could say no. "And I almost forgot. I have something for you." She put down the pitcher and disappeared into the house through the basement screen door.

"How about you, any summer vacations planned?" Tami asked me.

This is *our vacation*, I thought. "Nothing on the books right now," I said, not wanting to admit out loud how house-poor we were at the moment, how most of this year's summer-vacation savings had been spent on the outdoor furniture that had arrived a few days ago, our first big decorating purchase, and how the rest was going toward our dining room and hopefully a grill. Alyson's grill had me dumbstruck when we'd walked in earlier, a gleaming barbeque beacon shining proudly in the middle of their vast redwood deck. It wasn't merely a grill; it was practically a whole outdoor kitchen with a built-in sink and fridge and cocktail area and a rotisserie with something delectable cooking, a sweet and smoky aroma wafting through the still afternoon air.

Alyson returned with a light-blue paisley file folder, the fanciest file folder I'd ever seen. "Here you go."

I opened the folder and found a professional-looking Excel spreadsheet with columns printed across the top: *Name. Kids Names. Kids Ages. Home Phone. Cell. Nanny Cell. E-mail. Notes. Address. Husband.* Every box was filled in and the margins lined up perfectly.

"What's this?" I asked.

"It's the list I told you about so you can get in touch, set up playdates. A *Who's Who* of Suffern. Well, everyone who you need to know, at least. A lot of these people will be stopping by at some point today so you'll be able to match the names with faces. And I'll e-mail it to you so you can have it on your computer, with a link to join the Laurel Meadow Google group."

The names appeared in alphabetical order, and there I was already: *Almasi, Jessica,* right near the top.

"Do me a favor and send me your cell and your nanny's cell when you get a chance? And on the second page are the doctors and other contacts we talked about."

I turned to page two, amazed by the level of detail—this was a mom who had way too much time on her hands. Putting a list like this together, not to mention keeping it updated, required a crazy amount of work. "Wow. I can't thank you enough. This is incredible. Someone should pay you to do this."

"Someone should pay me to do a lot of things," she said dryly.

"Let me see that list," Tami said, grabbing the sheet. "C'mon, Aly, really? Claire Petrillo?"

"Without Claire you know we'd be doing twice as many Wednesday pickups."

"I suppose that's true," Tami conceded, twisting her lips into a pout. "But ugh, Michelle Upton. What a total poseur. With a capital P."

Alyson explained, "Michelle's husband Randy is the chair of the zoning board, so if you ever want to get an addition approved or move your driveway—"

"I don't care who she's married to, she's fucking annoying," Tami cut in. "She pretends like she's this laid-back crunchy-granola-yogi chick who couldn't care less about what she looks like when it's obvious she spends god knows how long putting together her drop-off out-fits, every day with a different pair of designer ballet flats and a matching bag."

Phoebe's old preschool had been full of faux–low maintenance moms like that. "I know the type," I said.

"I heard she's starting her own business. A wellness center in Pomona," Alyson said.

"Of course she is, women like her are *always* opening wellness centers," Tami said. "Look, if she wants to get her hair blown out three times a week, more power to her. I just wish she'd *own* it, y'know? I mean she's got a look, she's tall and thin and blond, although when you get in close it's like, yikes!—this chick's got seriously bad headgear. I mean, her face is actually kind of ugly. She has the pieces, but she's a definite near-miss."

Alyson shrieked and held a towel up in front of Tami's face. "Pay no attention to the bitch behind the curtain," she said with an embarrassed laugh.

Tami giggled and pulled down the towel. "Kidding! I'm kidding," she countered, but even though I had only known her just shy of an hour, I could tell she wasn't. She took a sip of her drink and scanned the list for her next victim. "Well, I'm glad to see Ivy's back in town. She's a doll. Seriously, you will love her," she said to me, and then turned to Alyson. "See? I can be nice."

"Well, I would hope so—Ivy is one of your actual friends."

"Is she the one you mentioned coming by later?" I asked.

"Yep. She and the kids and Drew are back from a two-year stint in London, fully funded on Drew's company's dime." Then Alyson shouted across the pool: "Jeff—people are going to be here soon. Can you get out and check on the pork shoulder? And maybe put on the first round of burgers?"

"Five minutes," Jeff called back.

"Where did you get your grill?" I asked Alyson. "It's really beautiful. We've been starting to look for one but there are so many, it's a little overwhelming."

"To be honest, I have no idea," she replied. "The grill was all Jeff, practically the only thing he cared about when we moved into the house. "Jeff," she yelled, "tell Jessica about the grill. And then put the burgers on."

Jeff waded over to the shallow end. "It's the Lynx Professional series. Was top of the line when we got it but I've had my eye on the new fifty-four-inch that just came out."

"Give me a break, Jeff, you just bought this one two summers ago," Alyson said.

Jeff ignored her and kept talking, standing forth like Marc Antony addressing Rome. "The most important thing to look for is performance, and the Lynx gives you the most BTUs per square inch of grilling surface. And I really like their three-speed rotisserie. But you should also take a look at the Alfresco. They have a sweet new model with a dedicated smoke burner right below its smoke box."

Wow, Jeff seemed to know a lot about grills. I hadn't seen the brands Lynx or Alfresco at our last trip to Home Depot and had no idea what a smoke box was. Aaron came over to join the conversation with Madison in tow and Phoebe kicking behind him.

"What do you think of the Weber Summit?" I asked.

Those grills had been my favorite for looks but Aaron had about fallen over when he saw the price tag topping two grand for the lower-end models.

"Webers are a piece of junk. You want something that'll last. I'm telling you, check out that new Alfresco, you will fall in love. I can go with you to the dealer if you want—Silver City in Spring Valley is the closest but I really like the service at Aitoro out in Norwalk; we could take a drive out there."

"Do they have that new outdoor fridge, the one that turns into a beer keg with the lever out the top?" Chris asked.

"The Kegerator? I just saw they have the DCS on sale for twenty-five hundred. That's an excellent price, Aaron. While you're at it, I would definitely pick up one of those. And if you buy everything at Aitoro, they can do the installation too. They worked with my stone guy to seal up the cabinets so the deer and bears don't get in."

The bears?

As Jeff went on about all of our requisite accessories, I could see the look on Aaron's face as he realized the little charcoal hibachi he'd envisioned wasn't going to cut it. Not by a long shot. If the Kegerator alone was $2,500, I could only imagine what the final number would look like by the time Jeff was through designing our deluxe backyard setup. Not that we needed beer on tap or the tippy-top of the grill line, but it was probably a good idea to at least consider Jeff's advice to go with quality products built to last.

Alyson interrupted: "Jeff, the burgers? Girls, c'mon, let's go in the hot tub while we have the chance."

Tami stood up and took off her cover-up, revealing a

bright white bikini. Her skin was tanned and I couldn't help but stare right at her cleavage as she adjusted the straps of her top. Her body wasn't perfect—she had the telltale mommy stomach paunch—but she was so confident showing it all, not seeming in the least to care. I hadn't put on a real bikini in years; a tankini that covered most of my stomach was the closest I had come, and even with that I was still self-conscious, especially the first time in a bathing suit in front of new friends. I couldn't seem to get my stomach to deflate to its pre-baby state, which had been far from perfect to begin with. But Tami's lack of inhibition made me feel more at ease and I followed her lead and took off my cover-up too.

The hot tub was raised five feet or so above the pool, high enough for a cascade of water to flow over the side—a nice design touch. The sun beat down on my shoulders and the bubbles made me feel almost too hot; I took a sip of my melting margarita and sank into the tub, feeling the water from the jets beat against my lower back in the perfect spot.

"Alyson tells me you work in PR for Broadway? Sounds like a dream job."

"Oh, I wouldn't say that." It had always bugged me how people thought PR was the same as advertising, but I never corrected them. "Have you seen any shows lately?"

"We don't get into the city that much and Chris prefers the movies. I saw *Lion King* a couple years ago. And my mother dragged me and my brothers to *Phantom* once."

Tourist shows, I thought. "Our agency handles *Phantom*. It's not one of the shows I work on, but this year for the first time I'm handling the *Radio City Christmas*

Spectacular," I said, figuring she might know it.

"I always wanted to be a Rockette," Tami said, stretching out her long leg so I could see her polished toes above the bubbly water. "Do you work full-time?"

"Yes, but starting yesterday I'm working from home on Fridays. To give me more flexibility, and not have to commute all five days."

Phoebe jumped in the pool, into Aaron's arms, and got water up her nose. As she started crying, my instinct was to get up and help, but Aaron quickly calmed her down. *Nice job.*

As I was about to ask Tami if she worked, she said, "My family owns a clothing company," and I was grateful to not have to ask. "We manufacture the crap people buy in places like Kmart and Sears. School uniforms. Stretchy pants. I go in when I can, but with the twins and now the baby, it's been a little sporadic, to say the least."

"Well, at least it's your family, you don't have to worry about job security."

"You would think so, although with my prick of an uncle now at the helm, sometimes I wonder."

Alyson reached for a towel and wiped the back of her neck. "Have you signed Phoebe up for any classes in the fall?"

"Beyond preschool, you mean? I hadn't really thought about it." I suddenly worried I'd missed the boat on something important I was supposed to do.

"You should put her in Susie's dance class on Saturday mornings," Tami said. "Brianna and Emmy are taking it again this fall. It's full but I know the director; I'm sure I can get you in."

"That would be great," I said.

"Perfect, then we could carpool," Alyson said. Along with list-keeper, she must also be the official carpool organizer.

An old song by Madonna started playing out of a speaker masquerading as a rock. "Oh my god, remember blasting this song driving down to Wildwood, Aly, senior year?" Tami exclaimed. "The weekend you finally hooked up with Glenn Stridel after four years of pining?"

"I remember. Most of it, anyway. Ancient history."

"I ran into him a few weeks ago at Sutter's Mill. He was back in town visiting his brother. Divorced, no kids, living in Hoboken."

"You're shitting me."

"Swear to god."

Jeff put a huge raft in the pool that looked like a race car, with big black tires and a wheel that actually spun around. "Daddy, I want a turn," Phoebe insisted. It felt good to be getting a break from responding to her every want.

Tami took off her sunglasses and placed them on the rim of the hot tub, squinting. "I heard a fucking horrible story yesterday," she said. "A friend of mine from Nyack told me a five-year-old boy was swimming in his pool after camp with a friend last week, and his nanny was watching them. He was a really good swimmer, and the kids were playing a game where they threw weighted plastic fish down to the bottom of the pool, and then dove down to get them. Like that submarine game you have, Aly.

"So the boy was diving down and getting the fish and on one dive his arm somehow got caught in a drain in the deep end and he couldn't get it out. He tried to shake it free but his arm was stuck and he got trapped under the water. The nanny jumped in and tried and tried to get his arm out but the suction in the drain was so strong she couldn't and the other little boy was standing on the side of the pool screaming and screaming and she told him to run next door and get the neighbor to help and the neighbor ran over and managed to turn off the drain pump but it was too late—in less than five minutes the boy had drowned, he actually drowned right there on a Tuesday afternoon in the pool in his own backyard."

"Oh my god, that's awful!" I said, getting the chills even with the hot water all around me.

"The whole town's a fucking mess, they can't get over it," Tami said, and took the last sip of her drink. "I think the parents are going to sue the pool company."

I looked down from our hot tub perch at Aaron and Chris chasing Phoebe and Aidan, playing sharks-and-minnows in the shiny blue water. "I'm gonna get you!" Aaron teased Phoebe and lunged toward her; she let out a happy scream and splashed to the side of the pool. "Base!" she cried out, but Aaron grabbed her anyway and raised her high above his head, ready to throw. "Stop it, Daddy, stop it!" she yelled, flailing her arms, her little pink floaties like swollen jelly beans. "I mean it!" she screamed. "You can't get me, Daddy, I was on base!"

I closed my eyes and took a calming breath. That delighted splashing could so quickly lead to stuck, submerged, drowned, dead, still, suspended forever. *Who by fire and who by water, who in his time and who too early*—the annual holiday chant ran like a ticker through my head.

"I'll bet that mom will never forgive herself for letting

her nanny watch the kids in the pool," Alyson said. "I never let the kids swim while Priya's here."

"But it could have happened even with a parent watching," Tami said. "Accidents happen."

They happen, I thought, *but not like that.*

"Do you really think so?" Alyson said, pulling herself out of the water to sit on the side. "We don't know the whole story—maybe the nanny went inside for an extra towel or to pee or check the charger on her cell phone. Maybe she turned her back for a second or two or three.

"A parent would have been watching," she continued, louder. "A parent would have jumped in faster and dove down quicker, pulled his arm harder, maybe even broken it in order to save his life. There is no way he would have died that day if a parent had been watching. Don't you think, Jessica?"

I wasn't sure what to say. Alyson was right—leaving your five-year-old to swim under a nanny's watch seemed like a huge mistake. But Tami was right too: accidents happen all the time. Kids climb on rock walls in the summer when their parents are away and Grandma's sleeping over; they slice their hands open on broken green glass and have neighbors drive them to the hospital for a line of six neat stitches down the middle of their palm. We had been lucky so far: no stitches yet for Phoebe. But I knew it was bound to happen one day, under my watch or not, although preferably under mine, a slip and cut or even a break and we'd rush through tears to the doctor and get it fixed, a story to tell Daddy at home that night with a new stuffed animal and a kiss good night on her Barbie Band-Aid. But the thought of a truly serious accident, of Phoebe falling, crashing, drowning, dying, god forbid, wasn't a place I ever let my brain go. I couldn't imagine how that mother could go on after getting the call that her son was dead.

They were both staring at me, waiting for my answer. "The whole thing's terrible, what an awful story," I said, not wanting to have to choose a side.

Every summer there was a story on the news about the danger of pools. *Watch your kids in the pool, you idiots*, the newscasters say with serious faces. *We're warning you, it happens*. And the drowning story would get passed like the flu from backyard to backyard, a friend-of-a-friend reminder to stay vigilant, or else.

"The shark's got you!" Aaron shouted, and threw Phoebe high up in the air, too high I thought, her arms and legs splayed in an aerial jumping jack, and then she landed with a splash, so hard she went under even with the floaties, but then she popped up laughing and fine, forgetting to be mad about the base. "Again!" she said.

I shuddered. Things I never had to worry about in the city—sharks-and-minnows, nannies checking chargers, and death by suction drain—all now present and at the front of my mind.

In the fading daylight, Madison lay across my lap, finishing the last of her bottle. I knew I should start to wean her off and get her to a sippy cup like the pediatrician had directed last week at her twelve-month check-up. But she loved it so much, especially when she was tired. She held the bottle with one hand and with the other played with a long blond curl next to her ear. She was my baby; I didn't have the heart to take her bottle away yet. Maybe next week. Or before the end of the summer.

A few families were still scattered around the back-yard, older kids taking turns jumping off the diving board, throwing around a Nerf football on the grass. I hadn't seen Aaron and Phoebe for a while; last I'd noticed they were on their way to the basement playroom, following Jeff who was talking about the refurbished original Space Invaders game he had bought from an arcade, no quarters necessary. When I asked Alyson what Jeff did for a living, she said he had an electrical contracting business, with something about deals with the MTA and Tishman Speyer and some other monolith builder. They certainly seemed to have the means. And from bouncing on the trampoline to driving behind the wheel in one of the mini electric cars in the driveway, Jeff seemed even more excited than the kids to be playing with the toys.

It had been a good day. A long day. Alyson and Jeff had introduced us around to their seemingly endless stream of friends, and I'd never imagined a day of pool-side meet-and-greets could be so exhausting. Smile, *Nice to meet you . . . Yes, right next door . . . A few weeks ago . . . Hold on a sec* to catch the kids running in two different directions. *Have you seen Phoebe?* There she was on her way to the swing set holding hands with Emmy, the fast new BFFs.

But I could barely remember any of their friends' names, how embarrassing. Dayna and Rob? Brian and Laurie? The one with her hair up in a ponytail who grew up in Bergen County . . . Heather? I had some serious homework to do, studying my new chart.

Madison shifted in my lap to tilt her bottle to get to

the last drop of milk and curled her toes into the crook of my elbow. She barely fit, she was getting so big, walking, running, now a toddler, not a baby anymore. And those busy little feet were certainly filthy: bath time. I put her down on the chair and started gathering our towels when Alyson came over and said, "You're not leaving, are you?"

"We'll probably have to get going pretty soon," I replied. "Although I may never get Aaron and Phoebe out of your game room. I can't thank you enough for having us."

"You can't go yet—you'll miss the make-your-own-sundaes coming up for the kids and of course watching the fireworks later, around nine." She bit her lower lip. "Tami and Chris are staying, and Ivy and the Wagmans and the Ryans said they're going to stop by. Why don't you run home and grab the kids' pajamas and stay? We're going to turn on *Toy Story* in the living room and have our nanny Priya watch the kids so we can hang." She stood, waiting expectantly for my answer.

There wasn't any particular reason why we had to leave—it wasn't like Aaron and I had any big plans for our Saturday night, and even though I was tired I didn't want to shun Alyson's hospitality. "Sure, why not?" I said. "I'll find Aaron and let him know."

I ran home to bathe Madison and put her in pajamas, and while I was there I threw on a sundress, grabbed a sweater, and freshened up my face. An hour later, Madison was sleeping in her stroller and Phoebe was zoned out in front of the movie with Emmy and a group of other kids. Aaron and I sat out on the deck in the warm evening air with

Tami and Chris and a few other couples who had also stayed for the party's extension.

"More wine?" Alyson asked, and I said, "Sure," as she poured me another full glass of pinot grigio. Over the course of the day, I must have had six, maybe seven drinks. More than I usually consumed in a whole week. The booze was certainly flowing—probably because it was free. If everyone was paying twelve bucks a pop like in the city, people would likely be drinking a lot less. But all those drinks spread out over the whole day, I barely felt tipsy. *Next time we'll bring a bottle of Absolut*, I thought. That sun tea kit gift idea had been stupid; when we arrived I saw she already had one out on the deck for the guests.

I leaned back on their comfortable outdoor couch, glad to have the chance to relax with adult-only company after a long kid-filled day, picking at the remnants of my red, white, and blue vanilla bean cupcake and watching Alyson walk around refilling people's wineglasses, looking relaxed despite a long day of hostessing. It all seemed so effortless for her.

I wondered when we'd finally be ready to throw our first party. After we bought more furniture. After we installed our shiny, new, mortgage-requiring grill.

"You play hoops?" Jeff asked Aaron. "A bunch of us have a run Tuesday nights down at the middle school."

Aaron had been telling me how much he missed his pickup game in the city. "I haven't played in a while, but yeah, I'd love to join," Aaron said. In the light of the citronella candle I could see his cheeks were red—red from sunburn, or maybe too much wine? Whatever it was, I could tell he was having fun. I reached over and squeezed his knee and he put his hand on top of mine and squeezed back.

Alyson's friend Ivy was sitting on a love seat across from us, chatting with Tami. She was wearing a low-cut halter dress and looked younger than everyone else by a good five years, with not even the hint of an eye wrinkle when she smiled. How to remember her name. Long dark hair, long like ivy; black hair, blue eyes, the combo I'd always wished I'd been born with. We'd met her husband when they walked in earlier, something with a D . . . David, Daryl, Dan . . . Drew. He was short and thick like a bull with kind of a square-shaped body, and a hairline just about ready to recede. I wondered what had brought them together.

I overheard her say, "And on the weekends we'd hop on the train and be in Paris, or in Brussels."

"What were you doing in London?" I asked.

"Drew's at JPMorgan and they asked him to go over to start up a UK trading desk. At first I didn't want to go, with the kids being so little and everything. Tanner was barely two and Ruby just a baby. And London! I hadn't ever traveled overseas before. The whole experience feels like it was a dream but it's sooo good to be back. Being here tonight, it's weird, it kind of feels like we never left. But enough about me. How are you settling into Suffern so far?"

Jeff walked over with a tray of shot glasses and a bottle of Avión Silver. "Where's Drew? Drew!" Drew waved from the gate next to the driveway with his cell phone to his ear. "Get off the freaking phone already and get over here!"

Jeff poured the shots and the tray was passed around.

When Drew rejoined the group, Jeff raised his glass. "Welcome back, Ivy and Drew, to the good ol' US of A. It's a good thing you finally came back, because to be honest, you were gone so long we almost forgot about you."

Everyone laughed.

"And to our new neighbors, Jessica and Aaron: thank god you're cool and not old and curmudgeonly like the ASSHOLES that live on the other side of us and always complain about the noise!" he shouted over his right shoulder.

I shrugged at Aaron—we hadn't met those neighbors yet.

Jeff continued, "And I wanted to give a special shout-out to everyone who's supported me these past few years on the village board. We've come a long way; we balanced the budget and built three new playgrounds. But there's still a ton of work to be done. So, to give us a voice on a higher platform, I've decided that a year from this November, I'll be asking for your vote to have me represent you on the Ramapo Town Council!"

A round of applause and a chant of *"Jeff! Jeff! Jeff!"* broke out. Alyson was beaming.

I whispered to Aaron, "What's the Ramapo Council?"

"No idea. Sounds like the tribal of elders."

I pictured Jeff sitting around a campfire and stifled a giggle.

"For the next fourteen months," Jeff went on, "I'll be planning gatherings to get your input on what everyone sees as our town's most pressing needs. Meet-and-greets, parties, and yes—fundraisers. I'll be looking for your support to help me champion our *numero uno* issue: to lower our goddamn taxes, once and for all. I know you're all with me on that."

Suffern's taxes were a lot higher than many of the

surrounding areas, but we had justified it as well worth it for the highly rated public schools.

"So raise your glass to good friends, good tunes, good booze, and a happy Fourth. Cheers!" And with that he downed the shot.

Shots weren't my favorite, the way the raw alcohol singed my throat and took me to that next stage of buzzed a little too fast. But the toast was in part for us and for Jeff's announcement and, what the hell, I wasn't driving—I clinked glasses with Aaron and closed my eyes and the tequila actually went back more smoothly than I thought it would.

While everyone was congratulating Jeff, I excused myself to find the bathroom. The guest bathroom near the kitchen was occupied, so I wandered in search of another, passing room after room—they had so many!—all decorated in varying shades of brown. The dining room walls were a deep shade of cappuccino with an oversized chocolate-brown table in the middle, next to a living room with creamy plush carpeting and an ivory sectional couch. A white couch, with kids? Off the living room was yet another room with bookshelves and sconces and velvety wallpaper with a gorgeous grand piano at its center. I was tempted to try out a few keys but didn't want anyone to know I was snooping. I hadn't played in forever; I doubted I could even bang out "Heart and Soul." Maybe we could think about buying a piano in a few years. We certainly didn't need a grand, but we did have room for an upright, so Phoebe and Madison could learn to play.

Alyson's look was a little traditional for me, but the finishes were high-end. And finished. *A finished house.* Not only was every inch decorated, down to the match-

ing tassels and valances; there was also beautiful greenery everywhere, plants and blooming flowers adorning
shelves and side tables, bringing nature from the outside
in. What a green thumb she had.

I poked my head in on the kids in the den and saw
they were watching *Dumbo*, that awful scene when the
pink elephants multiply and morph into scary-faced
ghosts. I'd never liked that movie, even when I was little,
so sad with his mother taken away in chains. But Phoebe
and the ten or so kids lounging on the couches seemed
perfectly content, eyes glued to the screen. Phoebe looked
zonked; it was way past her bedtime. I didn't see Alyson's
nanny, that was strange; maybe she was taking one of the
kids on a bathroom run.

"Hi, Phoebe," I whispered, and kissed the top of her
head. "Are you having fun, sweetie? Are you tired?"

"I'm thirsty, Mommy."

I picked up the cup closest to her on the side table. "Is
this your lemonade?"

"It tastes funny," she said. I took a sniff and then a
sip. Oh my god, it was spiked!

"Where did you get this?" I demanded. Phoebe
shrugged. "Don't move, I'll be right back."

I grabbed all of the cups on the table and ran into the
kitchen and dumped them into the sink, wondering how
in the world an alcoholic drink could have made it into
the kids' room. One of the parents must have left their
cup by accident. But Alyson's nanny was supposed to be
supervising—where the hell was she? Any kid could have
wandered off, let alone drank from the wrong cup. Then
I saw that on the kitchen counter, right next to the plastic bowl of Pirate's Booty, were two identical pitchers of

lemonade. I taste-tested each and found that one indeed was the vodka-infused batch. The same exact pitcher! I moved the vodka lemonade over to the grown-up drink table and as I started to pour Phoebe a cup of water, a voice startled me from behind.

"Jessica, right?"

I recognized Ivy's husband but couldn't recall his name.

"Drew," he said, extending his hand.

"Of course! Drew who just moved back from London." I was proud for remembering that detail in my befuddled state. I took a sip of Phoebe's water. "I lived in London once, for a semester in college."

"Which part?"

"Bayswater. Not exactly deep cultural immersion, but . . ."

"Our flat was across the park, in Knightsbridge."

"One of my favorite pubs was in Knightsbridge! What was the name . . . I haven't thought about that place in forever . . . It's at the tip of my tongue . . . Nag-something . . ."

"The Nag's Head." He took some ice out of the freezer drawer and dropped it in his glass. "Can I make you a drink?"

"No thanks, I'm good." *I have to get back to the drunken-toddler room.* "I can't believe you know the Nag's Head, that's so funny. I can still taste that cider."

"Ah, sweet Woodpecker." He smiled and I noticed an ever-so-slight space between his two front teeth.

"I've been dying to go back to London for a visit. I'm working on the marketing for this new show coming to Broadway in the spring that's debuting in the West End, and I'm *this* close to convincing the producer to put me on the list for an advance trip."

I knew I had no chance of making that coveted list. Still, it felt good to say I might. Although if they told me to hop on a plane tomorrow, I couldn't imagine actually going: I hadn't been away from Phoebe and Madison overnight, not even once since they were born. Aaron and I had attempted a weekend away almost two years before when I was a few weeks pregnant with Madison, but our grand plan to meet up in San Francisco after his meeting fell apart when my parents decided they weren't going to be able to come up from Florida to babysit after all. A friend's seventieth birthday party that they couldn't miss. And there was no way we were going to let Aaron's parents watch Phoebe after their last debacle, when we'd arrived home from a movie and found Phoebe still awake at ten p.m., unable to move her arm. We speed-dialed the pediatrician who phone-diagnosed a case of nurse-maid's elbow and gave us the choice of either spending four hours in the emergency room or being directed how to fix it ourselves. So I reluctantly put her on speaker and Aaron sat Phoebe in his lap and I held my breath and put one hand on her elbow and gave her wrist a quick turn and twist, and to this day I can still feel the pop of her ligaments moving back into place.

"Tami mentioned you had a cool job," Drew said. "We used to take clients to shows in the West End all the time."

"If you ever need house seats in New York, I can hook you up," I offered.

"I might just take you up on that."

I asked him what he did for work and he started to

explain about swaps and options and managed risk; I nodded and tried to follow but never could get a straight answer of what my friends in finance actually did. It sounded to me a lot like gambling with millions of dollars of other people's money. Albeit educated gambling.

"They convince you to go to London by saying it's good for your career but really I think they send guys away when they don't know what else to do with them," he chuckled. "But I made it there and back and here we are."

"Here we are. Happy to be here."

"Happy you're here. Welcome to the 'hood," he said, and reached out and gave my hand a squeeze.

Uh-oh, he's one of those touchy-feely guys, I thought, and started to pull my hand away, but then I felt him leaning in for a kiss on my cheek. *Ugh.* I stiffened, and just as I thought I was in the clear I saw him coming in for a kiss on my other cheek and I bobbed to try to avoid it and we awkwardly bumped noses. "Sorry!" I exclaimed, and I could feel my face redden as I realized he wasn't being inappropriate; it was the double European kiss, of course. Or was the double the French? Maybe that had been the triple.

"See you around, Dave!" I said way too loudly.

"It's Drew," he responded with a bemused smile.

"Right, sorry! That's what I meant—Drew."

I hurried into the den and was relieved to see Alyson's nanny was back. I almost said something about the cups but knew there was no way for it not to sound accusatory. Alcohol + kids = fired, no doubt, and leaving the cup was more than likely a parent's mistake, not hers. I handed Phoebe her water and told her I'd check on her in a few minutes and would be right outside if she needed anything.

I found Aaron still on the couch on the deck entertaining Alyson and Ivy. Drew wasn't there, thank god, I was so embarrassed about my gaffe in the kitchen.

"Who plays piano?" I asked Alyson. "Emmy's not taking lessons already, is she?"

"Huh?"

"The piano. In the library?"

"Oh, that's just for show," Alyson said.

I waited for her to laugh and tell me she was kidding, but she didn't. Before I could fully comprehend that someone might own a grand piano solely for decor purposes, a blond boy ran outside and whispered in Ivy's ear.

"The fireworks will be soon, Tanner, honey," she said, smoothing his bangs. "Go back inside and we'll come and get you when it's time."

Tanner. That name was a new one for me. It sounded like a cowboy name—Alyson had said Ivy was originally from out west somewhere, Minnesota or Arizona? She wasn't sure.

"I'm still so loving his little British accent," Ivy said. "I'll be so sad when that's gone."

Tami's husband Chris held up what I thought was a cigarette, but then I realized it was too thin and must be a joint. "Anyone want to join me?"

"Ooh, I definitely missed that in London," Ivy said.

"Jess? Aaron?" Chris asked.

"I'm good with wine," I said, and Aaron added, "No thanks."

Aaron had never been a pot smoker, turned off by the fuck-ups in his high school who had speedily moved from pot to cocaine and harder drugs and eventually into juvee, *Do Not Pass Go*. I hadn't smoked in years and really didn't miss it; pre-Aaron, I had only joined in on the occasion when a joint happened to be passed around at a party, and mostly afterward I didn't feel much of anything except ravenous for junk food and extremely tired, two states I generally tried to avoid. It seemed that as our friends started having babies, I'd seen it around less and less. In fact, I couldn't even remember the last time I was at a party where there was pot.

"Aly, you coming? I've got Purple Haze tonight."

Tami looked up in surprise. "Since when are you sharing the good stuff?"

Chris shrugged. "It's a holiday."

"I'll take a rain check," Alyson said. "Just don't light up right here with the kids still awake."

Ivy, Tami, Jeff, and a few others went with Chris behind some trees toward the back of the yard and soon I could smell the familiar scent in the air. Aaron wrinkled his nose at me but I thought, *If they want to do it, they're all adults.*

"I can't believe it's almost nine already. Almost fireworks time," Alyson said. "It's not quite Macy's, but the local fire department puts on a pretty decent show."

"Can you see them from here?" I asked.

"Most of it. But actually, the best place is on your lawn. From the hill in your backyard we can get an unobstructed view."

Our lawn. I felt like I had just won an Oscar: *And the award for the best view for the fireworks goes to . . .*

"Should we grab the kids and all walk over?" I asked.

The kids jumped up at the mention of the fireworks.

Phoebe was rubbing her eyes but still running on the day's adrenaline and way too many sugar cookies. *And possibly her first taste of vodka.* I decided not to mention that minor detail to Aaron—I wasn't absolutely sure she had tried it and I didn't want anything to ruin our night.

I carried Phoebe piggyback and led the other families on the path to our backyard, listening to them reminisce about last year's show, the cascading silver sparklers and the red ones, remember? In the shape of a star?

Aaron transferred Madison to her crib and then helped me quickly arrange our new outdoor furniture along with some blankets for the kids to lie on. Alyson sat down on one of my favorite pieces, the double chaise longue, and said, "I love this fabric," and I casually replied, "Oh, thanks," but inside was elated that she'd noticed, as I had spent way too much time at Crate & Barrel debating which fabric and pattern to go with. Aaron grabbed a bunch of beers from our extra fridge in the garage, I passed out some sweatshirts for people to borrow, and in an instant we did it—we were impromptu entertaining.

This is why we moved, I thought, looking around at our new friends and their families gathered together at our new home, waiting for the show to begin.

I felt the cool dew on my toes and the chill of the air and then heard a pop as the first burst filled the dark indigo sky. Aaron picked Phoebe up and put her on his shoulders and she squealed with delight, amazed by the spectacle above her. Aaron leaned over and gave me a kiss. "Happy Fourth," he said, and I felt warm and content and exactly where I was meant to be.

Two days later we were getting ready to drive into the

city for Liza's son's third birthday party at the Central Park Zoo. I had always wanted to throw Phoebe a zoo party—she loved the seal feeding show and pressing her nose against the glass to watch the polar bears swim below the water, and I enjoyed our outings almost as much as she did. But I had to peel myself off the floor when I looked into it and found out the lowest-priced party option cost five thousand dollars for up to twenty kids, plus you had to pay for all the food and adult admissions. For that amount of money we could throw Phoebe a three-year-old wedding.

While Aaron had the girls upstairs on a search for Ooh-ooh, Madison's stuffed monkey, I packed the diaper bag with extra wipes and snacks for the car and saw Emmy's white sweater neatly folded in a Ziploc bag on the kitchen counter. I had found it hiding under one of our patio chairs after our Fourth of July fireworks viewing with a light-pink *Emmy* name tag stitched inside. I washed it on gentle and hung it dry and had meant to drop it by Alyson's yesterday plus say a quick in-person thank you again for the party.

"Back in a sec!" I yelled to Aaron.

I found my way through the path connecting our yards and saw Jeff speeding out of their driveway in his white BMW convertible. *Nice car*, I thought, although couldn't picture myself ever driving one. Too fast. And I'd be too worried someone would scratch it in a parking lot.

Their back gate was open and I could hear the TV on through the kitchen screen door. I poked my head in and sang, "*Hel-lo-o!*"

I didn't expect to find Alyson sitting at the kitchen table with her head buried in her hands.

"Whoops—uh, sorry . . . Are you okay?"

She picked up her head and at first looked furious, like what the hell was I doing barging into her kitchen? But the anger vanished as she wiped her tear-stained cheek with her sleeve. "I'm fine."

She didn't look fine. With tired puffy eyes and raw red nostrils, she barely resembled the polished Alyson I'd met just days ago.

Remnants of the party—cups and bowls and empty platters—were strewn on the counter. And the door leading to the garage was left open, like Jeff had split in a hurry. A fight maybe? "Are you sure you're okay?"

She looked down at her hands. "No! I mean, yes, I'm okay. It's that . . . um . . . last night we . . . I . . . I had some bad news."

Bad news usually meant one of the big Ds: Death. Disaster. Disease. I didn't hear Emmy padding around the house. I hoped whatever bad news it was had nothing to do with her.

I took a step closer to the table. "Is there anything I can do?"

"It's just . . ." Alyson paused and let out a slow breath. "I had a miscarriage."

"Oh my god, I'm so sorry!" I rushed to her side but didn't know if she'd want a hug so I placed my hand gently on her shoulder.

Pregnant! I never would have guessed—she was so rail-thin. But it was probably very early. Now that I thought about it, I hadn't seen her drinking at the party; most of the time she was running around pouring everyone else's drinks. The cup in her hand must have been cranberry and soda, not vodka cranberry—of course, the pregnant drink. I had pulled that switch many times before I wanted anyone to know.

"I am so sorry," I repeated. A miscarriage, how terrible. Would she have to go in for a D&C? Probably not on a Sunday. I couldn't believe Jeff would leave here there alone. "Do you have any help today? Someone to watch Emmy? I can take her if you want," I offered, even though I had no idea how we'd be able to bring Emmy with us to crash Liza's party, not at $250 a head.

"Thanks, but Jeff just took her out for a while and Priya will be back tonight."

"Well, that's good, so you have time to rest."

I rubbed her back in a soft circle and could feel each vertebra of her bony spine. "It'll be okay," I said stupidly.

She looked far away, into the living room. "They were convinced the IVF would work, and it had this time, for a few weeks anyway."

I remembered the expensive IVF tribulations of Sharon and Dave, the shots and hormones and ups and downs. How devastating to lose a pregnancy after all that. And even though I barely knew her, it felt right to connect in that way only women who have gone through it can know.

"It happened to me too," I said softly.

She turned her head and looked surprised.

"I didn't have IVF but . . . it happened, after Phoebe."

I couldn't believe I had just said it out loud; Aaron and Liza were the only people who knew. I had never even told my parents—Aaron and I went in for my twelve-week checkup, giddy for the green light to tell everyone, and I still remember the silence as the doctor stared for too long at the fuzzy gray screen.

There's no heartbeat. I'm sorry.

That can't be, I have morning sickness, I'm healthy! And my first pregnancy was totally fine.

It happens sometimes.

But it doesn't happen to me!

It didn't help even a little when she told me there was likely something wrong with the fetus—*It's your body's natural way*—and did I want to check the tissue after the D&C? No, I didn't want to check, I didn't want to do anything except curl up and cry, but I couldn't, I had to go back to work and wear a maxi pad until the bleeding stopped; I had to change Phoebe's diapers and give her a bottle and wonder if I'd ever be brave enough to give it another try. From the moment I became pregnant with Madison, I was nervous, drinking juice every hour and turning over to make sure the baby moved inside. I didn't want to know if it was a boy or girl; I didn't want to connect with it until I knew everything was safe and fine. And thank god, when Madison was born it was all okay, my quiet secret behind me.

"I'm sorry," Alyson said, and I felt myself start to tear up again after all this time.

Pull it together, I told myself, *this isn't about you.* And then I heard myself blurt out, "When you're ready— if you want I can get you the name of this doctor my friend went to at New York Presbyterian. She has one of the best track records in the country for IVF."

Alyson looked uncomfortable and I knew I should have kept my mouth shut; it was way too soon. *Shit.* "I'm sorry, I shouldn't have said that."

"No, no, that's okay. I don't want to get into it but with Emmy I got pregnant without any help and now the doctors aren't sure what's wrong. We've done every test, most of it isn't covered—and this isn't the first time I've . . ." She trailed off.

I felt my cell phone buzz in my pocket. I was sure it was Aaron wondering where the hell I was.

"I have something for you, from the other day," Alyson said. She stood up slowly and returned from the other room with a recipe box.

"What's this?" I opened the lid and saw a stack of pastel index cards inside.

"It's tips from everyone at the party—your Best of Suffern welcome box. The best farmers' market, the best car wash, the best bakery for birthday cakes . . ."

My welcome box. I flipped though the cards and felt overwhelmed with gratitude, so touched that Alyson had taken the time to organize such a thoughtful gift. There were so many cards from so many people who didn't even know me, yet all cared enough to share. And I started to feel it—a part of a community, connected by closeness and kindness and the simple coincidence of choosing this particular house next to this particular neighbor who days ago was a total stranger and now I considered my friend.

"I can't thank you enough, really," I mumbled, feeling tears starting to spring again.

"This one's funny," Alyson said, pulling out a pale pink card with letters written in red Sharpie: *DO NOT USE LYNCREST DRY CLEANERS! They ruined my favorite coat!* "Sometimes the *Do Nots* are even more valuable than the *Dos*." I saw a weak smile start to emerge on Alyson's face and was glad that for the moment she seemed distracted.

But then my phone buzzed again.

"I feel so terrible to leave you here but we're driving into the city, and Aaron and the girls are waiting. We'll be home later and I can stop by to check on you or you can call me anytime. Day or night."

"Thanks, I'm fine," she responded, and then a serious look came over her face. "Promise you won't say anything about this to anyone? Not even Aaron? Jeff would kill me, sharing this kind of private—"

"Say no more. I promise. Believe me, I completely understand," I said, and I gave her a gentle hug before walking out the door, heavy with her sorrow and the reminder of mine and the added burden of having to keep it all inside.

I walked back along the wooded path in a daze and could hear Aaron's playful monster voice chasing Madison and Phoebe, laughing in our yard.

And then I looked down in my hands and realized that along with my welcome box, I was still holding the bag with Emmy's folded sweater.

CHAPTER SIX

I SAT BEHIND THE GLASS WATCHING PHOEBE in her powder-blue leotard next to Emmy and Brianna and nine other preschool ballerinas. *First position, second position, now relevé.* The gaggle of chatty moms around me was discussing the new pizza place that had recently opened on Franklin Turnpike and whether it was better or worse than Bella Vita. I thought both pizzas tasted like cardboard. I hadn't managed to find a decent slice in the months since we'd moved and found myself craving it, that perfect New York City combination of cheese and just enough tomato sauce, with a thin crust crunch that had never seemed elusive until it wasn't available right down my block anymore. When Liza and I met for lunch in the city, sometimes I made her go with me to Mariella's, a little hole in the wall near my office that gave me my fix. A Mariella's would do gangbuster business in Suffern.

Phoebe's pigtails bounced as she threw a pile of colorful scarves high in the air and Emmy ran under the cascade, giggling. The two had spent nearly every free minute together over the summer, and thanks to Alyson calling in a favor to make sure they were in the same class at school, the transition couldn't have gone more smoothly. Phoebe woke up excited every morning to go with Emmy to their "big girl" class; after school most days, the nannies rotated houses for playdates, and then Saturday mornings Phoebe had ballet with Emmy and Tami's daughter Brianna. We were settling into an easy back-to-school rhythm which we quickly found out included a robust social schedule for the grown-ups as well.

I shook the melted cubes at the bottom of my iced coffee and wished I had another, and a Tylenol. Last night's couples' night out had been fun but I should have said no thanks when they ordered that second bottle of Sancerre. *Table for ten, no, make it twelve* nearly every Friday and Saturday night, ceviche and steak and mojitos, sure, we'll take another round. This group liked to go out and party, more than Aaron and I ever did when we lived in the city, even before we had kids. *Sunday night early dinner, are you guys free?* The invites kept coming, and I kept replying yes, we can make it, what can I bring? My calendar felt happy to be overflowing with plans, but these groggy mornings were telling me I might want to think about slowing it down.

My phone itched in my palm. I had promised myself for once I wouldn't check it, that for forty-five minutes I could focus and watch my daughter dance. When Alyson asked if I minded taking the carpool again this week, I told her I'd be more than happy to—I'd be more than happy to drive them every Saturday morning to spend extra time with Phoebe. I knew I needed to set aside special mommy-time for Madison too, but Saturday mornings were reserved for Phoebe. Then why was it so hard to not glance at my phone for a quick peek, click, and scroll to see who might be looking for me? *Because toddler ballet class is fucking boring*, Tami had said out loud last week what I'd felt guilty thinking. And so far today Phoebe had only danced her way to minute fifteen. Still, I wanted to prove to myself I had the discipline to do it.

I put my phone in my bag and saw Carolann walking toward me. She hadn't been at Alyson's Fourth of July party but was one of the regulars around the table at the moms' after-drop-off coffee, part of my new Fridays 'working'-from-home routine. With nanny Noreen taking care of Madison, most Friday mornings I dropped Phoebe off at school and then met up with Alyson, Tami, Ivy, and a few other rotating moms at the diner. Over a latte and sometimes a bite for breakfast I caught up on the week's gossip and goings-on and then headed back to my home office for a few hours of work and, when I could fit it in, a run or a visit to the gym before afternoon pickup. From there we usually chose someone's house for a mom-and-kid playdate where we more often than not enjoyed an early happy hour while keeping an eye on the children. I loved Fridays working from home.

Carolann had a daughter at Laurel Meadow a year older than Phoebe, and a boy in kindergarten. "Irish twins," Carolann explained, only eleven months apart. Within seconds of being introduced, Carolann told me she was the preschool's volunteer coordinator and annual auction chairperson and would I consider volunteering on three different committees? The gift-wrap fundraiser desperately needed a coordinator. I told her I'd have to check my schedule and let her know. With work and the kids and everything else, I couldn't see how I'd find the time to fit in volunteering for the school. I hoped she wasn't coming over to ask me about that.

"Isn't this the cutest thing you have ever seen, Jessica?"

she said, and took off her glasses to wipe them with the bottom of her shirt. I couldn't figure out who she reminded me of, her hair cut in a layered bob with terrible highlights, like a toddler had taken an orange paintbrush to a cat. When she put her glasses back on I noticed a little gold embellishment on each side. The glasses and her nose that came to a point. And then it hit me—she looked like my seventh-grade English teacher, Mrs. Littman.

"Adorable," I said. *Minute eighteen down, twenty-seven to go.*

"So, Jessica, I wanted to make sure you had a flyer for my jeans party next week." Carolann was one of those people who always said my name. Maybe it was her way of remembering someone new? And there was something about her tone, formal and slightly disapproving, with the hint of a *tsk*. Yep, just like Mrs. Littman. *Remember, Jessica, that's a simile, not a metaphor.*

She handed me a postcard with a silhouette of three sexy women posed like on the mud flap of an eighteen-wheeler. *Jeans, Jeans, Jeans Party! Thursday, October 18—7:00 sharp!* "Jessica, you really should try to make it."

"What's a jeans party?" I asked.

"Do *not* tell me you have never been!" She dropped down on the bench next to me and asked, "Do you mind if I sit for a minute? A jeans party is like a trunk show of all the best designer jeans, but *way* cheaper than retail. And we never buy retail now, do we, Jessica? Plus, it will be a terrific mom's night out—there will be wine and refreshments and a ton of people for you to meet."

Of all the Suffern moms I'd encountered so far, I wouldn't have pegged Carolann to be the one to host a designer jeans party. Or a designer anything party. She usually wore sweats with a baggy zip-up hoodie that covered most of her body. Maybe she was a few pounds overweight but her clothes made her look even bigger than she probably was.

She put her hand on my arm. "So it is settled then. See you next Thursday night at seven o'clock, Jessica—you will want to be right on time for the best selection. My address is on the back."

"I'll definitely try," I said.

I had been invited to a trunk show once in the city, for a friend of a friend selling jewelry and donating part of the proceeds to some charity she was supporting. It was fun to steal away from work for an hour on a Wednesday afternoon, to sit on a white sofa drinking wine in a beautifully furnished apartment with a view of Central Park. But in between the smoked salmon hors d'oeuvres and my glass of chardonnay, there was a palpable silent pressure to make a purchase that I hadn't expected when I agreed to attend. With only fifteen people in the room, I felt obligated to buy a sea pearl choker that I only marginally liked. And being new to the trunk show circuit, I hadn't even thought to bring my checkbook or enough cash in my wallet to cover the $400 purchase, but they conveniently had a portable swipe machine accepting all major credit cards. I had vowed not to be snookered into another trunk show again, but knew I would be seeing Carolann at school and on my weeks of carpooling in the dance class waiting room, all year long. That was the genius to the home-show marketing scheme—the guilt factor to support your friends.

That week I received sixteen e-mail reminders: *SEE YOU THIS THURSDAY AT 7:00 p.m. sharp. xo, Carolann,* cc: *Alyson, Tami, Ivy,* and twenty other e-mail addresses I didn't recognize. I thought about the pile of pre-baby jeans in my closet I hoped one day to get myself back into. Maybe I could use a new pair.

After work on Thursday I drove to Carolann's house from the train station, almost missing the left off Route 202 onto West Gate Road. My headlights illuminated a mix of modest homes, split-levels and Colonials that looked like they were built in the 1970s. As I drove up to the mailbox marked *38,* I saw that the driveway was full. Cars were actually lined up the street along the curb. How many people had been invited? It was already almost 7:45 and I had missed the *7:00 sharp* window—it figured that the one weekday night I had plans, the train was delayed out of Secaucus.

I finally found a parking spot about five houses up and checked my face in the rearview mirror before heading in. I looked tired. I *was* tired. And I was going to have to summon up some serious energy to meet a bunch of new moms while participating in one of my least favorite activities, trying on jeans. What get-together would be next, a bathing suit party? Plus, it had been a less-than-stellar eating day. It had been a less-than-stellar eating month. I could still feel that vanilla mocha and everything bagel with cream cheese from breakfast and the pasta special I couldn't resist ordering at the Osteria al Doge client lunch. The not one, but two late-afternoon macadamia nut cookies I'd poached from the tray of meeting leftovers in the office kitchen. And the few remnant M&M's I had found at the bottom of my pocketbook on the train ride home. Maybe there'd be a table with jewelry or aromatherapy lotion or something that would enable me to participate without having to try anything on.

I was surprised at how self-conscious I'd been feeling lately. In the city I had never thought twice about what I threw on when I ran out of the apartment, but in Suffern, I felt a weird pressure to make sure I looked somewhat put together, especially in situations when I knew I might be meeting people. Like middle school all over again. *Is my bra strap showing? Is my shirt tucked in right?* At drop-off, at pickup, even at the supermarket on Sunday mornings, I often felt eyes all around me, little looks checking me out: the new mom. In a second I felt them scan my face, my hair, my clothes right down to my shoes. I didn't want to care what people thought, but a proud little part of me actually did, which was starting to bug me.

I riffled through my bag for cover-up and dabbed some under each eye. After a swipe of blush and a little lip gloss, I tested a smile in the mirror and felt somewhat better.

No one answered when I rang the bell. I heard voices inside and found the door unlocked. Two women were huddled in the cherrywood kitchen, chatting next to the fridge.

"Hi," I said with my new-mom smile. "Am I in the right place for Carolann's party?"

"Downstairs," said the taller one, gesturing to a door on the right, and then she turned her back to me and resumed her conversation.

Bitch, I thought, as I went down the steep carpeted stairwell to the basement, careful not to hit my head on the low beam. Over the loud din of female chatter I heard a man's deep voice call out in a Long Island accent, "Got a size twenty-seven True Religions for whoeva' gets 'em first." A frenzy of hands shot up like tentacles and grabbed for the prize.

Giant plastic bins overflowing with jeans were stacked and strewn all over the room with handwritten labels taped to their sides: *Joe's, 7 For All Mankind, Lucky Brand, Rock & Republic, Vince, Citizens of Humanity, skinny, stretch, boot cut, white, black, boyfriend.* Twenty, maybe even thirty women were kneeling, sifting, taking off their pants and trying on others, eyeing each others' backsides and nodding or nixing, looking in a line of temporary mirrors leaned up against the basement's walls while two men with slicked-back hair doled out the goods. I couldn't imagine wanting to be anywhere less than I wanted to be there.

I scanned the room for a familiar face and didn't see anyone I knew. In the bright fluorescent basement light I couldn't help but notice that every woman taking off her clothes had on fabulous underwear. Blue-striped bikinis, hot-pink boy shorts, sexy green hipsters with purple lace around the edges. Of course, the pair I'd thrown on that morning was my usual workaday beige cotton Hanes. With sixteen e-mail reminders, how could I have not remembered to put on a nicer pair?

A woman with a clipboard directed me to put my coat and bag in an adjacent room, and on my way back I spied a table off to the side with a platter of little cheese squares, piles of untouched cheddar and havarti with dill. Next to the platter were bottles of soda and seltzer and two open bottles of wine, and as I took a plastic cup and poured myself a pinot grigio, a woman next to me started piling up cheese and crackers on a paper plate. *Thank god someone else is eating*, I thought; I was starving but didn't want to be the only one digging in.

I picked up an orange cube and introduced myself. "Hi, I'm Jessica."

"Oh, hi, I'm Michelle," she replied, and shook my hand firmly. "Michelle Upton."

It was Michelle Upton, the "near-miss" from Alyson's contact list, at least according to Tami. I reflexively put my cheese back down on the table.

"Are you the new Jessica, Alyson's neighbor?"

"That's me." *The new Jessica.*

"I love your house," she said. Michelle had full lips and round cheeks but her face was far from the ugly mug Tami had described. And her hair, a shoulder-length mass of long curls, didn't look blown-out at all. "It reminds me of a big birthday cake, up on that hill."

"Thanks," I smiled. It always made me feel good when people complimented our house, although no one had ever said it looked like a cake before. "I remember Alyson mentioning you were opening your own business?"

"In about two weeks, finally, thanks for asking. It's Unami Wellness—nutrition counseling and yoga, but with a big emphasis on outdoor adventure. We're almost at the finish line now that the ropes course is in, and I'm close to inking a partnership with Eastern Mountain Sports to tie in to their hiking and biking classes. But that piece probably won't go live until the spring. Lots of time and a ton of stress, but after almost five years of planning, it's finally coming together," she said, and popped a cheese cube in her mouth.

The head of a wellness center who ate cheese cubes—that was my kind of wellness.

"Wow, five years?"

"From the time I came up with the concept to securing the financing, finding the right spot, and a thousand and one steps in between. It's been a hell of a journey so far and it's only the beginning." She took her phone out of her pocket and I smiled when I saw it had a crack in the corner of the screen just like mine. "If you give me your e-mail, I'd be happy to put you on the guest list for the open house."

Michelle seemed pretty calm for someone opening a new business in a couple of weeks. Yoga wasn't my thing, twisting into all those pretzel positions, but a ropes course sounded more intriguing than any of the classes on the schedule at Planet Fitness. If I could tap into some of her serenity, maybe her place was worth checking out.

I spelled out my e-mail for her and was about to ask her where Unami was located when Alyson appeared holding an armful of jeans. "Hey, Michelle. Hey, Jessica. Have you seen the box of jeggings?"

"I think they're over there," Michelle said, pointing to the far corner of the room near where I saw Tami staring impatiently in our direction.

"I've been looking for those, I'll go with you," I said quickly, and gave Michelle a little wave and followed Alyson, even though I had no interest in a pair of jeans that fit like tights. But I immediately felt mad at myself for running away so abruptly. So what if Tami had said she didn't like Michelle? She had seemed nice enough; I could have at least finished our conversation to decide for myself if we were simpatico. I reminded myself to try not to write off people so quickly from now on.

Carolann came over holding a clipboard with a list of names and what looked like a chart of people's purchases. "Can you believe this wonderful turnout? Jessica, I am *so* glad you made it! Are you finding everything okay?"

"Just about to start trying on," I said, hoping my name wasn't on Carolann's report card. *Jessica: zero.*

"Better hurry, the good stuff is going fast," she said, and ran over to help a group of women on the other side of the room.

"It's great to see her happy for once," Alyson said. "Peter didn't want her to host this party—he's been totally anti. Don't say anything," she whispered.

"Oh, no worries," I responded, and sipped my wine as Alyson turned around to admire herself in the mirror in her jeggings. She was so thin, without even a hint of fat on her thighs. *Too thin*, I thought. Even if all I ate for a whole entire year was iceberg lettuce and an occasional carrot stick, I could never achieve that level of thin. *She could use some extra fat to help her get pregnant.*

Alyson hadn't mentioned another word about her fertility issues after that day in her kitchen, and even though I was tempted to ask how things were going, I respected her wish to keep it private. It had been a lot harder than I thought it would be, especially not telling Aaron. But I'd promised. To let Alyson know I was thinking about her, every so often I sent her e-mails with decoy subject lines like, *Fabric samples—what do you think?* with links to Sharon's doctor, an acupuncture therapy website Sharon had sworn by, and a discount offer a friend of a friend had forwarded for a new book called *On Fertile Ground* with mind-body fertility techniques. Alyson never replied but I totally understood her need for distance; I just hoped she found my e-mails helpful and crossed my fingers she was on her way to getting pregnant again.

My stomach grumbled and I wished I hadn't left my piece of cheddar on the table. "What does Carolann's husband do again?"

"Peter was in operations at IBM over in Hawthorne but got laid off last year," Alyson said, then added in a hushed voice, "They've been really strapped for cash. Carolann told me they even talked about selling the house and moving back up near Syracuse, where his parents are."

"Ugh, Syracuse," I said, starting to feel guilty for not having shopped yet.

"But Carolann said there's no way she's moving up to that freezing hell hole. So she's thinking about going back to work. Did she tell you she started taking classes to get her real estate agent's license? Needless to say, when the jeans party came up, she jumped at the chance to host."

I started to feel uncomfortable knowing a bit too much. "Where are all of these jeans from?" I asked to change the subject. "Are they off the back of a truck or something?"

"Who cares where they're from, they're practically free. Come on, try some on. What are you, a twenty-nine . . . ish?" She sifted through a bin and threw me a few pairs.

"Jeans sometimes run a little small," I said, putting down my drink and feeling like I was fourteen again in the giant communal dressing room at Loehmann's, the mecca for discount designer bargains my mother used to drag me to. At Loehmann's they didn't have private dressing rooms, and I dreaded changing in front of the mirrored walls amongst the overweight ladies in big beige bras and girdles, with rolls of old stomach rippling out. They tried to squeeze into marked-down skirts, arguing about where to go for lunch and did you hear whose husband just dropped dead of a heart attack in Bronxville, poor thing? The lack of partitions somehow gave them permission to critique anyone changing around them; no one was safe from their watchful eyes and ongoing commentary: "Oh, that looks fabulous." "That material's pulling, Sheila, you can do better." "Gorgeous—did you see another in a size fourteen?" I would tuck into a corner and strip with lightning speed into my Jordache, Sasson, and Gloria Vanderbilts, zippered and button-fly. But no matter how quickly I changed, they always got their comments in. "Oh, she's got a lovely figure," they would say to my mother, and I'd feel my face get hot and wish I could melt into the floor.

"Shit, Jessica, those look amazing on you," Tami said, surprising me as she came up from behind. "Really."

I looked in the mirror. She was right. The smooth, dark material had just enough give and just enough rise to cover my stomach. In the back, strategically placed pockets flattened my behind. I looked about five pounds thinner. "Wow," I said.

"You should get them," Tami said. "You should get *two*."

"That's the spirit!" chirped Carolann, reappearing right next to me with her clipboard.

Tami then stripped off the pair of jeans she was trying on and bent over to pick up a new pair. I was shocked to see her bare ass and it looked like she didn't have on any underwear—how gross for a jean try-on party! But then down the middle of her butt cheeks I saw a thin sliver of red thread, like something straight out of the Frederick's of Hollywood catalog. I owned a few thongs but nothing even close to that skimpy. I had seen Tami in a bathing suit yet this was different—her butt cheeks, a G-string, right in my face—it was way more of Tami than I ever needed to see.

She turned toward me and I noticed she had a tiny monarch butterfly tattoo above her hip bone.

I blurted, "I like your tattoo."

"Thanks, hon," she said, zipping her pants up. "Do you have any?"

"Uhhh . . . no." The thought had never crossed my mind. Actually, it had once, at four o'clock in the morning during spring break in Cancún senior year, but the second Liza and I walked through the door of the tattoo parlor we totally chickened out. And thank god. A rainbow peace sign on my ankle would look ridiculous now.

Tami said, "It's for my mom who died when I was nineteen. Breast cancer—seven months, just like that." Then, without skipping a beat, she eyed herself in the mirror and said, "I never liked boot cut on me. I think I'll get the white ones. Do you want to try these before I put them back for somebody else?"

The thong, the tattoo, *just like that*—I couldn't even eke out a no.

Tami said, "Sorry, didn't mean to lay that on you."

"No, no," I stammered, "*I'm* the one who's sorry."

She flung the jeans over her arm. "No worries, chica. Let's grab these goods while we can and get in line to pay."

I reached for my pocketbook and then remembered

I'd thrown it in the pile in the other room. "I have to get my bag, I'll meet you."

I walked down the dark hallway and tried to figure out what it was that bothered me about Tami's reaction. Something seemed amiss in her too-casual way. What did I expect her to do, break down crying in the middle of a party about something that happened more than fifteen years ago? I had no idea what it felt like to lose a parent, fortunately; there was no way I could judge what was right or appropriate for someone who had experienced such a loss.

I opened a door to what I thought was the room with the bags and it took a second for my eyes to adjust and realize I had stepped into some kind of storage room by mistake. I flicked on the light and could tell immediately this was no ordinary Costco closet; it was more like a bunker, lined with floor-to-ceiling shelves stocked with gallons upon gallons of water and cases of oats and canned tomatoes and Carnation powdered milk. Perfectly lined up rows, ten deep. Huge plastic buckets and industrial bars of laundry soap. Peas, corn, Chunky Hearty Bean & Ham Soup, and oversized cereal boxes, and I literally jumped when I saw four gas masks staring up at me like skulls from the future.

I had read once in a magazine about people who were convinced the apocalypse would hit at any moment—"preppers," they called themselves, proud of their stockpiled survival supplies that not only included food but also arsenals of ammo and guns. But I had thought they lived in the back hills of Kentucky and northern Montana, not the suburbs of New York City.

Then I froze: there on the wall was a brown lockbox

that looked about rifle-size. *I am standing in a room loaded with guns*. Guns and Clorox and a ten-year sup-ply of Cap'n Crunch. *Holy shit*. I quickly shut off the light and closed the door, making a beeline up the stairs to get out of there.

At the checkout table I still felt shaken but managed to find my credit card and handed it to the man with the cash box. "Sorry, sister, cash only," he said.

I rummaged through my wallet and luckily was able to scrape together enough to cover it. I would have been happy to pay full retail for two pairs of flattering new jeans, but for the price of not even one, I had two, and besides stumbling into Carolann's bizzaro bunker, I was glad I'd come to the party after all.

"Let's get out of here and get a real drink," Alyson said.

Not pregnant, I thought.

A drink sounded good but it was getting late. "Sorry, I can't," I said. "Aaron's away in Austin and I have to get home for the sitter."

"Oh, come on, for one drink," Tami said.

"Ivy just sent me a text," Alyson added. "She's at Varka and already has a table."

I really wanted to. There wasn't any reason to rush home if Noreen could stay an extra hour. The kids were probably asleep already anyway. After a quick call to confirm and wearing my new jeans, I followed Alyson and Tami and a group of other moms out the door.

Varka was packed. *Who are all of these people out on a Thursday night?* I wondered as our party of five snaked through the crowd, looking for Ivy. I smelled perfume and cologne and passed men in tight black T-shirts and women in off-the-shoulder silk blouses, martinis in hand. Loud music blared from an outdoor patio. There were couples too, tucked away eating and drinking at tables leading up to the packed area by the bar. Since we'd moved to Suffern it hadn't occurred to me to go out for a date night with Aaron during the week—most nights we barely had enough energy to hike up the stairs from our couch to our bed, let alone leave the house. But it felt good to break out of my normal routine, in a crowded bar on a school night.

Ivy waved to us from two high cocktail tables pushed together toward the back of the bar. She was with a few women I didn't know. After meeting a Cheryl and a Lisa and another Jessica, I sat on a stool next to Alyson and caught an edge of their conversation while I scanned the room for a waitress.

"Not the book fair—then we have to sit there for the whole freaking day with that kid Jacob's mother and Lily's mother too," Alyson said.

"You mean Jacob, the kid who had lice last week?" Cheryl said.

Alyson nodded. "Second time this year."

"We could all help Carolann with the auction," Ivy suggested. "When is it, April? That usually doesn't get started until after New Year's."

Tami shook her head no. "Too much work. I warn you: steer clear. Carolann enjoys the heavy lifting, I say let her do it. If you have to volunteer, you want to choose something easy, like box tops collector. Or do what I do: raise your hand to take the guinea pig home for a holiday weekend—then with a change of newspaper and a little bit of water you're done with your obligation for the whole year. Just don't take my weekend, Ivy—it's Thanksgiving—or I'll have to fucking kill you."

I liked the take-home-the-pet concept but definitely didn't want to infringe on Tami's territory.

Another mom I recognized from the party joined the group. She gave Alyson a kiss hello and said, "Congrats, I heard Jeff hired the same campaign manager who worked on the state senator's big win last year. That guy's supposed to be amazing."

Alyson rolled her eyes. "Please, for one night, can we not discuss the election? I'm not sure I'm going to make it through another whole year of this ridiculous Ramapo Town Council crap."

I had thought Alyson was supportive of Jeff's political aspirations, or at least she seemed to be when we were out with the couples, nodding and smiling whenever he discussed his ideas for a new sewer system and additions to the police force. From what Aaron told me, Jeff enjoyed his public service side job and seemed genuinely interested in making a difference. I decided not to mention to Alyson's friend that it was actually Aaron who connected Jeff with his new campaign manager through a friend of a friend from b-school. And that Jeff was over-the-moon excited to have him on the team.

I turned to my right to find out what the other women were talking about, to see if it was more interesting than the usual school banter.

"... and I told him the stones on the patio were breaking and what we really needed to do was replace it, not just fix it. But then when I showed him the estimate for a new one, he completely flipped out. And I had thought the price was pretty reasonable for a whole new patio. He just doesn't have a clue what these things cost. That, and he's such a cheap bastard."

I definitely needed a drink before I could stick my toe into those waters.

Then Cheryl said to me, "So, Tami tells me you're from the city. We used to live on the Upper East Side in Normandie Court? I absolutely *love* the city. I can't wait to move back there when the kids go to college."

"Me too," the woman complaining about the patio said. "Counting the days."

"Where did they apply?" I asked.

She burst out laughing. "That's a good one! *Where did they apply?* My oldest just turned four so we've still got a ways to go."

How was I supposed to know she'd be talking about her plans to move fifteen years from now? Plus, the desperate note in her voice made me feel squirmy.

I looked up to see if I could find a waitress but there was still none to be seen. "Anyone need a drink?" A few hands shot up and I managed to squeeze through the dense crowd lined up four deep at the bar and returned a few minutes later with four Amstel Lights.

"Hey, Jessica—look over behind you. That guy is totally checking you out," Tami said.

"Yeah, right," I replied. "Very funny."

"He is, seriously! It's the jeans, I'm telling you."

I quickly turned my head and thought I caught a glimpse of a group of guys at least a decade younger than us leaning against the bar, looking in our direction and smiling. I had to admit it felt good being checked out in a bar. *Ha! I still have it.* I decided I would wear my new jeans every single day from now on.

Tami nudged Alyson. "Doesn't the one in the middle remind you of Dr. Mike from Miami?"

Alyson glanced at the bar and then shook her head. "I thought we agreed not to bring up that night since I almost cracked my head open."

Tami said, "Yeah, you almost cracked your head open alright. I hope they offer that sweet condo again at the auction this year—I could really use another break in South Beach. Right about now."

"When were you guys in Miami?" I asked. "My parents live there."

"Back over Memorial Day weekend," Tami said. "A bunch of us went on a moms' weekend away and it was a total fucking blast. We even convinced Ivy to fly her ass in from London—"

"How's your house decorating going, Jessica?" Ivy interrupted, shooting a strange glance at Tami. "I am sooooo jealous you have that beautiful brand-new house and get to do it all from scratch. Since we've been back I've been working on Drew to get the green light to redo our kitchen. And the master bath while we're at it."

"We're getting there, but it's a little slow," I admitted. "I've been looking for a dresser for Phoebe's room and a coffee table for the den." Not to mention the hundreds of other items on the list: pillowcases and drawer dividers and linen storage boxes from the Container Store. And curtains—I still hadn't ordered curtains. "It's been hard to find the time to go shopping. And there's only so much you can buy on the Internet. Returning's such a pain."

"If you want, I can introduce you to Frederico," Ivy said.

"Oh my god, Frederico's amazing!" a woman at the

other end of the table exclaimed. I couldn't remember
if she was Lisa or the other Jessica. "He did my friend's
whole house in Franklin Lakes. And get this—before she
hired him, she toured a few houses he decorated, found
one she really liked, and said, *I'm moving into my new
home in October, you have four months to make my
house look like this one.* Then she gave him a blank check
and said she wanted to literally walk in the door with her
whole entire house decorated. She didn't want to approve
one single item—she let him buy *everything*, sight un-
seen! Custom-made couches, all the beds and all the bed-
ding. Bathroom fixtures, tiles, artwork, picture frames.
Everything. Can you imagine?"

I couldn't. "What if she didn't like something?" I
asked. I knew a custom-made couch could run upward
of ten, even fifteen grand. Who in their right mind would
risk that?

"Anything that wasn't custom, she could exchange.
But guess what? She didn't return one single thing. She
kept it all, down to the knickknacks he put on the shelf
above the sink."

"That's crazy, I could *never*," Alyson said. "The year
we did our house, I can't even count how many hours I
spent with my decorator picking everything out."

"I'm sure Jeff can give you a count of exactly how
many hours you spent when he paid her hefty bill," Tami
said, raising her eyebrows.

Alyson gave her the finger.

"I think there's something freeing about letting someone else do it all," Tami continued. "Think about all the
time you waste just choosing one picture frame—I mean,
in the scheme of the world does it really fucking mat-

ter if it's silver or pewter? Shiny or matte? Etched or plain? All you need is for this decorator fairy to come in, wave his wand around, and voilà! Your whole house is done."

"Frederico's a decorator fairy all right," Ivy giggled.

"For enough money, you can pay anyone to do anything," Alyson said. "But I'd be much more stressed out wondering whether or not I was going to like what he chose. And it's not that hard: silver frame, matte with the etched edge, done."

Even if we could afford to hire a decorator, there was no way I would want someone to pick out every single item in our house. It wasn't about control—which I could tell it might be for Alyson—I didn't want to live in a showcase for someone's latest designs out of the D&D Building. I wanted to fill our home with pieces that we chose ourselves, that meant something to us. Some items we needed to buy new, of course. But I liked the idea of melding the old with the new and having the best of both, like buying a new lamp for our antique desk, one of the few pieces of furniture we'd brought with us from the city—our first big purchase as a couple, scouted at the flea market on Columbus and 77th the weekend we moved in together. Even though the wood was scratched, we fell in love with its curved edges and hand-carved details. Plus, the length couldn't have been more perfect. Aaron tested the drawers and noticed the edges were interlocking dovetail joints: the strongest kind. "Built to last. Just like us," he said, and then he turned to kiss me—a deep, thoughtful kiss that took me by surprise and just about melted me right into the asphalt. There was no way I was ever going to let some decorator tell me that desk wasn't right for our new "decor." It was nice of Ivy to offer, but I knew I wouldn't be calling Frederico.

Alyson took a long gulp of her Amstel and nudged my elbow. "See over there by the window? That's Nikki Thompson, the single mom I told you about. Her son Jayden's in the Threes again this year, the other class. He's got that borderline birthday and she held him back."

In the distance I could make out a woman wearing a long sweater, belted at the waist, smiling up at a good-looking guy with dark wavy hair. I liked her outfit.

"Divorced?" I asked.

"Haven't ever seen a dad at school," Alyson answered. "Or another mom."

Tami said, "We *think* she had IVF from a donor, but no one's really sure. Maybe that's her mystery man. I heard through the grapevine she might be having number two."

"Ooh, I'd love to have one more," Ivy said. "Ruby's turning three soon and every day I get sadder and sadder. She's my *baby*! Drew says no way but I'm not giving up so fast. Another baby and a new kitchen. Is that so much to ask?"

"I would die if I found out I was pregnant again," Tami said. "Another baby? No fucking thank you."

I couldn't believe Tami would say that with Alyson sitting right there! She had to know about Alyson's fertility issues. Or did she? Maybe Alyson was truly keeping the secret to herself, like I had when it happened to me. Or maybe Tami did know and was putting on a front so everyone else wouldn't suspect. I tried to give Alyson an empathetic glance without anyone noticing, but she didn't even look my way, her face a passive mask.

"I told Chris it's time for him to get a vasectomy but he's giving me a ton of pushback," Tami went on. "He says he's scared of the pain and of his balls blowing up like balloons. Which I actually heard does happen, but only for a day or two. So last week, I finally gave him the ultimatum; I said, *I gave birth to three kids and have been on birth control for—I don't know—the better part of twenty years. Now it's your turn.* And then I made an appointment to get my IUD taken out next Thursday and told him after then he's shut out until he gets the snip."

I finished the last drops of my beer. This moms' night out was yielding a lot more information than our usual playdates and coffees. Now I knew that my new friend was withholding sex to convince her husband to get a vasectomy.

"No more sex? You won't last," Alyson said.

"Me? *He* won't last. You'll see, he'll cave. Maybe you could convince Jeff to get one too—they can hold hands and go in and do it together."

A vasectomy for Jeff? Tami was really laying it on thick. Alyson played right along and said, "Yeah, maybe."

Cheryl said, "I don't see what's wrong with an IUD. I have one and I love it."

"I've actually been thinking about getting one," I said, surprising myself for saying so out loud. "But I heard it's uncomfortable."

"Not at all—well, maybe for a few seconds when they put it in—but after you don't even feel it. And then it's wide-open season for five whole years."

"I have one too," said the other Jessica. Or was that Lisa? "What I love is that it's not so final, like the snip is. Just in case you change your mind and want another."

Another pregnancy, another baby—I was with Tami on that one: not interested, not even a little. I was more than happy with two. And now that I was about to hit the thirty-five yard line, there was even more to worry about beyond unexplained miscarriages; there was also Down's syndrome and the heightened risk of autism and gestational diabetes. Maybe there was something in the water to mitigate those worries in Suffern because nearly every family we had met except for Alyson's had three kids. Some families even had four.

"I still don't think birth control should always have to fall on us; not at this point in our lives," Tami pontificated. "Let the man deal with it for once. Now let's do one more for the road and then I'm going home for one of my last good fucks before Chris is shut out."

I barely even flinched anymore hearing those words come out of Tami's mouth. No matter what we were talking about, Tami always found a way to bring up her prolific sex life with Chris. On the kitchen counter, in the front seat of their Suburban, multiple orgasms outside on the swing set—I'd never had a friend who talked about sex so much. My favorite was their forty-eight-hour rule: Tami told us she and Chris have sex every forty-eight hours no matter what. Every forty-eight hours! With Aaron's travel schedule, we were lucky to have sex once a week. And the most creative we'd been in recent memory was having a quickie on the floor in our home office, stopping in the middle to make sure we hadn't hit the power cord and screwed up the computer.

Aaron would have been furious if he found out I'd told my friends what we did together in our most intimate moments. I'd never shared those details with anyone, not even Liza. It had been one thing back in college to trade notes over breakfast about what went on in the sorority house the night before. But bragging about the orgasms your husband gave you . . . to me, that went over the line.

Luckily, part of Tami's candor routine didn't include asking us to dish out our own personal details. I wondered if Chris knew how much she told us, and if he was okay with it. I didn't see him often, though when I did, I couldn't help but think about him in all of those positions, entering her from behind in their new steam shower, hands tied up above his head with her Hermès scarf.

Tami came back to the table with a round of shots. "Drink up, girls," she said.

I wasn't sure if I could do a shot and be able to drive home. But I did only have one beer. Tami doled them out and made a toast: "To kick-ass new jeans."

"To kick-ass new jeans," we all said. How could I not drink to that?

"Ugh, what was *in* that, Tami?" Aly grimaced. "It tasted like turpentine. Next time, please, gimlets or something sweet."

Ten minutes later, I found myself clenching the steering wheel at ten and two, driving at exactly the thirty-mile-per-hour speed limit, praying a cop would not stop me. Maybe I was technically under the influence but I was pretty sure I wasn't DUI drunk; if need be, I could put my finger on my nose and walk in a straight line, no problem. If it ever came to that. It wasn't going to come to that. *Slow and steady, stay right in the lines now.* I never did eat dinner, that must be why I felt so light-headed after just one beer and a shot. But if a cop did stop me, he'd totally have to let me go, a responsible mom. In a pair of hot new jeans.

Despite driving home buzzed, I felt very focused, a more perfect driver than even on my road test. And as I pulled up our driveway, I realized it had been a lot easier than I ever thought it would be.

CHAPTER SEVEN

A FEW WEEKS LATER DURING MY MONDAY-afternoon marketing meeting, Noreen's number flashed up on my phone, but I was right in the middle of explaining to our client on the other end of the speaker box how inserting quotes from the *New York Times* and *Daily News* reviewers in the Radio City Christmas show's advertising could help boost ticket sales during the weeks leading up to Thanksgiving. When sales were slow, it always seemed to be the advertising's fault. And sales were slow.

"'A Beloved Holiday Tradition,' with the subhead 'Bigger and Better Than Ever!' right across the top," I proposed. "We could add a burst with a discount for the weekday performances and promote the offer online through *Playbill*'s e-mail list."

While I waited for the producers' response, Noreen called again. *Shit.* "I'll be back in a sec," I whispered to our graphic designer, and went out to the hallway to take the call.

"Jessica? It's me, Noreen." Her voice sounded shaky. "I have a big problem. I'm here with the girls and just got in a car accident."

I felt my heart stop and drop into my stomach. "Oh my god. Is everyone okay?"

She paused for maybe a second but it felt like an hour. "Everyone's fine but the police are filling out a report and an ambulance is here."

An ambulance! A wave of bricks hit my stomach and I couldn't breathe. *The girls were in a car accident. There's police and an ambulance and I am standing here in a hallway talking on the phone.*

"Where are you, Noreen? What happened? Where's Phoebe? Can she . . . talk?" Tears sprung from my eyes as I imagined the worst, her limp body on a stretcher next to Madison's.

"Hang on a sec," Noreen said. What did she mean, *hang on? I cannot hang on!* In the background I heard the sounds of traffic going by and a few muffled voices and then a man's voice on the phone.

"Hello, Mrs. Almasi? This is Officer Richardson." Authoritative and professional, even-toned. *This is how they tell you,* I thought, *this is how they break it to you.* "There was an accident, a collision at the corner of Spook Rock and Viola. There's extensive front-end damage to your minivan but I wanted to let you know that everything is fine, that your sitter and both your daughters do not appear to be injured. But as a precaution we're going to take them over to the Good Samaritan emergency room."

Mention of the emergency room instantly turned my tears into sobs. "The hospital?" I choked. *If everything is fine, why do you have to take them to the emergency room?*

"Take a breath, ma'am, a deep breath, now. Their car seats seemed to have done their job and kept them safe and strapped in, but it's standard procedure to have a doctor look them over to rule out any internal injuries or head trauma."

Head trauma?! Oh my god.

"The good news is they are up and alert and they want to be with your sitter. She's with them right now. Would you like to speak to—what's your name, little girl? Phoebe?"

A moment later, Phoebe's voice said quietly, "Hi, Mommy."

She could speak, thank god she could speak. She knew I was her mommy and she could speak. I tried my best to put on a cheery voice through my panic for her. "Hi, sweetie, how are you? Are you okay?" *Do you have a headache?*

"Noreen says when we get home we can have ice-cream sundaes."

Ice-cream sundaes—*what the fuck?!* "Wow! What a treat. I'll be there very soon and don't worry, Phoebe, okay? Everything's going to be fine, I promise," I told her to make it true. "I love you."

"I love you too, Mommy."

Her sweet voice made me even more upset.

Officer Richardson got back on the phone. "How long until you can get here, ma'am?"

"I'm in the city—I don't know, an hour?" I felt a million miles away. Should I take a cab? The bus? The train? And, of course, Aaron was away on a business trip in San Francisco, today of all days, San Fran-fucking-cisco on the other side of the country, and his flight wasn't getting in until late that night.

The officer asked if I had a pen to write down a few phone numbers and I sprinted to my office where I scribbled the ambulance cell so I could stay on while they rode the few minutes there, the number of the towing company, and the officer's contact information in case there were any further questions. I grabbed the piece of paper and flew out the door to make the train leaving in seven minutes, trying Aaron's cell on the way. He didn't pick up. "Call me, it's important," I pleaded.

The train felt like it crawled to Suffern. *An accident. I can't believe Noreen got in an accident. With the kids in the car! How could she have* done *that?* The policeman said they were okay and I believed him but I was still filled with the worry of a thousand unknowns. Staying on the phone wasn't enough, I needed to see them, to see with my own eyes they were all in one piece. And now we were stopped on the tracks between Allendale and Ramsey, waiting for a signal ahead of us to change. I wanted to scream.

Would they remember it? I wondered. At seventeen months, Madison was too young—she wouldn't remember anything about it. But at three, Phoebe might. *If I had been there, I would have been driving and this never would have happened.* Or would it? Add driving to the list of goddamned dangers of the suburbs. I just wished Aaron would call me back already. I tried him again.

Maybe one of my friends could get to the hospital before me, to comfort the kids and keep me updated while I was on my way. I tried Alyson but she didn't answer at home or her cell. *Who else, who else?* I scrolled through my contacts. I tried Ivy and she didn't answer. I searched for Tami's contact info and then I saw Alyson was trying to call me back. I told her what had happened and she said she'd leave Emmy with Priya and promised to call me back as soon as she arrived at Good Sam. I let out a shallow exhale, feeling so grateful to have a friend who would drop everything just like that to help me.

I left my car at the emergency room curb and ran into the empty waiting room. The nurse took me right back behind a curtain and thank god there was Madison bouncing playfully on Alyson's hip and Phoebe with the doctor's stethoscope on her ears, giggling at a knock-knock joke. *Banana who?* I rushed up and hugged them, and even though Alyson had reassured me on the way that they were both totally fine, I burst into tears.

Phoebe looked shocked. "You're crying Mommy," she said, and I hugged her even tighter.

"Yes, sweetie, I know, I'm just so happy to see you. I'm crying happy." I wiped my face with my sleeve.

Noreen stood up from her chair looking pale and scared, and between her profuse apologies I hugged her too. "It's okay, it's okay," I repeated, and now that I was there, it was, my angst and anger extinguished by relief.

Dr. Romanello ("Call me Connie") assured me the girls had checked out perfectly, and when I admitted I'd never felt so scared in my life and my hands were literally shaking, she asked if I needed a Xanax. If so, she could give me a few samples and call in a prescription.

"I don't know," I said. Did I look like I needed a Xanax? I had never taken anything like that before; the last thing I wanted was to be zonked out, immobile on the couch.

"You should," Alyson advised. "I mean, it's always good to have for . . . you know, just in case."

So thanks to Alyson and my new BFF, Dr. Connie, I walked out of the hospital with my unscathed children and a handful of little white pill samples tucked in my purse. Minus the two Alyson had asked for.

On the ride back to the house Noreen was mostly quiet. "Are you doing okay?" I asked.

"Forget about me, I'm just so relieved that Phoebe and Madison are okay. I am so, so sorry, Jessica, I really am," she said from the passenger's seat, and told me again how she had both hands on the wheel and more than two car lengths between her and the blue Taurus in front. "I don't think he saw the light was changing and then he slammed on the breaks and I ran right into him, and not even that hard!"

I nodded as she spoke, the twenty-three-year-old girl with bitten-down nails painted purply black who I entrusted with my children every single day. The person who might have gotten them killed. Killed! Was I crazy to let someone who was a total stranger until a few months ago be responsible for my children? Could I still bear to look at her every morning after such a huge fuck-up, even if it wasn't completely her fault? I didn't want to. But I felt like I had to.

"Accidents happen," I said, feeling nauseated as I said it. "But I appreciate how well you handled this, with the police and the ambulance and remembering to call the pediatrician. You must be exhausted." I had no idea how I'd be able to cancel the three meetings on my schedule the next day, but I knew I needed to be home. "Why don't you take the day off tomorrow?"

Noreen looked nervous. "That's really not necessary, Jessica. I'm totally fine."

"That's okay. Take the day to recoup. My treat," I insisted.

The rest of the day and into the evening I snuggled with Phoebe and Madison on the couch, wistful for the days of pushing a stroller to get wherever we needed to go.

I watched them watch TV, noticing their bellies rising and falling with each breath. Two new freckles on Madison's arm; a scrape healing on Phoebe's shin. When did she fall? They spent so many of their waking hours every day with Noreen, not me.

I can't believe I wasn't there today. And my not being there actually caused them harm. It could have been worse, I knew; thank god it wasn't. And I knew there was no way I could ever be with them every single minute to protect them for the rest of their lives. But for now, I had to do better. I had to figure out a way.

I smoothed Phoebe's hair as she watched the puppets on the screen and she promptly pushed my hand away with a "Stop it, I can't see!" I guess she really was fine, back to her normal obstinate self.

When Aaron got home after midnight I gave him the lowdown.

"I do not want the kids driven in a car by anyone except for you and me ever again," was his response.

"Oh come on, Aaron, that's ridiculous—their whole life is being shuttled from one place to another in the car. How do you expect them to get anywhere?" I imagined the neighbors gossiping about us, those crazy parents from the city who no longer let the nanny drive their kids, that weird family under car quarantine who now homeschool their kids and get their annual booster shots by a house-call pediatrician. "We can't hold them hostage in the house. Accidents happen—some guy stopped short in front of her. And it could have been a lot worse; let's just be thankful no one was hurt."

"I cannot even go there," he said. He sat down at the edge of the bed and rubbed the sides of his forehead with his fingers, the way he did when he was upset.

"I know—I worry every minute we're away from them," I said, feeling myself getting choked up again. "But I trust Noreen—we have to. It's the only way this is going to work."

He paused, apparently signaling his agreement. "How much damage to the car?"

"I don't know." I forgot I had to deal with the car tomorrow. "Do you know how much our deductible is?"

"I have to look it up; I think a thousand?"

Shit. "Maybe the repairs will be less and we can just pay out of pocket."

"Well, I would think Noreen would help cover it."

"Are you serious? If it's a thousand dollars, that's practically two weeks pay for her."

"Why the hell would we have to pay if it was her fault?"

I was too exhausted to argue. "I have to go to bed," I mumbled.

The next morning Aaron got dressed for work still complaining about the probable increase to our insurance premium. Alyson proved to be a total lifesaver again, offering Priya to watch the kids while I went to the collision shop where the car had been towed. The front bumper and part of the hood were bent inward, but all in all I didn't think it looked that bad. Boy was I shocked when the mechanic told me the repairs would be close to six thousand dollars.

"Are you serious, for that little dent? Is there any other way?" I asked, but he wouldn't budge and said we were lucky to only have to pay the deductible.

I had to leave the car there for nearly a week to get it fixed and Noreen said she could use her own car to take the girls to and from school and their playdates and classes. When Aaron asked me if I'd spoken to Noreen about contributing toward our costs, I told him that we'd be needing to look for a new nanny if we ever brought it up with her and I certainly didn't have time for that right now.

So, by the time that week's moms' coffee break rolled around, I needed to vent. "It's so frustrating that Aaron can't get it through his head why I won't ask Noreen for money to help cover the repairs."

We were sitting at our corner booth at the diner against the wide windows decorated with cling-on turkeys and cornucopias. Looking out on the busy Route 59 intersection, I saw cars following their morning choreography—left arrow, green, go, and then stop—marveling at how the giant masses of moving metal narrowly missed hitting each other every time.

Carolann took a sip of her tea and said, "I don't know, Jessica, I can see why he'd be upset. I mean she *was* the one driving your car. She should be responsible to pay *something,* don't you think?"

"No. I don't think so at all," I answered, surprised to hear that she felt this way. "Driving the kids is part of what's required for her work. Why would she think she's responsible to pay for something that happened on the job?"

"Plus, there's no way she could ever afford to pay," Tami said, backing me up.

Carolann persisted: "I think she could at least offer you a token to show how sorry she is for crashing your car. It's the principle, not necessarily the amount."

"How much of a token?" Tami asked. "Even a hundred dollars would be a lot of money to her, to any nanny. If it was me and my nanny offered to pay, there's no way I would take it. I think it sets up a weird precedent. If by accident she broke a glass or a vase or something in the house, it's not like I would ask her to replace it."

"But this is a car. *Your* car. It's not a glass: it's a thousand dollars. That is a lot of money for you to have to shell out for her mistake," Carolann said.

She wasn't getting it. "I don't think she feels obligated to pay anything at all. Nor should she," I said, moving my fork around my half-eaten omelet. "Although she did push me almost to my limit yesterday: she asked for gas money, for driving the kids in her car for the week."

"Jessica! She did *not* ask you for gas money!" Carolann cried.

"I gotta give it to her, that nanny has one hefty set of balls," Tami said. "I like her even more now."

"I thought it was pretty cheesy of her to ask," I said. "Even though we didn't discuss the details in front of her, she had to know we had an expensive week. If Aaron ever found out, he would totally blow a gasket. No pun intended, now that I know what a gasket is."

"On the bright side, at least you didn't have to get a rental car," Ivy said.

"Well, you didn't give her the money, Jessica, did you?" Carolann asked.

"Of course I gave it to her." *You are so maddeningly*

naive, I wanted to say. *She's taking care of my kids! Of course I want to keep her happy.*

"You could shave some off her Christmas bonus," Carolann said.

I'd really had enough of Carolann. Except for kids at the same preschool, we had little, if anything, in common. But she'd been friends with Alyson and Tami way before I came along. Except for my growing annoyance with Carolann, I loved going to the Friday-morning coffees; I couldn't make most of the in-class story hours and birthday lunches and felt like I needed that hour of female friend time to connect with the home and school world I was away from most of the week. It was true that most of our conversations were of the lighter variety, but they were good people and I was entitled to a little mindless fun once in a while. I felt lucky for my Fridays at home and my Suffern mom friends—I just wished I didn't have to spend my limited amount of free time hanging out with Carolann.

"It still kills me Aaron was away and missed the whole thing," I said, deciding to ignore her last comment. "Alyson, I can't thank you enough again for meeting me at the hospital, for *everything.* I couldn't have made it through that awful day without you." Yesterday I had flowers and a jumbo gift basket from Bliss delivered, but it barely felt like enough.

"I told you before, it's not a big deal," Alyson said, and I thought I saw her shoot a sideways look at Tami. Was she annoyed by my gift? She hadn't mentioned whether it had arrived.

"Well, um, anyway, thanks again," I said, trying to shake off her chill. "And I know it's silly but I'm still pissed at Aaron for not being there on the most stressful day of my life."

"Believe me, babe, I know how you feel," Ivy said. "Drew misses like half of our lives being away for work. Two weeks ago he phoned in from Paris on Tanner's birthday. I wanted us to go on a family vacation, maybe to Disney the week between Christmas and New Year's, but he's been working on some big deal and his schedule is so up in the air, it's impossible to make any plans. He's back in London right now and I'm alone with the kids until Sunday night. I'm fine during the week but the weekends really stink."

"You don't have weekend help?" Alyson asked.

"My mother-in-law is coming in tomorrow from the shore and staying over. She's great with the kids but then I have to deal with entertaining *her* all weekend. I wish my mother lived closer than a five-hour plane ride."

"You're on FaceTime with her like six times a day—for all intents and purposes, she's here," Alyson said.

Six times a *day*? My parents barely kept their weekly scheduled Sunday-night call, always running from tennis to bridge night and even spur-of-the-moment cruises to nowhere when the price was right. I was glad they were so busy living it up in Florida but it hurt me more than I'd like to admit that they didn't visit more often. They flew in once a year; we went to visit them every December for a few days before the flight and hotel prices went through the roof, and that was it. They seemed perfectly content with their distance and maybe that's what bothered me: it was the same distance I'd often felt in our house growing up. As an only child, I'd had more than my share of stuff: a room filled with board games and records and a stockpile of stuffed animals on my canopy bed. But most weekends I found myself pawned off at one friend's house or another while my parents played golf at their club, rounds of eighteen that rolled into cocktails and inevitably dinner as the phone would ring and I'd overhear, *Yes, we have plenty, she's welcome to stay,* my place at the table already set. Somehow I'd always thought that once they saw the adorable little faces of their next generation they'd feel that inexplicable grandparent bond I'd read so much about, that they'd be jumping on a plane any chance they could to spend time with Phoebe and Madison and mean something more than the smiling photo on the grandparent page in the *Who Loves You* book. Not the case so far. On their infrequent visits, Phoebe and Madison usually stiffened and cried at the sight of them, strangers invading with strong perfume and loud voices bearing presents with hundreds of tiny chokable pieces.

"FaceTime's not the same as seeing my mother in person," Ivy said. "I really miss her."

I noticed Tami looking down, typing on her cell phone, and immediately remembered Tami's mother wasn't around to miss in Arizona or Florida or anywhere anymore. It had to be excruciating for her to sit there listening to Ivy, and I took Tami's rare silence as a sign that she was hurting.

I searched the faces around the table to see if I was the only one who sensed her discomfort. Ivy was certainly oblivious. "Well, if we don't end up going away, maybe she'll fly in for Christmas. And as far as this weekend goes, I'm hoping Drew's mother can take the kids to the movies on Saturday afternoon so I can get a break.

Maybe even a manicure." She looked down at her fingers. "I know it's crazy but Drew has been overseas so much lately, sometimes I swear he's keeping another family there."

Tami looked up from her phone and said plainly, "I read an article in *People* the other day about a woman whose husband was traveling to Brazil on business a lot and it turned out he *did* actually have another family there—a wife and two sons."

"Oh, that is so not funny," Ivy said, and her face started to fall as the real possibility sank in.

Tami shrugged. "Shit happens when they're on the road." She glanced out the window, looking almost satisfied. And I started to see how with the skill of a surgeon, Tami took pleasure in slicing just deep enough to expose the pain and fears in others so she didn't have to feel it herself. She'd dig and jab and then right before you cried out she'd somehow convince you her blood-letting was what you needed to heal. It must have been how she stayed strong, how she barreled through.

Then Tami turned her focus to me. "I don't know, Jess, Aaron seems like he travels a lot too . . ."

For a second I felt defensive—could she seriously be insinuating that Aaron might be cheating on me? But I wasn't going to let myself be her next patient. "Yeah, right—I doubt Aaron's keeping a secret family out in San Francisco, the housing's *way* too expensive there," I said, and Tami laughed. "But that's where all of the tech VCs are, so he does have to go there a lot. He mentioned the other day his company might be buying out another web-mail company based in New York, so if that happens, he'll be in town more."

"Still, it must get lonely," Tami said.

"It does sometimes," I admitted, surprised at how good it felt to say so out loud.

"Although, honestly, don't you think it's almost easier when they're away?" Ivy continued. She certainly was resilient. Either that or a little more clueless than I'd thought. "When Drew *is* in town, it's so annoying how he always seems to find a way to walk in the door right as the kids are about to fall asleep. And then they're up for another hour."

Aaron always did that. "I know, it's like they're negative help," I said, but didn't mention that on the nights when Aaron was able to come home early, he had a way of making bedtime a lot more fun.

"Helping, not helping, home, away, whatever," Tami said. "Get yourself out and busy and find things to make yourself happy instead of sitting around complaining."

Tami had to be directing that comment to Ivy, not me. I wasn't a complainer, not usually, although with Aaron and the accident I had been the one who kicked off that morning's round of husband-bashing. But I certainly wasn't idle, every morning out racing, lugging, driving, diving, and ducking out of the way of low-hanging branches. My moods waxed and waned with the on-time trains and the people around me, whose tummy hurt and the software glitch in the website rollout and the typo someone didn't catch until after the flyers went to print. I tried to do what those mom-zine articles recommended, to fall asleep counting all the little things I should be grateful for, clean water and having enough to eat and two children who weren't injured, thank god, in a crash that left my car a mangled mess.

"What would really make me happy is more sleep," I said to try to lighten the mood.

Tami said, "What's been making *me* really happy lately is the Neutrogena Rejuvenator."

"What, like Neutrogena soap?" Alyson asked.

"No—it's the battery-operated facial cleanser. But you don't use it on your face. I swear, I can come with that thing in less than a minute, it's so fast."

That wasn't exactly the making-yourself-happy I thought Tami had been referring to.

"It's got that perfect purr and whirr and before you know it—*bam*, you're right there," she explained. "Plus you can keep it in your drawer and if your cleaning person finds it they think it's just something from the bathroom. I'm surprised you all don't have one yet: Chris has been spreading the word like gonorrhea to all the husbands around Suffern. I think he loves it so much because he's a lazy shit. But for once I'm glad he's lazy, I barely need him anymore now that I've got my new friend in hand."

"You are too much, Tami, honestly," Ivy said, blushing.

"Get yourself one, Ivy, and you'll be good to go even if Drew's traipsing around Europe."

"I *wish* Jeff would travel more," Alyson said.

"I would think the more Jeff's home the better your chances are to . . ." I almost slipped and said *make a baby*. Alyson's eyes widened. ". . . win the election," I said quickly. "It sounds like there's so much to do, so much on your plate with organizing everything for all of those fundraisers. You must be swamped."

Alyson kept a stiff angry lip and didn't say anything.

"We could send Jeff and Chris on a trip somewhere," Tami suggested. "Like Antarctica."

It would be hard to have sex every forty-eight hours from Antarctica, I thought. But knowing Tami and the wonders of Skype and with her new facial cleanser vibrator, she'd probably figure out a way.

"That's one way to get out of party planning," Alyson mumbled.

I noticed Carolann was caught in a stare out the diner window with the disgusted puss on her face that appeared every time Tami launched into one of her sex discussions. I didn't know Carolann's husband Peter well—she barely ever mentioned him, good, bad, or otherwise. The one time I sat next to him at a couples' dinner he talked about an ATV he was thinking about trading in for a new one and it took me more than a minute to figure out it wasn't "a TV" as in "a television," it was one of those four-wheel vehicles people drive on dirt roads. After my second glass of wine I was tempted to ask him if he was making room to park it in his nuclear-meltdown room, but then the main course came and I lost my nerve.

Carolann asked, "Is anyone interested in hosting the next Maliblu party?"

No one responded.

"You guys know Maliblu, that new peer-to-peer clothing line out of California? Jessica, you missed the party at my house last week but I'm looking for a few more hosts for the spring line."

"Sorry, but I'm way too swamped right now," I said, and then added tentatively, "You have to be careful with those home businesses. I had a friend who got roped into one back in college, selling a water filtration system. It all sounded good when she started but she had to put all this cash up front for the equipment and the sales materials and ended up losing a ton. When you look into it, a lot of these companies are set up like pyramid schemes."

Carolann pushed her glasses up the bridge of her nose. "Well, that is *not* how Maliblu works, Jessica."

Maybe I didn't like Carolann that much, but it infuriated me how these companies preyed on stay-at-home moms looking to make a quick buck. "Most of the time you can tell if something's fishy if they're holding onto your profits. Like the money from your last party—are they keeping it to cover your costs for the next season's clothes? If so, something might be up. Another sign is if they're not paying you out any cash until you find hosts for the next parties. That's the pyramid part."

Carolann stood up abruptly, threw two singles on the table, and announced, "I have to go."

"I just don't want to see you get hurt," I called after her, and I thought I meant it.

As the door swung shut Alyson said, "You didn't have to be so harsh, Jessica. Carolann's excited about working with Maliblu—they're expanding to the East Coast and she might be one of their team leaders."

"On commission, I'm guessing," I said under my breath.

"I'm not sure how it works exactly but Peter still hasn't found a job and, well, Carolann is very sensitive about money."

I had forgotten about Peter's work troubles and suddenly felt terrible. "I was just trying to be helpful."

"Maybe next time, try not to be so helpful," Alyson said brusquely, and gave me the same dismissive look I'd seen her give Emmy after she misbehaved.

Alyson had been so nice this week, helping me after

the accident. What button I had just pushed to switch her into mean-mode, I still didn't know—I felt like I was right back at the middle school lunch table with the cool girls from study hall. I thought they had invited me; I gave up my free period and switched around my schedule so I could eat with them, but when I sat down I saw one give the other that look—*What's she doing here?* I knew I had made a mistake, a bad mistake, but I didn't know how to fix it so I sat there gnawing on my cream cheese and jelly sandwich while everyone else ate tater tots and giggled about the bulge in the Spanish teacher's pants.

"I think Carolann might have actually made some money from Maliblu," Ivy said, breaking the awkward silence. "But it's always smart to look into these things to make sure they're legit."

I took a sip of my cold coffee to keep down the lump in my throat and tried to thank Ivy with a blink of my eyes.

Alyson ignored Ivy's comment and glanced at her watch. "I have to get to my core fusion class. Are you coming, Tam?" Sometimes she asked me if I wanted to join, but not today.

"You might have to drag my ass off the floor when I'm done, but yeah, I could use a good sweat," Tami said. "See you around, Jess."

CHAPTER EIGHT

I DIDN'T SEE MUCH OF THE MOMS over the next few weeks. With the holiday break and our annual trip to Florida to visit my parents, we were all busy with our families and out of our regular school routines.

I still felt lousy about what I'd said to Carolann and started several apology e-mails that sat languishing in my drafts: ~~Dear Carolann,~~ Hi Carolann, *Remember what I said about Maliblu in the diner?* ~~I didn't mean~~ *I'm sorry if I hurt your feelings.* They all sounded so trite. And so after-the-fact. If I was going to say I was sorry, I should have done it that day, or at least later that week—especially if I had known that once the New Year hit I'd be completely slammed at work and wouldn't have a moment free to worry about apologizing to Carolann or much of anything else outside the breakneck pace of deadlines coming from my office.

Two of the three new Broadway shows our agency took on ended up on my plate, including a new musical by an emerging producer-director, Marco Vera Cruz. Marco was known to be a raging egomaniac who thought the only good advertising ideas were the ones that came out of his own mouth—typical for most producers, but Marco was among the breed's most demanding. My boss

Sybil told me in no uncertain terms that keeping Marco happy—no, not happy, *ecstatic,* she had said—was my new top priority. If all went well with this first show, he could turn into a very big client. And it was up to me to make sure that happened.

With that directive, I found myself working more hours than I had in years. And to add to my misery, the only time Marco had open for our weekly status conference call was Friday mornings at the exact same time as my moms' coffee. I didn't have to be at the meetings in person, thank god, but as those cold January weeks ticked by, I became more and more bummed to be missing my once-a-week girlfriend gathering. I even started to miss being annoyed with Carolann.

Michelle had reached out to me a few times after we met at Carolann's party in the fall, but with her wellness center taking off like a rocket and my crazy schedule, it was our nannies who ended up getting together with the kids, not us. I had missed the Unami opening and felt bad that I still hadn't stopped by, but I subscribed to their e-newsletter and enjoyed scrolling through the pictures of women balancing on tightropes in their mittens and hats, cheeks flushed and ruddy with winter sweat. *One of these days*, I promised myself.

One night on my way home late from the train station Noreen texted me: *we r out of diapers*. Again. No matter how many stock-up trips we took to Costco, we always seemed to run out of diapers. In the city it had been no big deal, even late at night—we'd just walk down the block to the twenty-four-hour Duane Reade and grab another pack along with a decaf cappuccino from the corner café. Not so now. Once, in the middle of the night, in a truly desperate moment, I found myself out of Madison's diapers when she had the runs and like MacGyver, I made my own diaper with a plastic bag, some duct tape, and a maxi pad.

Noreen had been on her best behavior in the months since the accident but remained at the top of Aaron's shit list. He was still mad, not only about the money but the fact that she was still driving our kids around every day. I tried to explain how much we needed Noreen, how critical she was to keeping our two-parents-working-in-the-city lives even remotely doable. Not to mention how much Phoebe and Madison liked her. But that didn't sway him—once he made up his mind about something or someone it was near impossible to change it back.

Noreen was going to have to step it up and help me not only manage the diaper and wipes inventory but also baby shampoo, another essential that always seemed to run out in the middle of bath time. The one instance when I'd tried to surreptitiously substitute our shampoo for their usual No More Tears formula resulted in both girls screaming, "My eyes, my eyes!" loud enough for Children's Services to hear.

I sighed as I turned into the CVS parking lot; there was always so much to keep track of. Most of the time, I felt like I had it under control, more or less. As long as I wrote it down, it usually got done, eventually—flu shot appointments, snow boots, a throw rug for our room, toddler underwear, toothpaste, finger paints, buying and mailing an anniversary card for Aaron's parents, ordering the *Hands Are Not for Hitting* book. But in the midst of my recent work deluge, more often than not I found myself making my weekly list and then losing it, not for the life of me remembering even half of the important and not-so-important tasks I had written down. I was beginning to feel like the somewhat-organized working-mom life I was trying to lead was held together by a pen and a thread and a Post-it note.

One thing that had fallen off the list lately was a date night. I had hoped Aaron and I might be able to meet up in the city to grab a bite after work sometimes before heading home together, but his company had recently acquired a competing software provider with a huge client base and his office moved to a bigger space, downtown on Franklin Street in Tribeca. Aaron was promoted to managing director, a big step for his career, but now he was working a zillion more hours and his commute was up to almost ninety minutes, and often more, with traffic. Even when he wasn't traveling he got home very late—ten, even some nights after eleven. He was turning into a weekend dad. And a weekend husband. He promised it was temporary, that in a few months, once the dust had settled and operations were running smoothly, he wouldn't have to be in the office as much or as late. And while I was thrilled his company was doing so well and the payouts he had been promised for so many years were finally starting to come in, I would have traded that money to see him more.

At CVS I was in luck: one pack of Cruisers left on the shelf in Madison's size. On my way to the checkout line I walked past the deodorant and shaving cream and contact lens solution and did a mental scan of our medicine cabinet to figure out if we needed anything else. The whole center aisle had been besieged by Valentine's Day paraphernalia—red and pink and silver Mylar balloons

next to stuffed bears and bunnies and puppy dogs, bins of
Sweethearts begging *HUG ME* and *BE MINE* and bags
upon bags of red and silver Hershey's Kisses. Russell Sto-
ver chocolate hearts, from giant to jumbo sized, wrapped
in shiny hopeful cellophane. Even ChapStick had a special love-potion cherry flavor.

I wondered what, if anything, Aaron might have
planned. I hadn't made a reservation for dinner anywhere
and doubted he had, either. We had always agreed that
Valentine's Day, like New Year's Eve, was an overblown
holiday—not worth paying extra for the crappy prix fixe
menu. But you still wanted that kiss at midnight even if
you were home watching *Dick Clark's New Year's Rockin'
Eve*. And while I no longer needed a fancy dinner out on
Valentine's Day, I still longed for that token, or card, or
bouquet. Even the Whitman Sampler wasn't looking half
bad. Next to the chocolate I spied a stack of boxes of
those tiny cards I used to tuck into my classmates' decorated Valentine's mailboxes in elementary school, carefully choosing the night before which boy would get the
kitty cat declaring he was the *Purr-fect Valentine*. Even
though I knew Phoebe and Madison were too young to
really appreciate it, I picked up two Winnie-the-Pooh Valentines and planned to stop at the Italian bakery for special Valentine cupcakes before the big day.

At the end of the aisle was a gigantic display of a
beautiful woman with an airbrushed clear complexion,
smiling while cleaning her face with a tool that looked
something like an electric toothbrush. *Introducing the
new Neutrogena Rejuvenator. As Effective As a Professional Facial in Your Very Own Home!*

There it was, Tami's new sex toy, on sale for $29.99. I

didn't own a vibrator, I'd always been too shy to buy one. But like Tami had said, this was a facial cleanser. And Aaron was traveling . . .

Just as I was about to casually take a box off the end of the display, I spotted Ivy's husband Drew right in front of me putting one in his basket.

"Looking for that just-had-a-facial feeling, Drew?" I teased, squeezing his arm from behind.

"Hey, Jessica," he said, looking as embarrassed as if he was fifteen and I had caught him buying condoms.

I know what you'll be doing tonight, I thought. Lucky Ivy. I hadn't had a chance to grab one and unfortunately it was too late now.

"Ivy has you out running errands?" I offered my most innocent smile.

"Yeah, a long list," he said, waving a handwritten note. "You're all dressed up." He eyed my skirt. "Going out on a date?"

"Yeah, right, a date. Coming from the office. Aaron's on the road, yet again. I'm surprised to see you're in town."

"All week."

"We should make plans for dinner one night, the four of us. If we could ever get our schedules to align. Maybe this Friday even," I thought out loud.

"I'd love that. But I'll see you tonight at Jeff and Alyson's party, right? Save you a spot in the hot tub."

Alyson had e-mailed me a half hour ago to confirm I had this weekend's ballet pickup covered and hadn't mentioned anything about a party.

I hesitated and then babbled, "No, uh, I can't make it tonight. My sitter has to go to a class and Aaron's away and I have a meeting tomorrow morning that I have to be up early for."

"That's too bad. Their annual winter fiesta's always a great time. Let me know about that Friday dinner, *Joanna*." He grinned at our little wrong-name private joke, giving me shit from our first meeting, and then leaned in and gave me his usual double-cheek kiss goodbye.

My mind raced as I stood in the line to pay. Maybe it was just a small group and that's why we weren't invited—it wasn't as if we socialized with them every waking moment. But what had Drew called it, their *winter fiesta*? That sounded like a party to me. What if it was a bash, a huge catered affair, and for some reason we were left off the list?

I walked outside with my bag and a raw wind hit my face. I zipped up my jacket and wished I could press a button and fast-forward to spring.

An hour later during bath time, I sighed to Phoebe and Madison, "I am going to ask you nicely one more time," but they kept splashing each other with the remaining inch of water left in the tub. I said louder, "Why is it that no one hears me unless I raise my voice? One, two, TWO AND A HALF . . ." and they finally got the message and scrambled up and into their butterfly-hooded towels with terry antennae.

"I wanna watch TV! Pleeaaasse, you promised," Phoebe whined.

"TV! TV!" Madison echoed. At eighteen months, *TV* was one of Madison's favorite words. *TV and a cookie, Mommy?* I had to stop letting them watch so much.

"No TV! It's after eight thirty already, way past your

bedtime." Way too late to just be finishing their baths, but it was my fault for not getting started earlier. "Pajamas, book, teeth, bed. That's IT." How little fun I sounded as those words from the female generations before me now channeled through my own lips and passed on to remain dormant in my daughters until a tired bath time thirty years in their future. I wanted to be more fun, to imprint bubble beards and play dress-up and snuggle under the covers, but after three days in a row of putting the girls to bed by myself, I was completely wiped out and depleted of even my backup supply of patience.

After they were finally asleep, I started to get ready for bed. Through the bathroom window I could see dollops of snow starting to stick to the grass; six to eight inches were due by morning. How was I going to manage to dig out in time to make the train? And would Noreen be able to make it over to watch the kids? I wished for once I was the one out to dinner with investors at the Four Seasons in Chicago and Aaron was the one left home to deal.

Contacts out and the remnants of the day's mascara wiped clean with an Eye-Q pad with moisturizing formula promising to keep the delicate skin around my eyes young and smooth. I studied the small lines starting to form at the corners. Only in full smile did you actually see them, I tested, as well as an extra line or two around my mouth where my smile had been. *Why wasn't I invited to Alyson's tonight?* She couldn't still be angry about that day at the diner. We hadn't seen each other a lot lately, come to think of it, but when I did run into her, she didn't seem mad. Maybe Drew had it wrong. Who has a party on a Wednesday night?

If only I hadn't run into Drew. If Noreen had remembered to buy the diapers herself that afternoon, I'd be blissfully unaware of any party that might or might not be happening that I may or may not have been invited to.

I stared at my pale winter face in the mirror. I wish I'd bought that Rejuvenator—for its intended use, if nothing else. In high school I used to whip up elaborate masques from *Seventeen* magazine. *Ingredients Found Right in Your Kitchen!* My favorite was raw egg whites, frothed on my oily "t-zone" forehead, nose, and chin; then, lightly beaten yolks rubbed in circles on my cheeks and dabbed lightly under my eyes with my fourth finger only, as instructed. After fifteen minutes the crusty egg layer would crack and reveal lines on my cheeks, a prescient map, quickly washed away with a cool water rinse, leaving my skin taut and smooth and, I hoped, on my way to beautiful. My skin, my face—it was still the same as my teenage me, the same but older and getting older by the day. *The snow will be accumulating an inch an hour.*

I grabbed my tweezers and plucked an errant gray hair peeking out from my side part and hunted for any other strands of brown starting to turn. I hated finding the long, witchy ones lurking in the back where I couldn't see. I didn't want to start coloring my hair; I wanted to look natural. But I also didn't want to look old and gray. Or with stripes in my hair, like Carolann. *I'm sure she was invited; why not me?*

I put on my robe and slippers and went downstairs. The light cast night shadows on the still-bare walls, waiting for me to fill them with carefully selected art and mirrors and professional family portraits I'd had no time to book. I stepped into the kitchen and thought I heard something, a bang from the basement and a brush or a rustle from underneath the floor. *It's just the heat turning on,* I told myself. That or another field mouse—that's what they call them out here, field mice, *aren't they cute?* But I didn't think so; country mice and chipmunks scampering across the stones of the patio scared the evening bejeezus out of me, along with the rest of the nighttime creatures surrounding us in the woods. But what if the groans from the floorboard were something else, someone lurking, waiting for that perfect unsuspecting moment to jump out and strangle me? All the way out here, who would hear me scream?

I flipped on all the lights and told myself to stop watching cop shows, to get my mind busy and go through the pile of papers and junk mail accumulating on the kitchen counter. Orange & Rockland Utilities: $986. For one month! Our heating bills this winter had been positively shocking. Gymboree sign-up for Madison, coupons for an oil change. I just didn't have the energy to decide what to sort and what to toss.

And then I heard the unmistakable sound of dance music coming from outside. I opened the patio door and sure enough, through the falling flakes a loud bass beat blared from Alyson and Jeff's backyard, sharp and clear in the frozen night with only the bare trees between our houses. A spike of laughter and a splash and a chorus of playful female screams. It was definitely a party, a Wednesday-night hump-day hot tub special. "Turn it up!" I heard Tami's voice shout. *Everybody dance now.* Everybody but me.

After months of playdates and nights out and countless hours of pretty intimate momversations, I had thought we were friends. Okay, so maybe none of them were my perfect match. But we were more than proximity friends, weren't we? More than just there for the kids and the carpools after school. I'm out of the loop for a few short weeks and now I'm Jessica on the list with a big fat *L for Loser* next to my name? Or even worse, just forgotten?

I didn't want to care. I didn't want to be in my thirties and still mired in petty friend shit paranoia. But they were my only friends in Suffern and I needed them, not only with pickups and drop-offs and to be there in the ER with me, but also to hang out with, to talk to and share with, and to let loose on occasion when the daily grind wore me thin. To help me feel included in the social scene of a town I still felt like I hadn't fully settled into after all these months, one foot always running for the train. *Give it time,* Liza had told me when we first moved, *it takes time to find your place.* I thought I had found it in an easy walk next door but I couldn't help wondering if I didn't know these women as well as I thought; maybe I was the tagalong they rolled their eyes at when I left the table, and now that I wasn't around as much it was a convenient time to dump me.

Tiny pellets of ice hit my cheeks and I let them sting; I wanted it to hurt for being so stupid to think all this time they might have actually liked me.

I needed a dose of old-friend comfort, that deep-down connection only possible with someone who's known you for a long time. It had literally been months since Liza and I had seen each other and I missed her terribly. She had been away on a vacation in Utah skiing with Richard and the boys and then jetted off to Asia for work, always traveling to exotic locales to source trends and check on production for her latest designs. I remembered our last e-mail exchange, trying to pick a date to meet up for lunch. She might be back now. I went inside and dialed her number and was thankful to hear her voice.

"Hey, Jess, how's it going?"

"Shitty," I said. "Aaron's been away for three days and I'm totally burnt. And my hair is turning gray. How are you?"

"Jess, I am so sorry but I can't really talk right now." Voices bubbled up in the background and I heard someone giggle. "I'm running out the door meeting some friends down at The Standard and I'm late. Can I give you a call tomorrow, or maybe Friday?"

"Yeah, sure, call me tomorrow," I said and hung up, feeling worse than before, like I was stuck in a remote penitentiary deep in the Yukon. When it snowed in Manhattan, life went on, people went out, even more awakened by the novelty of the cold white blanket. I wished I was out with Liza and her friends downtown, out in life, infused with energy in the place I used to be, with people who wanted to be with me.

I opened the dishwasher to unload but it was too soon and the hot steam hit my face. Burning my fingers, I took the dishes out anyway and then crawled upstairs to bed.

CHAPTER NINE

WE NEED YOUR HELP!!! THE MASS GUILT E-MAIL from the Laurel Meadow PTA shouted in my inbox a couple of days later, and for once I didn't automatically press delete.

Parent volunteers were desperately needed to help solicit items for the upcoming school auction less than two months away. If we didn't hit our donations goal, the e-mail warned, the school was in danger of not raising the $25,000 it needed to cover essentials for our kids like playground equipment and assistant teachers in each class.

I hadn't volunteered even one minute for the school all year. My working-mom alibi was more than legitimate, but all the parents had been told we were expected to do our share, and so far my only share had been the required once-a-month gluten-free pretzels for snack time, and when our turn had come around I'd even forgotten to buy those.

Tami may have talked a big game about trying to be involved as little as possible but there she was, *VP of Party Planning,* with Alyson right underneath *Carolann, Auction Chairperson.* Was my lack of school involvement one of the reasons for my missing hot tub party invite?

That would be insane. But not completely out of the realm of mom-pressure possibility.

Twenty-five grand did seem like a boatload of money for our little preschool to raise. A moment later I found myself e-mailing Carolann with an offer to help, at least with a donation of a few pairs of theater tickets.

Great! she immediately wrote back. *Come to the auction meeting next Thursday night.*

Somehow, by the end of that meeting and half a carafe of white sangria (*Bar options taste test!* Tami had insisted), I had signed up to be cohead of donations with Ivy. Carolann handed us a list of the past donors and items, restaurant gift certificates and high-end vacation stays and spa treatments and kids' mini-golf birthday parties packaged with pizza and balloons and three hundred other donations we were responsible for soliciting. As I flipped through the single-spaced, ten-page list, I knew no matter how lonely or guilty I might have been feeling, adding this huge job to my already overloaded schedule was one of the worst remedies I could come up with.

For two weeks straight, I stayed up well past midnight doing my penance, typing donation-request e-mails and writing up package descriptions for the catalog. Aaron couldn't believe the number of hours I was putting in (*For the preschool? Really?*), but I found myself starting to enjoy the challenge of hunting down the decision-makers and turning their maybes into yeses. Twenty dollars' worth of lunches at Subway? No problem. Liza said she'd donate one of her limited-edition Kate Spade totes. I called in a huge favor with Marco's company manager for a private backstage tour to go along with a pair of opening-night tickets and felt like I was on a roll.

But my donation-garnering skills were nothing compared to Ivy's—she'd walk into a store holding her daughter Ruby's hand and flash a smile, asking if they would please consider donating a gift certificate to help support the education of tomorrow's future? No one could say no to her.

I almost mentioned the hot tub party one afternoon when I was picking up Phoebe from a playdate at Alyson's but I knew there was little upside to pressing for the truth about my missing invite. She seemed a little distracted that day anyway, snapping at Priya for not folding the towels just so. I decided it was best to chalk it all up to an oversight versus a blatant snub and finally let it go.

Besides, I didn't want anyone to think my new fervor for volunteerism might not be rooted in anything but the purest of altruistic intentions. So I continued my experiment of how few hours I could actually sleep and still function—finding out after a brief yet brutal bout of bronchitis that the answer was five—and convinced myself it was all worth it to feel included again.

Valentine's Day fell on a Saturday and when we asked Phoebe where she wanted to eat, she said Firehouse. I couldn't believe she had even remembered it.

Back when we lived in the city, whenever we asked her where we should go out to dinner she always picked Firehouse, a bar-restaurant located a few blocks from our apartment—probably because she got to play with real dough while waiting for her personal pan pizza and the waitress always hung up her crayon-colored masterpieces on the wall behind the bar. Pre-Phoebe, it had also been one of Aaron and my favorite spots, the place where our coed football team used to squeeze around an outdoor

table crowded with hot wings and cheese fries and pitchers of Bud Light to dull our weekend-warrior pain, reliv-
ing the incredible plays of the day and feeling lucky to be
buzzed and bruised on a Sunday afternoon with nowhere
else to be but right there.

Even though it meant a drive back into the city on
a nonwork day, we hadn't been back to our old neighborhood since we moved. And while Firehouse wasn't
exactly the white-tableclothed, slightly more upscale Valentine's dinner I was hoping for, I was excited Phoebe had
picked it—and especially thankful she hadn't chosen her
current favorite restaurant, Chuck E. Cheese.

We found a spot at a broken meter two blocks up,
and when we walked in I wondered if we had made a
mistake in coming. While the rest of the restaurants we
had passed were already crowded with dressed-up couples dining together, Firehouse was empty except for a
few men at the bar peering up at the Knicks game. As I
was about to suggest redirecting to Patsy's Pizzeria down
the block instead, Aaron must have seen the look on my
face and said, "It's way early, Jess. And look, we can pick
any table we want."

Phoebe picked a booth in the back. We ordered two
Miller Lites and two Shirley Temples, "With four cher-
ries!" said Phoebe, and we put in for the girls' pizza. Big-
screen TVs played sports from every sightline and real
fire helmets and jackets hung on the walls—nothing had
changed a bit, which was comforting but also slightly un-
settling to me. "It feels funny being back here," I said.
"Almost like we never left."

Aaron nodded, looking down in the menu. "Should I
get the chicken burrito or the burger?"

I sighed; I wasn't in the mood for bar fare. But I found one of my old favorites on the menu, the buffalo chicken salad and a side of cheesy waffle fries. While the girls started coloring their firedog sheets, I took a sip of beer and started to relax.

"I feel like I haven't seen you," I said to Aaron.

"You're seeing me now," he responded with a wry smile. "Hi."

I noticed he hadn't shaved. Not that it mattered for a dinner like this, but he had a few days of scruff going and his eyes looked a little more tired than usual. Maybe it was the dim lighting. "Are you thinking about growing out your beard again?"

"My beard? I don't know," he said, and bent over to retrieve Madison's fallen yellow crayon.

"You should." I liked it when Aaron grew a beard: a short one, groomed close to his skin. A beard added a shade of sexy to his boy-next-door cuteness. As long as he didn't shave it into another goatee. The summer after Phoebe was born he had decided to try one out, and I hated how the hairy outline turned his smile sinister, like a villain in a Saturday-morning cartoon.

His eyes drifted to the basketball game behind my head. "He shoots, he scores!"

"He scores!" Phoebe echoed, and then held up her scribbled-in coloring sheet. "Daddy, what do you think?"

"I love it, cutie, I love it."

Madison was still concentrating on her drawing and I was amazed how carefully she was able to keep the colors in the lines. "Keep it up, Maddie," I encouraged her, and reached over to steal a cherry from her drink.

Aaron and I talked through a few house items including the three a.m. research I had finally completed for some more reasonably priced possibilities for our still-not-purchased outdoor grill. "We have to put in an order soon if we want to have everything in place by June."

"We have to decide *now* for June?"

"I know, but if we still want to use Jeff's stone guy we have to get on his schedule. You wouldn't believe how busy these stone guys get once the spring hits. At least that's what Alyson told me. Have you talked to Jeff lately?"

"He keeps e-mailing me about basketball but it's been impossible." I knew with Aaron's insane work schedule he had only made their weekly game a handful of times. And I didn't even want to think about our gym membership. Our amortized cost per visit was probably up to triple digits by now.

"Alyson said something the other day at the auction meeting about all the husbands going to a Knicks game at the Garden in a few weeks. You didn't mention anything—are you going?"

"We'll see. I think I have to be in Chicago that week. I finally landed a meeting with that guy who said he might be interested in joining the board. Could be big."

He had been chasing that contact down for a while but I really wasn't in the mood to talk about work. "Back to Chicago," I said coolly.

"If it's a lunch, I might be able to make it a day trip. We'll see."

"I forgot to e-mail you, we have plans for a couples' dinner next Friday. Jeff'll be there, so you can ask him about the stone guy then—and also Ivy and Drew. I think our reservation's at 7:30, at Brady's."

He made a face.

"What? I thought you liked Brady's the last time we were there."

"I just don't understand why we have to hang with these people every single weekend. Isn't there anyone else for us to go out with?"

"What are you talking about, *anyone else*. These are our friends." *These are our* only *friends*.

Aaron grumbled and finished off the last few bites of his burrito.

After dinner, I revealed Phoebe and Madison's Pooh Valentines and chocolate heart cupcakes and they squealed with delight. Cards weren't Aaron's thing; they never had been, and on most birthdays and holidays I was fine with it. I knew card-buying was not on the same allele as athletic ability and I had chosen sports prowess over sentiment. Aaron had some romantic in him, deep down; in my night table I still had a few little love notes he had scribbled on flower deliveries in the early months of our relationship. I looked across the table: it was our ninth Valentine's Day together and he was staring off into the World Series of Poker reruns on the screen. I slipped a red envelope to the edge of his fingertips. "I got one for you too," I said.

"Thanks." He looked down at the card and then up at me. "You're not mad I didn't get one for you, are you?"

"Don't be silly. Open it." I forced a smile but couldn't help feeling a small pang of sadness to be the only one at the table sans Valentine.

He smiled at the joke inside, dating back to our honeymoon. "You're the best," he said. Not *I love you*?

"I think we need a night away." The idea had just popped into my head but all of sudden I wanted that night. Badly. "The two of us alone, without the kids. Maybe in an inn somewhere upstate."

"We have a whole house. Why do we need to go to an inn?"

"We used to go away for weekends. To Newport. Cape May. You used to surprise me on Fridays after work, remember? Pick me up in the car and not tell me where we were going?" *Back when we were romantic.*

"But I want to be home on the weekends to see the kids. And you, of course," he added. "And when they're asleep we're alone . . ."

"Yeah, until Phoebe comes marching in at two in the morning and ends up sprawled across our bed, kicking me all night."

"I don't kick you, Mommy," Phoebe said. "I'm sleeping."

Aaron smiled. "She's so damn cute though. Aren't you, Phoebe? Madison, you can't fit that whole cupcake in your mouth at one time."

"Milky, Mommy," Madison said, and I dug into my bag for her sippy cup.

"I can't even remember the last time we spent a night away together," I went on. "Before Phoebe was born. Almost four years ago. You've been traveling so much and I . . ." I felt myself starting to get upset but held it in.

Aaron peered at me across the table with a tender-hearted expression that usually turned me into putty. But I wasn't feeling it, not even a little.

"Are you okay?" he asked. "You don't sound like you tonight."

He was right. I hated the way I sounded, the nagging wife, and on Valentine's Day no less. I wanted to tell him that I *was* mad that he didn't get me a card. And that I was tired of him jetting off to Chicago and California all the time and making me feel like one of those lonely and needy women I swore I'd never be.

"I'm just burnt out," I said instead. "I shouldn't have taken on all this auction stuff with everything so crazy at work." *And I miss you. I miss us,* I thought, but I didn't want to say it out loud. Not with the kids; not at Firehouse. "And I hate how it gets dark so early. I wish it was time to turn the clocks ahead already."

"Now I know what to get you for Valentine's Day. Vitamin D."

"Very funny. I'm serious, Aaron, let's put a weekend on the calendar, in March sometime. I could ask my parents to come up and watch the kids, or even your parents. Or Noreen could sleep over, we could ask her."

"Noreen is NOT staying over," he said. "Look, if you want to go away together—of course we can do it."

"Promise?" I felt my mood starting to soften.

"Do you want me to pinky swear? Yes, yes, I promise. Now let's get these sugar-riled kids in the car. We still have a damn hour's drive to get home."

CHAPTER TEN

WE WERE LOLLYGAGGING AT THE FRONT DOOR of the school one Friday when I was actually able to make it to pickup, and I asked if anyone wanted to go to the Clark Recreation Center playground. The mid-March air was still a little chilly, but all winter we'd been confined to basement playrooms and I figured everyone would jump at the chance to play outside. It was definitely warm enough for a run around a playground. "I read in the *Journal News* they just finished renovating it," I said.

"You actually read the *Journal News*?" Tami said. "You and my eighty-year-old great-aunt Lucille."

But Tami had to take Connor to the pediatrician and Ivy had a meeting with her kitchen designer and Alyson wriggled her nose and said, "No thanks."

On our way to the car, on a whim I texted Michelle to see if she and her daughter might be free. But she quickly texted back, *Sorry, try me again next time*, she was stuck waiting for the plumber to fix one of the locker room showers.

I had already mentioned the playground possibility to Phoebe and didn't want to disappoint her. So even though it was just the two of us, I decided to go anyway.

On the drive over Phoebe was quiet. "Maybe next time Emmy will come," I said.

"Emmy's not my friend," Phoebe replied matter-of-factly.

"What? You play with Emmy practically every day. Of course she's your friend."

"She said Lexi's her new best friend." Lexi was a new girl who had recently moved to Suffern and joined their class.

"That can't be," I said, wondering if Emmy was actually capable at age three of saying something so mean. "You know what? I'll call Emmy's mommy when we get home. I'm sure it'll all be fine. Plus, you have lots of friends. What about, um . . ." I strained to remember the names of some of her other classmates—*shit!* I was not in the playdate loop. "Like, Brianna?" I glanced in the rearview mirror at Phoebe staring out the window looking sad. "Anyway, we're going to have a great time today. Madison's with Noreen this afternoon so it's just you and me. It's a mommy playdate!"

That made her smile.

I expected the playground to be overrun with kids, but as we entered the gate I saw only a few children scattered on the huge wooden adventure area with bridges and tunnels and poles to climb. Along the perimeter sat rows of empty big-kid swings and a giant slide which I thought looked too tall for Phoebe, but she ran right up, undaunted, and screamed out happily as she slid down. I took in a breath of the fresh air and gazed at the beautiful view of the mountains behind us and felt happy we came.

A few women sat chatting on the benches. I walked toward them and could hear they were speaking Spanish and I immediately thought, *Nannies*—and then chided myself for making that snap assumption. At the play-

grounds in the city I used to hear a million different dia-
lects, Spanish and Portuguese and Russian and German,
spoken by mothers and nannies and grandparents. Since
when had I let my ears start to cloud my brain?

I watched Phoebe climb up to the rings. "Be careful!"
I shouted. But she swung easily from rung to rung and
then ran over to the line that had formed for the slide and
patiently waited her turn. I couldn't believe she was three
and a half already. Going on four. And that Madison in a
few months would be two and in preschool herself come
September.

A few minutes later, I felt my phone vibrate in my
pocket. I saw I had missed two calls and my office was
trying again. I quickly picked up to Megan's exasperated
voice: "Aren't you joining us on the call?" My silence spoke
my question and she said, "You know, the call to review
the final plan for opening night? Marco just asked if you
were on."

I had totally forgotten. "Yes, of course—I'll hang up
and dial in right now. But I'm not in a quiet place—why
don't you take the lead?"

I redialed into the conference line and said a quick
hello before putting myself on mute. I stood there holding
the phone to my ear, craning to hear the six other people
on the line with the playground noise around me. I saw
Phoebe run back up the ladder of the slide.

"Mommy, look!" she yelled, waving from the top. She
was up so high, *Too high*, I thought, and as I waved back
I held my breath for what seemed like a very long second
before she sat and slid down safely.

"Mommy has to work for a few minutes, sweetie," I
called over to her. "Please be careful."

I did a quick scan to get a lay of the land. The playground was fenced in—beyond the swings, there were picnic tables and, from what I could see, only one exit. Phoebe would be safe to run around for a few minutes while I quickly listened in on the call.

But the conversation dragged. Indecision about the color of the table skirting—should it be black or navy? The garnish on the drink special—a lemon twist or lime? Did we confirm an alcohol sponsor yet? *No*. What's the holdup? Then Marco insisted on going down the guest list line by line, discussing who had and who had not yet RSVP'd. His focus on the most minute details was excruciating—our agency had thrown these parties a million times—there had to be a way to get off the call without the telltale beep of my departure.

"Mommy, I need you," Phoebe said. "I want to go on there." She pointed to the monkey bars, which were a good four feet off the ground.

"One more minute," I promised, reflexively putting my hand over the mouthpiece even though I was on mute. "Let me finish this and I promise we'll go on the monkey bars. I can't believe you're such a big girl and you can go down that slide all by yourself. Let me see you do that again."

A proud look spread across Phoebe's face as she realized what a big girl she was.

"What do you think, Jessica?" I heard Marco ask.

I quickly got off mute, hoping a child would not scream at that moment. "Sorry, I've got a bad connection here. Can you repeat that?"

He asked his question again about whether four people up front with the press list was enough, and he sounded annoyed. Even though I thought four was too many I quickly said, "Yes, that's perfect," and put the phone back on mute, reminding myself to listen more closely and how unprofessional it would be to be outed on a call from the playground. But he kept talking and talking—it felt like the call was going on forever, like it was the longest conference call in the history of all conference calls. I looked at my watch—it had been almost thirty minutes already—how much longer could we possibly discuss the freaking party?

Phoebe ran over to me again. "I need you, Mommy," she said.

"Just one more minute, I'm really, really sorry, sweetie, I'm almost done. One more time on the slide, let me see you do it one more time."

Instead, she ran over to the adventure area and started climbing in and out of the wooden tunnels. For a second I lost sight of her but then spotted her little pigtails bobbing in and out again.

Less than a minute later she came over again and I could tell from her grimace that she was getting impatient. "MOMMY! I SAID I NEED YOU!" she yelled.

And as I was about to open my mouth to give her yet another hollow promise of almost being done, she spread her legs apart and I saw a dark wet shadow emerge down her pants and then a puddle pool at her feet.

Out of my peripheral vision I noticed two women looking over, at first with pity and then disapproval. *Serves you right*, I heard them thinking. And they were right. There I stood, the bad mom in the playground, phone glued to my ear instead of paying attention to my child. And now she had peed.

"I've got to go," I said into the muted receiver, and hung up. Tears were streaming down Phoebe's face as she tried to suppress embarrassed sobs.

"I am so, so sorry," I said, kneeling down and wiping her tears with my sleeve. I hugged her tiny body close to mine, stroked her matted hair, and whispered, "I think we have a change of clothes in the car. Let's go and get cleaned up and then we'll come right back. And I promise—this time I truly promise—I will play with you."

I left Phoebe's wet clothes next to my phone in the backseat, and together we returned to the playground. This time I was going to keep my promise to Phoebe and for once I didn't care how Marco felt about it.

A little boy who looked about Phoebe's age started on the swing next to us. "Higher, Mommy, higher!" Phoebe shouted, which prompted the boy to say to his mom, "Higher, *más alto, Mamá!*"

"Looks like we have a little competition here," I said to the mom, who was wearing jeans and a royal-blue fleece almost the exact same color as mine. "This high flier here is Phoebe. And I'm Jessica."

She smiled warmly. "I am Lupita."

Lupita's hair was pulled back in a low ponytail except for a few dark spirals that bounced around her face with each push. "Hold on tight, Samuel!" she said, and he pumped his legs and flew up higher still. I tried to explain to Phoebe how to pump her legs, and before long she started to catch on and Lupita and I fell into an easy rhythm of chatting and pushing the kids.

Lupita told me she had been a high school history teacher in Mexico, near Monterrey, and was working to-

ward her PhD when the violence of the drug wars esca-
lated and she fled to the States to join her brother and
his family in Suffern, about three years ago. But when
she arrived, she found out her teaching degree would not
transfer and was now attending SUNY Rockland Community College to repeat all of her undergrad credits on
her way to becoming recertified. She hoped one day to
continue on to graduate school here, but she wasn't cer-
tain it would be possible. For the moment, she was working at her brother's restaurant to support her studies and
Samuel, who would be turning four in the fall. No mention of a husband, and I didn't ask.

Phoebe and Samuel finished with the swings and sat
on the edge of the sandbox. Samuel was taking plastic
dinosaurs out of a small backpack and showing them to
Phoebe one by one. "This is a triceratops," he said, and
set it carefully on the sand in front of her. "And this one
is a baby apatosaurus."

"He's so bright," I said. "Where is he in school?"

"Sometimes he goes to the day care at the church, and
my sister-in-law's mother looks after him when I am at
work or at class. And next year he can start pre-K."

"Mommy, look, a stegosaurus!" Phoebe exclaimed.
We hadn't been to the dinosaur exhibit at the Museum
of Natural History in ages and I was astonished she was
able recall its name.

"Have you been to the Museum of Natural History in
the city?" I asked Lupita.

"No. But we have read about it."

"Oh, you have to—Samuel would love it. We used
to live a few blocks from there and it was practically
our second home. Not many people know but there's

this great spot downstairs, the Discovery Room. It's a hands-on area where they give the kids archeology tools and aprons and have docents to help explain what they 'find' digging in the sand. And then after you can look at beetles and butterflies and bees and other creatures under a microscope."

"Dead ones, I hope," she chuckled.

Aaron and I had loved taking Phoebe to the museum, even if she was too young to absorb it all. Sometimes we'd go twice in a weekend to say hi to the dinosaurs and African elephants and half-zebra okapi, all displayed in the same still-life tableaus as I remembered from my visits as a child. And my favorite, the big blue whale, suspended over our heads in the beautifully renovated Hall of Ocean Life. Every time I stood underneath its giant peaceful body I marveled at its gentle greatness and how much there was in the world for Phoebe yet to explore.

I felt sad all of a sudden as I realized we never took Madison to see the whale, at least not out of her infant stroller. We'd moved before we had a chance to show her the walruses and the giant squid—before we had a chance to spin with her until we were dizzy like we had with Phoebe, pretending we were airplanes on the wide-open carpeted floor.

The sun started to set behind the mountains and I could feel the temperature take a dip. Phoebe then said what she usually felt around four thirty p.m.: "Mommy, I'm hungry."

"Why don't you come to the restaurant with us for a snack?" Lupita suggested.

Phoebe peered up at me with big eyes. "Please, Mommy?"

We still had about an hour before I had to get home to relieve Noreen—it was a little random but Phoebe was having such a good time so I said, "Why not?" and we followed behind Lupita's car to downtown Suffern and found a spot on Lafayette Avenue near the movie theater.

I had walked on Lafayette many times before but had never noticed the cozy restaurant with gold tablecloths and a sign on the window that read, *Se Habla Español.* Lupita gave a kiss on each cheek to the hostess and introduced me to her brother who worked there, and shortly thereafter the kids were munching on cheese quesadillas and I was sipping a cup of strong and delicious Mexican coffee, feeling warm and comfortable. Phoebe looked positively smitten as she and Samuel leafed through a dinosaur sticker book together.

I asked Lupita about the classes she was taking—two this semester, one about child psychology and another on the history of Rockland County.

"You know, we've lived here almost a year and I'm embarrassed to admit I know practically nothing about Suffern." From my online research back at the time of our move, I remembered that George Washington had once slept in Suffern and this was its claim to fame.

"That is more than most people know. This block we are on right now was actually an important crossroads back during the Revolutionary War. And besides Washington, other famous people from that time ate and stayed at John Suffern's Tavern. Look at the street names: Lafayette Avenue for the Marquis de Lafayette, of course Washington Avenue. Alexander Hamilton and Aaron Burr were both here too, in the years before their duel. Sorry, I know I'm probably boring you with all of this."

"Not at all." I loved being right here on the same street as our nation's forefathers, part of history's living continuum.

"My history professor is visiting this year from Ithaca College. His specialty is in early American politics and he asked me to help him with research for a paper he's working on. I've been spending many months with my head in the library and Suffern's museum in the municipal building around the corner. Sifting through old books and property records, reading about all of the people who passed through here and lived here two hundred years ago."

"What's the paper about?"

"How politicians, even back then, maligned their opponents in the media to influence public opinion and win elections. Back in the early days, they used newspapers and political pamphlets, and today there are of course more choices, with TV and the Internet. Bashing your opponent worked then, and it still works now."

"Gossip always sells papers." I told Lupita how I worked with the media, and although not in politics, I was very much aware of how the ebbs and flows of eyeballs affected the market. And, I admitted, I still preferred to read the actual newspaper on my train ride into the city; despite being the recipient of more than a few curious stares, I liked the feel and the turn of the pages, and I liked seeing the full-page ads we placed, which still worked to sell theater tickets.

"I have been reviewing the case study from back in 1804 when Alexander Hamilton used the paper he founded—then the *New York Evening Post*, now the *New York Post*—to slander Aaron Burr to try to prevent him from winning the New York gubernatorial race. There was much bad blood between them: years before, Burr had won a senate seat from Hamilton's father-in-law and that is when their feud started. Hamilton said Burr was absent of any moral fiber; Burr publicly stated that Hamilton was not fit to be Washington's secretary of the treasury. In fact, the words that were ultimately printed in the *Post* and other papers of the time, whether or not they were true, directly led to their infamous duel."

"The *Post* has certainly done a good job since then staying true to its gossip roots," I said. "Have you seen *Hamilton* on Broadway?"

"I have heard of it, but no, I have not."

"Oh, you would love it. It's all about the Hamilton-Burr feud, but it uses rap to tell the story in this very cool and contemporary way. It's been a huge, huge hit—sold out for ages—and has completely infiltrated pop culture too. That's an incredibly rare thing for a musical to do. Most people couldn't care less about what's on Broadway these days."

"I have always wanted to see a Broadway show. Maybe *Hamilton* could count as research," she said. "My professor has a hunch that Hamilton and Burr were connected in some other way through Suffern; the records I have found so far show they might have actually both been here at the same time. If only I could find the time to lock myself in a room for a week with nothing else to do but research. Unfortunately, most of the documents are not yet digitized, and it is very slow work. But as I know you know, there are many things more important than work vying for our attention." She smiled and tousled Samuel's hair. "It's hard to focus sometimes but my professor said he will give me coauthorship of the paper, which could be very important for me, to submit it to the journals and perhaps have a published piece."

I admired Lupita's drive and passion. "I *know* you will get it done. And I want a signed copy when it's published!"

A text from Noreen popped up on my phone: *R u coming home soon?* We were forty-five minutes past the time I'd promised—whoops—I had been so engrossed in Lupita's story I had completely lost track of the clock.

"I wish we could stay but I am so sorry, we have to get home for the sitter. Phoebe, it's time," I announced, and felt just as disappointed to be leaving as Phoebe looked. "Maybe we can meet up at the playground again next week?" *And sometime soon take a trip to the museum,* I thought; even though we had just met them I could somehow imagine us exploring the halls together, and with Madison along this time too.

"Here," Samuel said, holding out the stegosaurus figurine for Phoebe.

"That is so sweet, you don't have to do that," I said, but Phoebe was already clutching the dinosaur.

"Thank you," Phoebe replied, without any prompting.

"We promise to take good care of him and will return it the next time we see you," I added. "Hopefully soon."

Lupita and I exchanged contact information and I held onto Phoebe's hand on the short walk back to the car. The gaslight streetlamps lining the block were now glowing, each with a banner proclaiming the village's motto, *Tiens a la Vérité—Hold onto the Truth—1773,* sketched in a blue and white crest.

Hold onto what *truth?* I wondered.

Like Lupita had said, the papers, the news, the gossip, even history—who knew what was actually true. It was so refreshing to discuss something other than the usual daily dribble for once, to stop and think about how the facts we think we know are woven through malice and motives and the passage of time. Headlines and scripts, even dinosaur fossils: we never really know for sure what is truth, what is fiction. So much is written and posted and printed to suit the powerful, the rich, and the influential, even today. I always prided myself on reading the *Post* with a grain of salt, but I so rarely took the time to question the *New York Times*, the *Wall Street Journal*. The stories on the eleven o'clock news.

I clicked Phoebe's car seat latch tight and could feel the past swirling around us in the early-evening chill. Washington, Lafayette, Burr, and Hamilton—names from two hundred years ago, and yet we're still talking about them, still wondering about the truths and lies and secrets that might be hidden in the streets and sidewalks of Suffern, still smiling through Hamilton's ten-dollar visage.

I jumped as the phone on my desk rang. It was Sybil. "Can you come in here a minute?" she asked. I walked down the long hallway to her corner office, wondering if I was about to be berated for dropping off the conference call last week. I had left Marco a message apologizing but hadn't heard back. *An emergency*, I'd tell her, I would tell her Phoebe had a medical emergency and that's why I had to go.

"Have a seat," she said, glancing up from her computer. Sybil sat at a big glass desk with floor-to-ceiling windows behind her that presented a breathtaking view of Times Square. She and her partner Larry Glancy had come a long way from the early days of their budding Broadway advertising agency run out of a tiny back office in a theater off Eighth Avenue. Twenty years and almost fifty employees later, they were at the top of the industry, but new competitors were constantly sprouting up, eager to snatch their clients. While I waited for her to finish typing, I eyed the photos on her credenza—arm in arm with the mayor; backstage with Matthew Broderick; on a boat with her husband and two grown sons. *As long as she doesn't take away my Fridays,* I thought nervously. No matter what, I had to protect my Fridays at home.

"I would like to discuss the marketing presentation today for Marco." She took off her glasses and placed them on her desk. "Are you ready to nail this?"

Sybil wasn't the kind of boss who usually found the time or need for a pre-presentation pep talk. I wondered what else was going on.

"It's all under control. I triple-checked the deck this morning," I lied; the untouched draft sat on my desk. "You and Larry will kick it off, and then I'll take everyone through the research and the details of the plan. We'll blow him away."

"Good, that's all I wanted to hear." She looked back down at her computer, my signal that we were done. As I stood up to leave she asked, "So, how are the kids?"

Here it comes, I thought. Sybil very rarely asked me about my children. She was one of those highly successful women who built her career by working nonstop, well before the conception of work-life balance.

"They're great, thanks for asking," I said warily, but then added without thinking, "I think Madison's starting up a little early with her terrible twos."

"I remember those days," she said with an inward smile. "I can't believe mine are all grown up already. It all goes so fast—enjoy it while you can."

"I will," I said, as a fast-forward filmstrip of Phoebe and Madison from bottles, to braces, to bridal gowns raced through my head. *Way too fast*, I thought, and could feel myself actually start to swoon. There was no way I was going to let myself pass out in front of Sybil. She'd probably think I was pregnant again. Which would have been medically impossible given the state of Aaron and my sex life lately. "Let me know if you need anything else," I said quickly before turning for the door.

What did that mean, *Enjoy it while you can?* Was that some code signaling her plans to let me go?

Back in my office, I racked my brain for what could be up. My review was in a month—technically I was up for a VP spot, but I thought a promotion was doubtful. Was it possible she was thinking I wasn't keeping up?

No way, I told myself. All of the shows on my docket were doing great, and if anything, I had been going overboard lately to prove I could still get it all done. Plus, she needed me—I was the point person for our top two accounts, and now Marco. But ever since becoming a mom, in the back of my mind I worried there would come a day Sybil would call me into her office to tell me she actually did notice all of those times I was on the phone making pediatrician appointments and running out early, that my head wasn't fully in my work the way it used to be and that she had hired someone else, someone younger and

unencumbered. If I had to defend myself, could I prove I
was still delivering?

I tried to make sure I attended all of the important
staff meetings. But I had skipped most of the Broadway
League's last road conference, the place where new relationships with producers were spawned and incubated,
networking in the hallways before lunchtime group sales
panels and schmoozing over cocktails at Joe Allen. I
knew it was important to be attentive to our clients—and
until recently, I'd always felt I had that piece covered. But
in Sybil's eyes, new business was even more valuable. If
she was questioning my worth, bringing in more clients
would be my only insurance. Finding and cultivating new
business would take a ton of extra work, work I didn't
even know if I was capable of. I'd have to scour my list
of contacts and set up breakfast and lunch meetings with
the few people I knew at production companies; spend a
lot more weeknights in off-off-Broadway theaters, sitting
through tedious hours of new shows working their kinks
out in development.

Before Phoebe was born, I used to love being the
first at the workshops and previews, sitting up front in
comped house seats with a backstage pass granting me
stage door access after the show. Now, whenever invites
came up for tickets or after-work cocktails, unless it was
absolutely required I opted to hop on the train to get
home instead, for story time and kisses good night.

Hop, jump—more like sprint. Going in the morning
was usually okay, but coming home was turning into a
nightmare. State budget cuts had put a serious crater in
my perfect express schedule and now if I missed the 5:38
the next three trains were all locals, and my as-advertised

less-than-an-hour commute was now turning out to be more like an hour and twenty. Every day around 5:15 I found myself debating whether or not I could speed through the copy in the eight minutes I had remaining before I would miss that train; copy I knew I should proofread at least one more time before passing it along to the art department if the ad had a chance of going live online that night. More often than not I went with it as is, with a note to call me if they had any questions, and then I'd run down the subway stairs crossing my fingers an A or C would be waiting on the tracks with its doors sliding open so I wouldn't miss my golden 5:38, the only train that would get me home for mommy time.

There was no way Sybil was going to promote me with that level of sloppy oversight. But I hoped she'd also noticed all the times the producers called with their inevitable late-afternoon emergencies—*Quick, change the headline and the photo for the taxi tops.* And it was my job to be at their service—*Sure, we can do that, we can absolutely make those changes*—and then I'd frantically scramble to figure out who could call in a favor with the ad rep to extend the deadline and which designer could stay late to finish it and then e-mail it back for final approval, watching the clock tick past six and sometimes past seven, and by the time I finally pulled into the driveway my heart hung heavy, knowing my children were already long asleep.

I told myself to shake it off and stop beating myself up. Maybe Sybil was just feeling a little nervous about the presentation, worried that the hot young producer might catch her off her game. But I knew Marco, and I knew with the right finesse, I had a shot at convincing him to give our agency a bigger share of his producer pie. Maybe today was the perfect opportunity to wow him in front Sybil and Larry and prove that I was VP material.

Twenty minutes was all I needed to review the deck, thirty tops. Plenty of time to prep, and then I could focus my energy on the hundred other things I needed to get done before the meeting at four.

CHAPTER ELEVEN

THE AUCTION INVITATION SAID *SEMIFORMAL*, but as we stepped down the stairs into the Sacred Heart Church basement, I knew immediately I had overdressed. The men were in their usual suburban uniforms—untucked button-down shirts and jeans. And most of the women were in jeans too. High heels and jeans. Like any other party, any other day.

"I told you I didn't need to wear a sport jacket," Aaron said, giving me a look.

Just because your company's new personalized e-mail product got a bad review on CNET a few days ago doesn't mean you still have to be in such a foul mood, I thought. "It's not such a big deal, you can just take it off," I said.

It wasn't like I could take off my little black cocktail dress, unless I wanted to parade around all night in my boob-to-thigh ultra-support Spanx like a hermetically sealed sausage. Although I did like the way the material smoothed out my stomach and my hips—so far, it was worth the loss of circulation. I was just thankful for the built-in pee flap.

I found Alyson and another mom I faintly recognized from Phoebe's class at the entry table with a *Hello My Name Is* sticker on her chest: *Robyn.*

"Hey, Jessica. Hi, Aaron," she said, checking us off on her list and handing us our name tags. "Nice dress."

"Thanks," I replied, feeling a little better. "You don't think it's too dressy?"

"No, you look great."

"Okay, volunteer assignments," Alyson cut in. She flipped through her spreadsheet. "Aaron—meet Jeff and Chris over at the bar in the back. You're all under strict orders to get everyone good and wasted so they'll bid their asses off." She grinned and I couldn't help but notice her teeth were gleaming like luminescent Chiclets. Was it the lighting or had she just come from a seriously high-octane teeth whitening? "And Jessica—you'll be selling glow necklaces for the heads-and-tails raffle—go ask for Wendy in the office and she'll set you up."

Glow necklaces? I had signed Aaron and me up to bartend together and had been looking forward to it all week. "Are you sure that's right?" I asked her. "I'm almost positive I—"

"Do you have *any* idea how long it took me to put together this schedule?" Alyson snarled.

You don't have to be so nasty, I thought, but I wasn't going to stand there and fight with her about it, especially not with the line of people forming behind us. I summoned my dutiful auction-committee smile and said, "Whatever you need me to do."

"Before you run off," she smiled sweetly at Aaron, "what credit card will you be using for your purchases tonight?"

Aaron handed over our Visa for a preauthorizing swipe and she gave us our paddle, number 64, telling us to be sure to write it on the bid sheets at the silent auction tables and remember to raise it often during the live auction, which started at 8:30.

"Bid wildly!" Robyn said. "It's all for the kids!"

I whispered to Aaron, "How much do you want to spend tonight?"

"I don't know, a couple hundred? If it's stuff we need, we might as well buy it here as a donation."

Aaron gave me a peck and went off to find the bar and I headed to the office to find Wendy. She explained my job was to sell twenty-five-dollar glow necklace raffle entries to win a dinner for two at Marcello's, an upscale Italian restaurant in town. "You need to sell forty—and that'll be a thousand dollars for the school!" She placed a huge sandwich board over my head that read, *BE A WINNER!* and filled my wrists with the glow necklaces. I felt like one of those vendors at the circus. A vendor wearing four-inch pumps.

I bit my lip as I stepped out onto the floor. I hated direct sales. Develop a social media strategy, edit a radio spot, even e-mail an auction donation request, fine. But face to face, asking people for money—I hated the possibility of flat-out rejection. A leftover scar from my Girl Scout cookie days, no doubt—*Good try, Jess, here's your patch for participating,* while my friends went home with arms full of stuffed animals and clock radios and other top-seller prizes.

I scanned the room in search of a familiar face and realized I didn't recognize most of the people milling about. I took a deep breath, at least as deep as I could breathe in my full-body corset. It couldn't be *that* hard to sell parents raffle tickets to raise money for their own kids' school.

I approached a couple standing near the silent auction tables, studying the bid sheets. Music blared from the speakers a few feet away so I had to shout, "Want to buy a glow necklace?" They stared at me blankly. "It's only twenty-five dollars for a chance to win a dinner at Marcello's." I held out my sheet for them to sign.

"No thanks," the woman responded politely, and walked away.

Shit, I thought to myself, *how am I ever going to sell forty of these things?* I desperately wished I could Jeannie-blink myself to a spot behind the bar pouring martinis next to Aaron.

Across the room I spied Tami with her arms glowing like mine and several people lined up, signing her clipboard. Maybe she'd have a few tips for me—or better yet, take my whole sheet.

"The room looks amazing!" I complimented her. She had completely transformed the church basement into a bona fide retro dance club with colorful uplighting and high cocktail tables with fiber-optic centerpieces and even a disco ball suspended from the ceiling.

"Thanks," she said. "We'd better rack up a ton of freaking cash tonight to make all this goddamned work worth it."

"Speaking of . . ." I pointed to my blank sheet. "So far I got one big fat no from that couple over there and I feel like crawling under a rock."

"Who?"

I pointed to the couple, now in line for a drink.

"Oh, the Brenners. Screw them, cheap bastards. The trick is to hit up the dads standing near the bar, like that group over there who's already on their third round. And then don't ask—give them a little flirty smile and say you need their autograph. They're so lit they'll sign anything you put in front of them and you'll be done in, like, fifteen minutes."

"I'll give it a try," I said.

I spotted Drew standing alone near the bar and put my hand on his arm. "Hey, handsome, how's about helping a girl fill up her bid sheet?"

"I'd be happy to fill you up," he played along. He snatched the pen and filled in ten of the slots, just like that.

"Oh my god, I love you. That is such a huge help!" I said, and gave him a big bear hug. I felt his hand grab my ass and squeeze it toward his hard groin.

"Now when do I *really* get to fill you up?" he breathed heavily into my neck. He reeked of Scotch and Tic Tacs and expensive cologne. "You're so hot in this dress I can't stand it."

I broke myself away. "Ha, not funny, Drew."

He stepped in closer and whispered, "There's an alcove behind the rectory, no one will even notice we're gone." And then I felt his tongue flick in my ear.

Ew, oh my god, he wasn't kidding. I stammered, "You . . . you are definitely drunk and I'm sorry if you got the wrong idea, but . . ."

The hungry look on his face abruptly switched to raw anger. "You bitch, always coming on to me." And then he turned and slipped into the crowd.

My mind raced. All of his flirty jokes and touches I had thought were just his way—I never responded with anything that would have made him think I was interested. Had I? The lewd whisper, his hardness against me

. . . He'd better be wasted, so wasted that tomorrow he wouldn't even remember. But I'd remember. And I had no idea how I'd ever be able to look at him across the table at another couples' dinner again, let alone face Ivy.

I hurried to the other side of the room and found enough people to sign the rest of the raffle sheet. Aaron still had ten minutes to go on his bartending shift so I perused the silent auction tables, trying to focus on the packages in front of me while keeping an eye out to avoid running into Drew.

Wine basket with ten bottles of Italian red—minimum bid $150. Casino Night at the Parkers, Friday, June 30— $100 per person. I didn't know the Parkers and had minimal interest in a basketful of wine.

At the adjacent table, *Silent auction 2: On Fire!* I was surprised how high Carolann has priced some of the packages. *Yankees box seats 6 rows behind home plate—opening bid $500.* There were three bids already for those. *18k gold Tiffany diamond anniversary band— $700.* Two bids there. I found my donation of the tickets and backstage tour to Marco's new show and was disappointed to see no one had bid yet. *Opening bid $200.* Huh. It was worth a lot more than that. I wrote our name in on the first line to help start things off.

Then a package caught my eye: *Saturday-night stay in a suite at the Mayflower Inn, Washington, CT.* I'd been reading about the Mayflower for years on the "best of" lists in all the travel magazines. No kids were allowed at the Mayflower—an ideal spot for the romantic getaway Aaron had promised and still hadn't planned. I picked up the pen and wrote, *Almasi #64,* next to the $200 opening bid and hoped it wouldn't go much higher.

"Nice place," Carolann's husband Peter commented, looking over my shoulder.

"Hey, Pete, how's it going?"

"Carolann basically abandoned me so I'm just cruisin' around."

She's probably pretty damn busy running the party, I thought, but said, "She did some job pulling all of this together, don't you think?"

"Hey, babe," Ivy interrupted. She was wearing a skintight skirt so short it barely covered her ass. Only she could pull off a dress like that and look fabulous. Drew was such an asshole to need anything besides her. I looked for him over her shoulder as she hugged me hello and didn't see him, thank god. "Where's Aaron?"

"Still bartending."

"That was so nice of him to volunteer ... I told *you* to sign up for bartending," she turned and said pointedly to Drew. There he was. He looked right past me and mumbled something about needing to be out of there by 10:30 at the latest.

"Come get something to eat with us, Jess, I'm starving!"

I don't want to get something to eat with you, your slimeball husband just hit on me. But I didn't want her to suspect anything was wrong. "I really should go find Aaron, he'll be done any minute."

"He'll catch up with us. Peter—you too. Come," Ivy insisted, and then she grabbed our hands and led us toward the food.

Local restaurants were positioned around the room, offering "A Taste of Suffern" specialties donated for the event. Linguine puttanesca from Marcello's. Chicken fingers from Sutter's. A mountain of sushi from Koto. I piled my plate with spicy tuna and veggie rolls and was about to add some rice and beans from the chafing dish at the next restaurant's station when I noticed that the apron-clad chefs manning the Mexican food table were Lupita and her brother. We had texted a few times over the past few weeks but hadn't yet nailed down a second meet-up.

"I can't believe you're here, it's such a small world!" I greeted, leaning over the trays of food to kiss Lupita hello.

"It is good to see you! I had no idea this event was for Phoebe's school."

"Ivy—this is my friend Lupita and her brother Felipe. Felipe owns Solé. Have you been there? The food is fabulous. They have *the* most delicious quesadillas. Here, you should try some."

Our stop to say hello was backing up the food line, so after promising to bring Aaron by to meet them later, I followed Ivy, Drew, and Peter to a nearby cocktail table to scarf down a few bites and then quickly extract myself. "That's such a coincidence they're here," I said.

"How do you know those people?" Ivy asked.

"I met Lupita at the playground. You would really like her. She has a son the same age as Phoebe and she's taking classes at RCC for her teaching degree, which she actually already had from Mexico. You'd think there'd be some kind of transfer program, but I guess not."

"And make it easier for some illegal immigrant to take our jobs?" Peter snapped. "Have you seen the lineup of day laborers down by the bus stop in the morning? Suffern's been overrun. They should all be sent back to where they came from, damn wetbacks."

My eyes widened in disbelief. I had never heard anyone talk this way. On TV maybe, or flipping past those right-wing radio talk shows. I was so stunned I couldn't speak.

"That's what Jeff should focus his campaign on," Drew added. "Clearing those spics the hell out of here."

"Shut up, Drew," Ivy hissed.

Maybe Peter was still having trouble finding a job, but that was no excuse. And Drew agreeing with him! What a dick. I couldn't just stand there without letting them know what they said was unacceptable. I wanted to scream that Lupita and her brother were a hell of a lot more interesting and intelligent than they were or ever would be. That I had a more thought-provoking afternoon that one Friday with Lupita and her four-year-old son than at all the tedious nights out with them I'd had to endure. I wanted to say all that and tell them right to their faces what hateful imbeciles they were, yet all that came out was a shaky, "They donated their food and their time tonight to help our school."

They donated their food?! How about, *Go fuck yourself?* Or at least something to make sure they knew I didn't agree with their awful diatribe. Why was I was always so weak, so afraid of a confrontation? Smoothing it over and sweeping it under to appease a bunch of people I don't even like? I hated that feeling of wanting to fit in, of *needing* to fit in—worrying if I said the wrong thing I'd once again find myself outside with my nose pressed against the glass. I had a trove of comebacks rotting on a shelf in my consciousness, of no good to anyone except to remind me of how many times I'd failed to say what I should have.

Peter looked unfazed, staring out toward the bar, and Drew had a smug expression on his face, as if he couldn't care less about my opinion and felt not the slightest discomfort.

"Where have you been?" Carolann walked up to us and demanded, clutching her auction chair clipboard in one hand and a walkie-talkie in the other. The angry look on her face reminded me of that day she stormed out of the diner; I hoped I hadn't somehow messed up the raffle ticket sales.

But her ire was directed toward her husband: "I asked you to do one thing tonight, Peter, to handle the sound guy. And now you're standing here eating? No one can hear the announcements—please go fix it. Now."

Peter left the table with a Neanderthalean grunt.

Ivy asked Carolann, "How are sales going so far? It looks totally jamming in here."

"So far, so good, Ivy." Carolann turned down the dial on her walkie-talkie and smoothed her pants several times as if to regain her composure. "We hit an all-time record attendance of over two hundred guests. And a last-minute donation just came in from one of the teachers: two months of summer camp at Ramaquois. I better see that paddle raised sky high tonight, Drew."

"Don't you worry," Ivy answered for him.

A voice over the loudspeaker announced, *"Silent auction 2 will close in ten minutes."*

"Pete got that fixed pretty quick," Drew said dryly.

"I have to run and check on the bid sheets. Save me a seat for the live auction," Carolann said and dashed off, leaving me alone with Drew and Ivy.

"I have to check on our bid sheets too," I said, and

turned to follow Carolann, hating myself even more for walking away without the guts to stand up for what I knew was right.

Two other couples had bid on the Mayflower Inn package and the bid was up to $300. I really wanted that weekend away on our calendar. I paused and then scribbled, *#64—$350,* and went to find Aaron.

Parents were congregating like moths in front of the bar. I tried to squeeze my way toward the front and waved to catch Aaron's attention.

"Hey, Jess," he said, "glass of wine? Gin and tonic?" Jeff handed Aaron two shots and he passed one to a guest and then tilted his head back to down the other. He certainly seemed to be enjoying his little volunteer assignment.

"I'm bidding on a night at an inn for us," I told him. "We're at $350 right now. How high do you think we should go?"

"Jesus Christ, $350 for one night?"

"It's a fancy inn, up in Connecticut. Five-star. And like you said, it's a donation for the school. Tax deductible, remember?"

He scooped some ice into a cocktail shaker. "Well, I wouldn't bid much more than four. Does it include breakfast at least?"

I grabbed a glass of wine and ran back to the table. *#26—$400.* Ugh. I grabbed the pen and wrote in *$450* and stood hovering a few steps away to protect the sheet from any last-minute spoilers. A couple strolled by casually, glancing down at the bid sheets near mine. I willed them to pass—*Keep walking, keep walking*—but at the last second the husband picked up the pen and my heart

sank. I looked down at the sheet: #26 had drawn an arrow skipping their bid all the way up to $600. I wanted
so badly to scribble in *$650* but knew Aaron would be
mad if we paid over six for something he barely wanted
to pay four hundred for. And I didn't have time to run
back to try to convince him.

"Silent auction 2 is officially closed!" the announcer
said. A volunteer came and quickly grabbed all the bid
sheets off the table and it was over. We had lost.

I stood there for a moment, smarting in my defeat. I
hated losing. And I was even more upset that once again,
our romantic weekend away was back to just a wishful
thought. I took a swallow of my wine to push down the
lump I felt welling up in the back of my throat and saw
Alyson walking toward me.

"Hey, Jessica, I've been looking for you. I need to talk
to you about something."

"Sure," I said, figuring she was about to hand me another volunteer task. *Please, god, anything but the cleanup committee.*

"So. You know Noreen's accident in your Outback?"
she began.

"How can I forget my kids' first trip to the hospital?
Well, their first after being born." I smiled weakly at my
own joke but Alyson didn't.

"It's hard for me to tell you this, but . . . last week
your nanny Noreen was at our house with Phoebe and
Madison for a playdate, and from the top of the stairs I
overheard Noreen and Priya talking—and I heard Noreen say she was texting while she was driving, and that's
why she got in the accident."

"That can't be," I said, but felt a shiver up my back.

"I wasn't sure whether or not to tell you, but I thought if it was me, I would want to know." Alyson leaned over to give me a hug, transferring the full weight of her secret onto me. "If you need someone to watch Phoebe and Madison while you look for a new nanny," she whispered, "let me know and maybe we can work it out with Priya."

I stood there frozen, feeling the grains of sushi rice churning in my stomach. My nanny, texting while driving my kids? I didn't want to believe it but deep inside I knew it must be true. I should have listened to Aaron, I should have fired Noreen right after the accident. How could I have trusted a twenty-three-year-old liar? Who has been putting my kids in serious danger for the past six months? The enormity of my mistake spread throughout my body like poison and I shuddered, sick with guilt.

We'd have to get rid of her right away. I'd need to take a few days off next week and try to patch babysitting coverage together. Write up a job description and post it on one of those nanny sites and send out an e-mail to the school's Google group asking if anyone knew of someone looking. A new nanny. *Fuck.*

I ran back over to the bar to find Aaron. "I need to talk to you," I said.

"Uhhh, I'm a little busy." He nodded to the long line and proceeded to spill the cocktail he was pouring all over the table. "Whoops," he said, tripping over the rubber mat at his feet as he grabbed for a bar towel.

"Come on, you've been bartending for almost two hours. It's not even your shift anymore, it's enough already!"

"Did we win?"

"Did we what? You mean the inn? No, we didn't,"

I said, suddenly feeling angry to be reminded of losing again.

"That's too bad. What'd it go for?"

"I don't know. Six hundred."

"You should have bid more, it would have been fun."

"More! You barely wanted to spend *four* hundred!" I wanted to explode.

"Y'know, the guy running the bar said at the end of the night they sell the extra liquor. We can pick up a few bottles of vodka." The way he slurred—*afewbottlesofvodka*—made me realize how far gone he was.

"I don't care about the freaking vodka, Aaron!" I pictured sharing the news with the auction committee: *And what did you buy at the auction, Jessica?*

Oh, we grabbed a few bottles of discounted vodka. They'd probably kick Phoebe right out of the school.

"There's something else I have to tell you—in private." I took his hand and pulled him into to an area behind the bar where the wine and supplies were stored.

"Mmmm, in private," he said with a goofy smile. He grabbed my waist and leaned over to try to kiss me. His breath smelled fermented and sour.

"What are you doing?" I pushed him away. "This is serious. We have to fire Noreen! Alyson just told me Noreen was texting while she was driving Phoebe and Madison in the car. You were right—we never should have kept her on after the accident. I can't believe what an idiot I am." I looked up to check his reaction but his eyes were caught in a stare about four inches above my head. "Did you even hear a word I said? I was wrong about Noreen and you were right and we have to fire her."

He draped his arms around me in a sloppy hug. "I

forgive you . . . and I won't say I told you so . . ." His voice trailed off. For a second I thought he might have fallen asleep on my shoulder. He was so drunk I wondered if he would even remember having this conversation. But goddamn it, did he have to say *I told you so*?

"We should go home," I said, even though I didn't want to.

Aaron's head popped up. "But the party's barely started." He held onto my forearm and dragged me toward the empty dance floor.

There was no way I was going to let him embarrass us out there. I diverted him to the side and literally ran into Chris and Tami standing next to the giant cardboard "giving tree," its branches covered in green construction paper leaves with donation amounts for books and supplies for the school library.

"Hey, dude," Aaron said to Chris, and as he leaned over to give him an awkward hug, he fell right into the tree, sending it crashing to the ground and scattering its paper leaves everywhere. It was official: the drunk at the party was my husband.

"Anyone have a leaf blower handy?" Aaron joked as he tried to get up and slipped on a piece of paper stuck to his shoe.

I said through my gritted teeth, "We are leaving. Now."

"I have to take a piss," he announced loudly, and stumbled away.

I stood there, humiliated, and closed my eyes, hoping someone would gently shake my shoulder, *Good morning, sunshine, time for school,* and this night would be a calamity way in my future.

I heard Tami direct Chris to follow Aaron. Then she took my hand and led me back to the bar. She cut the line, grabbed a mixed drink off the edge, and handed it to me. I drank it down like water and helped myself to another.

"Feel better?" she asked.

"No," I replied, feeling more numb than angry. Or maybe the Spanx had finally cut off my entire body's blood supply.

"Chris'll get him cleaned up. Happens to the best of us. No worries."

No worries. As if just like that, with a wave of Tami, presto, they're gone. As if.

"I can't stay here," I said, and as I turned to flee I could feel the dam in the back of my throat give way and I couldn't help the tears and the words from pouring out. I told her everything: how Aaron hadn't even wanted to come in the first place tonight, how I had to practically drag him even though I told him how important it was to me and he had no idea how hard I'd worked through months of not sleeping and begging for all these donations but he didn't seem to care, he didn't compliment me on my dress and he hadn't complimented me on anything lately. We'd barely seen each other, we were always working and running and I'd stopped counting how many weeks or months it had been since the last time we tore it up between the sheets. And how our bathroom ceiling was all warped, how the goddamned builder forgot to install a fan and now we had water damage, how he'd started to fix it but he couldn't come back until the Thursday after next and how were we supposed to take a shower with the ceiling all ripped up? It was a brand-new house, it was supposed to be perfect but it wasn't, it was far from perfect. I cried about work and Marco and my fucked-up train schedule and how I didn't know how much longer I could keep it together. And now, on top of everything, I had to find a new nanny.

Tami handed me a tissue and when I looked up, both Ivy and Alyson were huddling with us too.

"I am so sorry, I can't believe I'm standing here in the middle of the party bawling my eyes out. Carolann is going to hate me for ruining her night."

"We cleaned up the tree before she ever saw it," Alyson said.

"*The live auction will begin in five minutes*," the announcer said over the PA.

"Well, this has been fun," I said, trying to force a smile. "I think it's time for me to collect my wasted husband and end this fabulous evening."

"You're not going home now," Tami said. "The live auction's about to start."

"Sorry, Tami, but I can't sit through—"

"Come on, Jessica, Aaron will be fine. Don't let him ruin the night we all worked so hard for. Go splash some cold water on your face and meet us over there."

"You should stay, Jessica," Ivy echoed.

They were right: I shouldn't let Aaron's bad behavior ruin our night. Plus, I didn't know if I could muster the strength to load Aaron into the car and deal with him at home.

After the bathroom, Tami waved me over to the semicircle of white folding chairs set up in rows in front of a stage. Ivy moved her purse off a chair for me and Alyson handed me a glass of wine and said, "Now, this is the fun part."

The lights dimmed and the auctioneer did his best to quiet the crowd.

Carolann made a few welcoming remarks, including a heartfelt thanks to Ivy and me for all of our donations work. Then Jeff took the microphone and thanked Carolann for volunteering as the auction chair and then launched into a long, rambling speech about the importance of our school to the community. It was obvious he was using the stage to posture for the upcoming election. It did not at all seem like the appropriate place or time for his speech. Alyson must have thought the same because she looked royally pissed. Finally, after the head of the school spoke, the auctioneer took his place behind the podium to start the live auction and Carolann slid into an empty seat next to us.

First up was a one-week trip to Disney with a room at the Grand Floridian. "Do I hear $900?" said the auctioneer. The bidding was lightning fast with paddles popping up like whack-a-moles and in less than a minute the trip was sold to bidder 128 for $4,500. Wow. That was some serious moolah.

Carolann was through the moon. "That went for two thousand over value! We are going to have a record year!"

I clapped along with the others, took a sip of my chardonnay, and glanced down at the list of "priceless" items I was never going to be able to buy. *Chef's dinner in your home. Palisades Mall shopping spree.* Then Tami pointed to package #5—*Weekend getaway in May: Kiawah Island, South Carolina. Three-bedroom beachfront house (sleeps eight), plus spa and pool access at the Sanctuary Resort. Two nights. Value: $2,200.*

"You're coming," she said.

I wasn't sure what she meant.

"Last year we all went to South Beach, this year it's Kiawah. And you're coming with us for a moms' weekend away."

There it was: my coveted invite to the inner circle. The words that, for so many months, I had longed to hear. They looked at me, grinning and expectant, but a voice inside me wondered if the real reason they were asking was out of pity. They must have thought I was about to go off the deep end. "That's so nice of you to invite me, but I can't accept . . ."

"You most certainly can. You are wound seriously tight right now. We've all been there and we get it, believe me. What you need is a break—a *real* break."

"You'll feel so much better after a couple of days of relaxation—without Aaron, without the kids," Ivy said. "Last year we had like the best weekend *ever*. And there's plenty of room, I looked up the pictures online last week and the house is ginormous."

"But you do have to come ready to par-tay," Tami added. "I mean, if you're up for it."

I had no idea whether Aaron was free to watch the kids that weekend but there was no way I was going to miss my chance this time to prove I was up for it. Plus, I'd never been to South Carolina.

"Oh, I'm up for it all right," I said, starting to feel better already. "Thank you, guys. Really. I can't tell you how much this means to me."

"So with five of us now going, it'll be more like four, five hundred a person, tops," Alyson said. "Plus the airfare, but if you have miles, the travel's free. What's your paddle number, Jessica?"

Shit—wait—I thought they were inviting me as a guest, not inviting me to *bid* with them.

Before I could think about backpedaling, the auctioneer announced, "Package #5. Spend a weekend in May, two nights, three days in a beautiful Kiawah Island beach house. Let's start the bidding at five hundred dollars."

"Five hundred!" Tami chirped, raising her paddle high in the air.

"Do I hear one thousand? Is that a paddle I see in the back? Lift it higher so I can read the number: paddle 18 for one thousand. Now let's get it up to fifteen hundred. Do I hear fifteen hundred?"

"Holy shit, he's going fast," Tami said, and she raised her paddle. "Fifteen hundred!"

"That's fifteen hundred dollars, going to help support your kids at Laurel Meadow. Now two thousand, who's in for two?"

There was a pause and I saw Tami cross her fingers on her lap.

"Only fifteen hundred dollars for a lovely beach-front house on Kiawah Island? World-class golf, tennis, and boating, with access to the legendary Sanctuary Spa. Come on, people, I want to hear two thousand. There it is in the back, two thousand!"

"Who the fuck are these people bidding against us?" Tami said, craning her neck to try to see. "Okay, here it goes, guys." She raised her paddle and shouted, "Twenty-five hundred!"

"That's twenty-five hundred right here in the front row! Now three thousand, do I hear three?" He scanned the room with his hand but no one raised a paddle. "Going once at twenty-five hundred . . ."

Tami sat back confidently and whispered, "This trip is ours."

"Twenty-five hundred once. Twenty-five hundred twice. Last chance for twenty-five hundred. Anyone for twenty-seven fifty?" he tried. Tami smiled and licked her lips, tasting her win.

And then #18 shot up like a dagger. "Three thousand!" a man's voice shouted.

Tami looked up at the auctioneer in wild disbelief.

"Going once at three thousand for paddle 18. What do you say in the front row? Do I hear four? A weekend in gorgeous Kiawah Island, three thousand going twice . . ."

"Shit, we're not going to get it," Tami said with urgency in her voice.

"Let's all throw in another couple hundred," Alyson said.

"Yes, yes, yes!" Carolann said. "A couple hundred more each should do it."

"We already bid on like four other packages," Ivy said. "Drew's gonna strangle me!"

"Give me a break, Ivy—in Drew's world an extra zero or two is barely a rounding error. Okay, Jessica?"

I wasn't going to be the one to say no.

Tami quickly raised her paddle. "Four thousand!" she called out.

A round of applause rippled through the audience and the auctioneer paused to let the excitement percolate. "That's *four thousand dollars*. Outstanding! Now let's really raise the roof for your kids. Do I hear forty-five hundred? Yes—there it is—paddle 62, a new bidder for forty-five. Now who's going to get us to five, do I hear five?"

"Five!" Tami yelled without a pause.

Oh my god, we're up to a thousand dollars a person.

"Fifty-five hundred!" paddle 18 shouted.

Without even a prompt from the auctioneer, Tami stood up and raised her paddle high above her head. She said firmly, "Six. Fucking. Thousand. Dollars." And with that, she turned around and stared back in the vicinity of the other bidders with a look I would never want to be on the receiving end of.

"Six *thousand* dollars!" the auctioneer announced, leaving out Tami's f-bomb. "Six thousand going once. Six thousand going twice." Not a word from the others. "Last call for Kiawah Island . . . SOLD to the blonde in the front row for six thousand dollars!"

We all jumped up and hugged like we had just won the jackpot on *Family Feud*. My glass of wine went flying, drenching the row of parents behind us. So what if it cost over a thousand dollars? So what if Aaron was going to be furious? It felt so good to finally be a winner.

CHAPTER TWELVE

THE TRAVEL PLANNING E-MAILS STARTED EARLY the following morning and flooded my inbox for the next several weeks leading up to the trip. Seven, twelve, fifteen e-mails a day, reply all, even more including texts. *8am flight out of Newark to Charleston, or what about the 9:45 out of Kennedy? The 7a, definitely the 7!!!* Alyson circulated a spreadsheet with a list of endless on-site activities, afternoon tennis clinics, and three-hour kayak excursions in the Kiawah River. The relaxing beach weekend I had envisioned did not at all include a 7:30 a.m. Beach Butt Blaster class.

But I didn't want to be the spoilsport, and definitely not a lazy one. I wrote back, *Sounds good! Up for anything! xoxo,* and marveled how we were spending more time planning the trip than we would actually be there for. After the seventeenth e-mail about how many pairs of sandals we were packing (*Two. Three. Six including flip-flops!*), I was starting to wonder if I could handle three whole days and two nights with this group.

When I told Liza I was having second thoughts about going even though I had spent over a thousand dollars on the trip plus five hundred for the airline tickets, as most of Aaron's frequent flier miles were on American and we were flying Delta—not to mention the two hundred I paid for my own donated theater tickets, which no one else had bid for—Liza reminded me that first of all, it was essentially a donation to the school. And secondly, it was a weekend on the beach at a five-star resort, not an Outward Bound survival expedition. Not only was I going, I was absolutely required to have my thousand-plus dollars worth of fun. And did I know how lucky I was? A similar trip at her private preschool auction in the city had sold for five times what we had paid.

Aaron couldn't have been more enthusiastic, constantly reminding me how much I deserved my weekend to relax. I knew he was overcompensating for his auction-night behavior which I was still angry about, even though he had apologized profusely and had sent me flowers at the office and, I'd noticed, the recycling was sorted neatly in the bins in the garage. He did seem genuinely excited to take care of Phoebe and Madison, though, refusing to hire a sitter and compiling a lengthy list of "best-ever daddy-time" activities I knew he wouldn't be able to get even halfway through. He was trying and I should have been happy.

But I wasn't. I trudged in and out of the house through our dull daily sameness, back and forth to the city, two tired parents in our long-running roles with barely a passing peck good night. Maybe Aaron thought he was being supportive, but every time he told me how excited he was for me to go on the trip, I felt like he was pushing me away. I wanted to feel excited about going, I wanted to find a way out of our funk of the mundane, but I knew that fix needed to start with us, and I didn't know how. All I did know was that it was going to take a lot more than white roses and neat newspapers to get us back to the relaxed and easy happy we used to be.

A few days before the trip I stopped into Solé on my way home from the train to say a quick hi to Lupita, and forty-five minutes later found myself sipping a warm café con leche surrounded by the hustle and buzz of the early dinner patrons. She was telling me about her exams and papers due now that her school semester was ending, and her plans to visit a cousin in Trenton before she started her advanced child development summer class.

"Did you ever finish that paper about Hamilton and Burr?" I asked.

She sighed. "Almost. The deadline for submission to the *Journal of American Studies* is next week. Just when I think we are done, my professor now has me chasing one more lead. He has been running me ragged with all of his theories and conjectures. If you can believe it, I am meeting tomorrow with a descendant of Aaron Burr's, a cousin who lives not far, in Bergen County."

"You're kidding, right?"

"I know, it seems crazy, but no, she is for real. I should not be complaining; the work has been very interesting. Entertaining, even." Her eyes shone with the gleam of excitement that comes right before revealing a secret. "I may be close to discovering something new about Hamilton and Burr and the first American political sex scandal."

Hamilton's sex scandal had been news to me when I saw the Broadway show. I had known that Burr was the one responsible for killing Hamilton in the duel, but hadn't realized that Hamilton had an affair and ended up

publicly spilling the beans about it in order to prove he
didn't steal money from the US Treasury.

"Sounds juicy," I said. "What is it?"

"I promised not to share the specifics until after my
meeting, but it involves Maria Reynolds, Hamilton's mistress."

Lupita went on to explain how back around 1792,
some reports claimed that in an effort to damage Hamilton's reputation, it was Burr who arranged for Maria,
a very attractive woman, to flirt with Hamilton on a trip
of his to Philadelphia, and to make sure she took him to
bed. It worked; Hamilton and Maria had a three-year
affair. Maria's husband John blackmailed Hamilton in
exchange for keeping quiet, and not long after, Hamilton
was questioned by Congress as to whether his financial
dealings on behalf of the country were above board. That
was when Hamilton revealed his affair with Maria,
actually using their love letters as proof of his fiscal
innocence.

"American history was *way* more boring when I was
in school," I said, smiling easily.

"Whether or not Burr hatched the Maria Reynolds
affair scandal has not been proven. In the end, Hamilton's career was not tainted, which must have made Burr
even more angry. Burr himself had many indiscretions
and was also known to be a philanderer, and Hamilton
took to the press to spread slander about him."

"I swear, you could be talking about two men in politics right now and it would sound the same. It's unbeliev-
able to me how history keeps repeating itself. There was
Marilyn. Monica. Now you're telling me this story about
Maria."

"Even before then: Jefferson had Sally, Benjamin Franklin had many. Grover Cleveland, FDR. Practically every elected official in France. Cheating was, and still is, the norm. The same egos that drive them into office make them believe they are above it all and will not get caught."

"But you'd think with how fast news gets around these days people would have a little more restraint."

"We want our leaders to be perfect but in the end they are just people, like the rest of us. Although their affairs do get a lot more press." Lupita took a slow sip of her coffee. "So we will see if this Burr descendant has anything of interest tomorrow. I cannot wait to put this project to bed so I can spend more time with Samuel. He keeps reminding me we still have not visited the museum with the dinosaurs. Once he gets an idea in his head, he cannot let it go."

"Driven, like someone else I know." I smiled. "We definitely have to pick a day."

"How about this weekend coming? Maybe Saturday?"

Ping-ping-ping, three texts came in. *Check out my new beach hat! So sexy, I love it. 2 more days, can't wait!*

I tucked my phone deep in my bag. "Sorry—I won't be here this weekend. I won a trip at the auction to Kiawah Island in South Carolina with a bunch of moms from Phoebe's school."

"That sounds like fun."

My bag vibrated, *ping-ping,* and I couldn't help thinking back to that night at the auction and those awful things Drew and Peter said. I knew Ivy and Carolann didn't necessarily share their husbands' prejudices, at least I didn't think they did, but by association I felt embarrassed about going away with friends married to people who were so shallow and rude.

"I'm actually kind of nervous," I said. "I haven't ever been away from Phoebe and Madison overnight before." That was a secret I still hadn't told anyone.

"Not even for one night? Your kids are very lucky."

I'd never thought about my predicament in quite that way. "I guess."

"You will see, the time will go fast. And it will be nice to be away and relax with friends."

"I hope so," I said, and as I was about to complain about the jam-packed activity schedule and the early flight out on Friday and our new nanny having to come early so Aaron could fit in a few meetings, it hit me how incredibly spoiled my gripes were sounding, even inside my own head. I was so fortunate to have the means to fly away for the weekend and stay at a fancy resort. Lupita was right—it would be nice to be away, to have fun on a beach for a couple of days, and it was high time I stopped complaining about it. I hoped I hadn't sounded snobbish bringing it up. "Can we plan for the museum the weekend after?"

We put it on our calendars, and as I got up to leave I reached into my bag for money for my coffee and Lupita said, "Stop, do not be silly, you are family here."

Warm water cascaded from an extra-large showerhead, flowing through my hair and down my back with the perfect amount of pressure. I could already see tan lines on my shoulders after just a few hours in the sun. My chest and stomach were touched pink and I smiled as the water continued its stream through the triangle between my legs. Even my thighs looked toned, good and sore from a late-afternoon beach run. I leaned my head back to feel the warmth wash over me again, lingering in the pleasure of an unhurried shower, wondering when the last time was I had taken one without rushing and worrying that in the two minutes I normally gave myself to quickly wipe away the grime, someone would get hurt, fall down the stairs, hit their head on the coffee table, or burst through the door in desperate need of a cookie or some apple juice or to untangle the twisted rubber band in a doll's matted hair.

I closed my eyes to listen to the *shhhhh* of the running water, and even though I did miss the girls, I felt relieved to have a respite from the usual home frenzy. Aaron would be back from work soon to relieve Samina, and when I'd called to check in earlier, everything was fine. Thank god for Samina. It had only been a few weeks, but with her youthful fifty years of mothering and nanny experience and calm demeanor, the house was so much more peaceful than it had ever been with Noreen. How perfect that Alyson's nanny Priya had a friend who was looking for a new gig. And bonus, she turned out to be a terrific cook too. It would have been so much easier if we'd found her to begin with, if we'd been able to avoid the whole Noreen ordeal culminating in those agonizing predawn hours the night before I fired her: Would she cry? Yell? Stomp out the door, furious? It had turned out to be the right decision not to give her a specific reason, to keep it professional and brief. *We need to make a change. Sorry for the short notice.* And with two weeks' severance in her hand and a bewildered look on her face, Noreen had walked out and it was over, just like that. And the kids barely noticed she was gone.

I opened the coconut conditioner Ivy had brought for us to share and inhaled the sweet, tropical smell of vacation. Bumble and bumble Super Rich, the kind I always wanted to buy but couldn't stomach spending the twenty-eight dollars a bottle. I poured an indulgent handful and massaged it into my hair, immediately feeling the silky-smooth results. I decided to leave it in for a few minutes to see just how soft my hair could actually get and nudged the dial even closer to *H*, feeling a hot chill as the water rained even hotter, so hot I could barely stand it, and as the steam rose I breathed it in deeply and for once felt cleansed, inside and out.

I stepped out of the shower and wrapped a towel around myself, tucking the edge in snugly under my arm. Everyone's toiletry bags were on the vanity counter and a few were left open: intimates on display. Secret roll-on; Bulgari body lotion; Advil; eyeliner; Dulcolax; Lotrimin; Maybelline Great Lash Mascara, like I used to wear in high school; Excedrin Migraine; the pill; tweezers; hairspray; Close-Up toothpaste. I didn't know they still made Close-Up toothpaste. Cosmetic vestiges of our teenage selves hidden in little zippered travel bags decorated with bright stripes and paisley florals.

One other bag was slightly open and I knew I shouldn't but found myself gently unzipping it to see what was inside. Behind the floss and the nail polish remover in a side compartment I saw two pill bottles with *Buproprion* and *Lexapro* typed on the labels above *CAROLANN REYNOLDS, 38 West Gate Road, Suffern*. I didn't know what those drugs were for, but all of a sudden I felt terribly guilty. I quickly tried to set the bag back in its exact spot on the counter, but I was still worried as I stepped into the bedroom to get dressed that Carolann would be able to tell someone had been snooping.

Ivy and I were in the smaller bedroom on the ground floor with two twin beds and a Jack-and-Jill bathroom, which connected to the master suite where Carolann and Alyson had claimed the king-sized canopy bed. Tami had taken the whole upstairs loft for herself with a huge porch overlooking the ocean. Even though Carolann and Alyson's room was much larger, there was no way I would have ever considered sharing a bed. It seemed weird to me to sleep in the same bed with a friend—and I was looking forward to my two blissful nights of long, late, uninterrupted slumber.

I sat on my bed and picked up my phone. No messages from work. Good. I opened up Safari and typed in *bupropion* and a long list popped up on the screen. *Brand name: Wellbutrin. Used to treat depression and seasonal affective disorder . . . Lexapro: Helps alleviate excessive worrying that interferes with daily life.* I thought back to all the times I had been so annoyed with Carolann, so impatient and short, all those months while her husband Peter was out of work. I felt awful. Maybe her depression was serious, something she'd been struggling with for a long time. Or maybe she was just using something to take the edge off. Either way, I would have handled things differently with her from the beginning if I'd known, watched what I said instead of being so blunt. I wished someone had told me. But maybe it was a secret. Maybe no one knew, except for me.

"Are you done with the shower?" Alyson interrupted

my thoughts, and I jumped at the sound of her voice in the bedroom doorway.

"Yep, I'm done, go ahead," I said, quickly clicking off the phone. "Just wanted to make sure no one at the office is looking for me."

Music started blasting from the living room, signaling the official start of happy hour. Time to get dressed, time to forget I knew anything about Carolann and her antidepressants. I opened my suitcase and took out the three night outfits I'd brought for our two-night stay, and couldn't decide which one to wear. I tried on my aqua and peach batik dress and put on a white tank underneath to cover the plunging neckline. Not that I had any cleavage left to worry about showing or hiding anymore. What once had been a nice set of Bs was now down to a couple of deflated As after breastfeeding two babies, and in order to fill my shirts I had to wear padded bras. I even had a white cotton one in my current rotation, which, the salesgirl said, was technically a training bra.

I looked in the mirror and wasn't happy with the dress. I took off the tank and rummaged through my bag to find the new "chicken cutlets" bra I'd bought for the trip—no straps, with sticky stuff to attach it to your boobs. The directions said to lean forward so your breasts hang, and then stick the cutlet underneath while you push toward the middle. I tried it, and a small ridge appeared in the V of my dress. I tried the other side, and adjusted it a little so my faux cleavage would be even. I liked it—instant boobs!—and in a moment of abandon, I chose my high-heeled sandals instead of the flats I usually wore.

Tami entered the room wearing a bright yellow halter

dress that showed off her real cleavage and also her tan. She looked beautiful. "Do you have any lip gloss?" she asked.

"I think so," I said, thinking it was a little strange to be over thirty and still be sharing lip gloss. But we were sharing a house for the weekend and sharing a bathroom, what was a little lip gloss between friends?

"You've got to try this thing I bought on our liquor run." She held up what looked like a fat green test tube. "It's called Suck & Blow. This one's green apple."

I took the tube and she explained, "I blow from one end and you suck in the Jell-O shot from the other. It's a total rush, like inhaling a great big vodka-soaked gummy bear."

"Sounds pretty gross but I'll try it." I held the "suck" end up to my mouth and Tami stood in front of me and held the "blow" side.

"Ready?" she asked. "One, two . . ." and then she blew forcefully. A wad of slimy sweetness flew through my mouth so fast I could barely taste it, and I felt the alcohol singe my throat as it went down.

"Water! Chaser! Fast!" I coughed and ran into the kitchen.

I heard Tami laugh and say, "Let's try the watermelon next!"

Soon we were all showered and dressed and gathered in the living room, double height with a fireplace, a dining table, and sliding glass doors that led from the open kitchen to an outside deck. It looked like a page ripped out of *Southern Living*, the comfy, white slip-covered couches and rattan furniture accents and framed photos of starfish and sailboats on the walls easy on the eyes and making no personal statement whatsoever.

I moved aside one of the blue and white throw pillows shaped like a shell and sat down on the couch next to Ivy with a cold Corona Light. Tami was initiating Carolann with a passion fruit Suck & Blow, which she proceeded to spit halfway across the room.

"Spit—take!" Tami said, doubling over in laughter.

"That is positively vile, Tami!" Carolann said, wiping her mouth with her hand. "Where is that mojito mix we bought? I'll make us a batch of those—right after I throw the rest of these things out. *Blech!*"

"Don't waste them!" Ivy said. "I'll do another before we go to dinner."

Alyson sprung up from her seat. "Shit, I just remembered—I forgot to cancel my personal training session with Antonio."

"Is that the new guy at Planet Fitness who teaches the boot camp class?" I asked.

"More like booty camp," Tami teased, raising her eyebrows. "Whatever it takes to stay motivated to exercise."

"Staring up at Antonio's gorgeous face for an hour every week would definitely keep *me* motivated," Ivy said. "His wait list is a mile long—I can't believe you landed a spot with him, Aly, you're sooo lucky. He's from Spain, right?"

"Brazil," Aly mumbled, looking genuinely worried. "I have to see if he can fit me in for a makeup next week. Be right back."

"Seriously, Aly?" Tami said. "We are not here to worry about home shit, even good-looking shit like Antonio. Stop being so uptight and let it go."

Alyson ignored her and shut the bedroom door. It did seem a little ridiculous for her to waste precious vacation time rescheduling a personal training session, but knowing Alyson and how anal she was about her workouts, I could understand how she'd feel better with it on her calendar for the following week.

I reached out to touch the stack of diamonds on Ivy's finger. "Can I try on your rings?"

"Sure," she said.

I took off my gold wedding band and squeezed her rings over my finger, holding out my hand to admire the intricate designs of the bezel-set stones. "They're beautiful. Are they white gold or platinum?"

"Platinum. This one was my push present after Tanner was born. And this one with the sapphires was after Ruby. They look really good on you."

"They do," I said, imagining what it would be like to walk around with a stack of beautiful diamonds on my finger every day. *It would feel pretty fabulous*, I thought. Not that anything was wrong with my matte-gold hoop, passed down from my great-grandmother. I loved my ring. But adding a thin diamond band above it and maybe even below for a little update . . . it was a little extravagant, but with Aaron still in apology mode, it might be a good time to do some shopping. Although it seemed ridiculous to even think about spending so much money on a piece of jewelry.

But, like Tami said, that was home shit and we were away. For one weekend, I could let it all go. I finished off my beer and took another out of the fridge.

Alyson came back into the room holding a Sephora shopping bag. "Okay, guys, I brought us all a little something. Just for fun." She dumped out a pile of makeup containers, fake eyelashes and body glitter and a palate of beachy-colored blushes and eye shadows entitled, *Cabana Glama—Your Destination Makeup Kit,* with instructions typed in curly script describing how to *glam it up* on your *vacay.*

"*Helloooo, hotspots!*" I read aloud. "Oh my god, Alyson, this is hilarious. *Take your tan sexy self and your flirty come-hither peepers out on the town. You'll have some kinda hunky asking for a sunset stroll in no time.* Where in the world did you find this?"

"Oooh, I love this color!" Ivy exclaimed. She dipped her pinky in the gold glitter and dabbed it on her eyelids, and then took the insert from my hand, "*Get ready to party and explore the hottttt local scenery.* Oh, I am definitely ready now!"

"Ivy, send me over some of that Cocoa Pizazz," Carolann said, giggling. "And a set of fake eyelashes, please."

I hadn't worn fake eyelashes in god knows how long. But what the hell. The sparkly blush didn't look half bad. Tami paraded around the room in an exaggerated catwalk, singing, "*Hands in the air like you just don't care,*" and soon we were all up dancing with the music blasting, our private party of hot moms ready to roll.

We piled into our SUV rental for dinner at the marina just a few miles up the road. The restaurant was packed with Friday-night revelers, but luckily Alyson had called to reserve us a prime table on the upstairs deck with a view of the water. Fishing boats and speedboats and a couple of white yachts sat side by side, still for the night, and as the sun dipped behind the lowlands in the distance, I felt a welcome breeze cut through the humid air, turning the daytime into evening.

"I had *the* best time today," Ivy said.

"You falling off that banana boat? Priceless," Alyson said, smirking.

"It was so huge and slippery, I could barely keep my legs around it. I feel like my thighs got some workout trying to ride that thing."

"That's what *she* said," Tami joked. Big Yellow, we'd named it, and kidded the whole time that the banana boat didn't *resemble* a huge, inflatable yellow penis—it looked exactly like one. I had never been on a banana boat before and loved speeding through the open water, jumping over the waves as the sea sprayed in our faces, pulled by a completely insane driver who thought it would be hilarious to go even faster every time he heard us scream. And it was—it was more fun than I'd had in a long, long time, a whole hour spent laughing and flying free, singing "Day-O" at the top of our lungs. "*Come, Mister Tally Man, tally me banana . . .*"

"I'll tally *your* banana right here," Tami had kept the joke going the whole afternoon, and now, "*Daylight come and we* don't *want to go home*," was our official weekend theme song. Ivy had already downloaded it as her new ring tone.

The waitress brought over a round of Red's famous frozen strawberry daiquiris and we ordered a Southern feast: crab cakes with avocado and key lime mustard and the jumbo platter of coconut shrimp. Jalapeño hush puppies and fried calamari. Two orders of three-cheese quesadillas. Every bite tasted so good; melted cheese and crunchy tortillas dipped in spicy mango salsa danced on my taste buds, salty and sweet.

"Look at that guy over there," Tami said to Alyson. "Doesn't he look like Matt Graziano?"

A few tables away a group of men about our age, maybe a little younger, sat at a long table crowded with food and buckets of Palmetto beers on ice. The one sitting at the head took a bottle to his lips and I noticed his expensive watch and thick platinum wedding band. My eyes automatically did a ring scan of the others, and from what I could see they were all married. Married and wealthy, in Italian golf shirts that fit just right, with faces tanned playing rounds of eighteen. A typical table of Kiawah golfers.

"Which one?"

"Wearing the Boston Red Sox hat," Tami said, looking toward one of the best-looking guys, blue eyes noticeable from across the room.

"You're right, he *does* look like him. A slightly younger version," Alyson said.

"Who's Matt Graziano?" I asked.

"My seventh-grade boyfriend. The first guy I went to second base with, behind the stairs before Mr. Foy's English class."

I quickly tried to recall the name of the first guy I went to second base with, although it had been at the end of ninth grade, not seventh. In seventh grade I had barely rounded first, let alone thought about second. It was Phil someone. Phil Ran . . . kowsi.

"And third base too," Tami reminded her. "We used to call Matt the 'Italian Stallion,' remember?"

"Of course I remember. It's pathetic, but if you can believe it, to this day I *still* know his birthday. March 30. And during the maybe three weeks we were boyfriend and girlfriend, he turned twelve and I bought him an Adidas half-shirt. ADIDAS: All-Day-I-Dream-About-Sex. Remember that?"

"Who doesn't?" Tami said.

"I have not heard that in forever!" Carolann chimed in.

I hadn't heard of that, ever, and wondered what else I had missed in seventh grade.

Alyson looked out toward the water and continued, "Sadly, it ended when he kissed me right after he ate a bag of Doritos. No wonder I can't forget him. For years I couldn't even look at a bag of Doritos without getting the heebie-jeebies."

We all laughed, but silently I wished I still had a friend from middle school to remember my firsts with. My adolescent experiences seemed a million lifetimes ago, tucked away in attic trunks next to old report cards and yellowing papers still marked with gold and red stars. I still had Liza to reminisce with about our college days. I knew we'd always be close, but keeping up with her was turning out to be a lot harder than I'd thought. And whenever I felt a twinge of loss about it, I tried to remember the refrain I learned at sleepaway camp around the campfire: *Make new friends but keep the old, one is silver and the other is gold.* Time to focus on the silver, to connect with my friends right in front of me and build new experiences and new firsts together. So far we'd had our first banana boat ride. And our first Suck & Blow Jell-O shots. Not exactly life-long-memory material, but it was a start.

The waitress set down our dessert menus and from downstairs I heard the electric twangs of a band starting their sound check.

"Look at this picture Chris just texted me," Tami said, passing around her cell. It was Jeff and Drew's heads, passed out on what looked like Alyson's dining room table, with a bottle of spilled red wine dripping down onto her white carpet. *Don't tell Aly,* the message read.

"Ha!" Alyson said.

"Aren't you mad?" I asked. I wondered if Aaron was home putting Phoebe and Madison to bed like he said or if he was at Aly and Jeff's house with the other husbands. Shit, that reminded me—I had forgotten to call. And it was already past nine, too late to say good night to the girls. I'd have to call first thing in the morning and send Aaron a text later.

"Oh, it is definitely a fake, Jessica," Carolann said, sipping the last of her daiquiri. "Although the wine looks pretty real on the carpet. Last year in Miami we spent half the time thinking all the photos they sent us were real. But then we figured out they were staging them, just to mess with us."

"This time we know better," Alyson said. She grabbed Tami's hand and walked over to the golfer table. Alyson did a subtle toss of her hair as she spoke to the one in the Red Sox hat, and then he and another guy stood up and posed next to Tami—first with their arms around her shoulders and then crouching down eye level with her breasts, sticking their tongues out fraternity style. Whoa. Maybe Chris had a sense of humor that would find those pictures funny, but I knew if I sent Aaron photos of me like that, even as a joke, he would be furious.

"Good one," Ivy said, giving Tami a high five as they sat back down. "We'll have to come up with some more."

"Yeah, good one," I echoed, and tried to think of a picture to surprise Aaron without going as far.

Alyson said, "Let's get the check and head down to

the bar. My Matt Graziano look-alike says the band is supposed to be rockin'. Plus, I owe them a round of shots."

"What about dessert?" Ivy asked. "That key lime pie looks sooo yummy."

"If you want it, go for it. We can meet you there," Alyson said.

"I'll share the pie with you," I said to Ivy, and was glad I did. We dug our forks into a plateful of sugary goodness topped with real whipped cream and set in the most delectable graham cracker crust. I had forgotten how good food tasted when given the time to savor it. Even if I had to roll myself home on Sunday, every morsel was worth it.

"You know, I came like *this* close to not coming this weekend," Ivy said, looking down at the remnants of our dessert.

"Second thoughts?" I asked, wondering if she felt the same as I did in the weeks leading up to the trip. Now I was having so much fun I couldn't believe I had even been nervous about it.

"No, it wasn't that—I've been looking forward to this trip for weeks. But Drew pulled some BS last night about a big deal of his that's closing and how he wasn't going to be able to look after the kids this weekend. He literally had my ticket in his hand and said he wasn't going to let me get on the plane."

Not let her? I wanted to shake Ivy and say, *What the fuck are you doing with this asshole*? Maybe she was in denial. Or maybe it was something deeper that kept them together. Like the safety his money provided. I really didn't know. All I did know was Ivy was going to have to be the one to say she'd had enough of Drew before I could even get close to saying anything about his behavior, and for a minute I thought that's where she might be going. "You must have been furious," I finally ventured.

"I was. Sometimes I just don't know . . . But there was like no way in hell I was going to miss this trip. So I scrambled and got our nanny to cover most of it and I told him to call his mother for the rest." She sounded angry, but looked more hurt, and just as I thought she was about to start to cry, her face brightened and she said, "Fuck it! I'm here now."

"You're here now," I repeated. "It wouldn't be the same without you."

"You're so sweet. Thanks." She gave me a hug. "Now let's go dance our asses off!"

By the time we made it downstairs, there was a line to get in. The bouncer stopped us at the door. "IDs, please."

There was nothing that made me happier than still getting carded. I gladly reached into my purse and handed him my license. "You just made my entire year," I said, instantly feeling twenty again as I stepped inside.

We snaked through the crowded room with crab traps and nets and other nautical relics hanging from the walls. Alyson waved us over to the giant oak bar with names and messages graffitied all over it. *Laurie & Bill—4-Eva. Gamecocks Rule!*

"Another round of Absolut lemon drops, please. Make it twelve," she told the bartender who looked barely twenty-one himself. He shook the concoction and poured it across the long line of shot glasses. One of the Boston guys laid down a fifty-dollar bill but Alyson said quickly, "I've got it on our tab. Next round's on you for sure."

"Cheers," Tami toasted, and we downed the shots, sugar masking the vodka's bite. It seemed like we'd been drinking practically nonstop since noon but I didn't feel even the slightest bit buzzed. Probably too much food in my stomach absorbing it.

"Jessica, Ivy, this is Brad, Steve, Sean, Colin, and was it Darrell? Donny? Whatever—I'm never going to remember the rest of your names or who's who, so you'll just have to figure it out."

Before I could say hi, Tami grabbed my hand. "Come on, dance with me, I love this song."

"Give me a minute," I said. Even though the bar was crowded, the dance floor was still pretty empty, and to get out there in front of everyone, even strangers, I definitely needed more to drink.

Tami took Ivy with her instead and they started dancing together seductively, well aware of everyone's eyes on them. Tami was having a great time playing it up. She casually let her fingers graze Ivy's arm and twirled her around, most likely whetting the girl-on-girl fantasies of every guy in the room.

"So are you all on vacation?" a voice from my right asked. I looked up and recognized one of the guys from the table. He was tall, over six feet, with broad shoulders and reddish-blond hair.

"Yep," I answered. "And you? Wait—let me guess. You played the ocean course at Kiawah today."

"Close. Oak Point today. Ocean tomorrow." He smiled and continued: "We come down every year with our families. Rent a couple of houses for the week, do some fishing, hit the beach. And I'll admit, we do try to get in a little golf along the way."

And your wives are where, exactly . . . ?

As if reading my mind, he said, "We switch off a few nights with our better halves for babysitting duty."

"I think they call it *parenting* when it's your own kids," I teased.

Tami signaled it was my turn to come out on the dance floor but I shook my head no and mouthed, *Not yet*. Carolann and Alyson and some of the other guys joined them, but I still needed another drink. I turned around to get the bartender's attention. "One Miller Lite."

"Two," the nameless golfer said, and proceeded to lay down a twenty.

I was about protest and started to reach for my money, but then said, "Thank you," instead. It felt good to have someone buy me a drink in a bar. Besides, he was married, I was married—it was safe.

We stood for a moment, sipping our beers and watching the dance floor. The band was pretty decent, playing a mix of classic and Southern rock.

"What do you do?" I asked, figuring he would say investment banking or law or something to do with owning real estate.

"I work in the theater industry."

"No way!" I exclaimed. "I do too. I'm at an ad agency in New York, Becker Glancy. Do you know it?"

"Of course I know it, it's a great shop. I produce shows for Stages in Boston."

Stages in Boston was among the top Broadway production companies in the country, next to the Nederlanders and Shuberts in New York and San Francisco. They used SpotCo, our biggest competitor, for their advertising, and Sybil had been trying to woo them as a client for years. "Wait—what was your name again?" I asked.

"Steven. Steven Masterson."

I know exactly who you are. "Next you'll tell me your brother is Sky," I said with a smile, and put my hand out to shake as my brain went straight into agency sales mode. "I'm Jessica. Jessica Almasi." What a coup it would be to come home with Stages in Boston as a new client. But we were on vacation, after all, not at a work event. "Do you know Eric Winters?" I asked. He was a highly regarded GM in the Boston area we had done a project for a couple of years before.

"Of course, he's a good friend. We worked together on a show last month."

"Great guy. Please tell him I say hello when you see him."

Our game of Broadway geography continued awhile longer and we found we had a number of industry connections in common. In the tight-knit theater world, business was all about relationships, and a strong bond between an ad agency and a producer could last for decades. The hardest part was getting the intro to the decision makers and there I was, hanging out having a beer with the lead producer at a hugely successful production company, and so far I could tell Steven and I were hitting it off. I wondered what the holdup had been with Sybil—maybe she *was* getting too old to relate to the next generation of talent. I certainly couldn't picture her out drinking Miller Lites in a dive bar in South Carolina.

"Is it true you've got a revival of *Follies* in the works for the fall?" I asked over our second beer. I could feel those earlier lemon drops mixing with the alcohol and I reminded myself to slow it down a little. I didn't want to let myself slip into inebriated territory with a potential client.

Just then Tami came back, and I could tell from the look on her face that this time she was not taking no for an answer. "Whatever you guys are gabbing about cannot be as important as Lynyrd Skynyrd. I mean, it's Lynyrd fucking Skynyrd!" she shouted, and then dragged both of us out on the dance floor packed with steamy bodies pressing toward the band. The lead singer roared into the microphone, "*Gimme three steps, gimme three steps, mister,*" and practically the entire bar yelled back in unison, "*Gimme three steps toward the door!*" The words flowed out of my mouth, forever imprinted in my brain back in college thanks to a mixture of alcohol and repetition at every frat party. Bowie and the Allman Brothers still lived in my head for the same reason, and when the band moved on to them, I belted their lyrics out too, in perfect unison with everyone else in the room. Bruce came next and then the Rolling Stones. Song after song, we all knew the words, everyone on the floor sang out loud, remembering it all together to the beat of the drums and the rhythm of the bass guitar.

"*I'm just looking for clues at the scene of the crime. Life's been good to me so far . . .*"

Steven leaned over. "Was that the Eagles or Joe Walsh? I can never remember." The hair on his forehead was wet with sweat and his eyes were practically glowing.

"Joe Walsh. Solo album," I said definitively. Joe Walsh had always been one of my favorite artists, a legend and a rebel in a perpetual drugged-out haze. Hazy like I was starting to feel, as throughout our marathon dance set refreshed drink after drink kept somehow appearing in my hand.

And then Carolann, who looked particularly hammered, hoisted herself onto the bar. She threw her arms up and gyrated her hips and the crowd went berserk. Carolann! Up on a bar! Not a second later, Tami and Ivy jumped up with her.

Alyson said, "Come on, Jessica."

Even though I was well on my way to wasted, I was not going to dance on a bar, especially not in front of Steven. "Nope, I'm good right here," I said.

"You're getting your ass up there whether you like it or not," Alyson insisted, and pushed me toward a stool to step up on, and before I knew it, Ivy had my hand and was pulling me up too.

The lights were shining in my eyes and all I could see was an undulating mass. The band tore into a set of AC/DC and the pitch of the room thundered even higher as we all screamed out together: "*She was a fast machine, she kept her motor clean, she was the best damn woman that I'd ever seen.*" Up there on display I felt powerful and sexy, fueled by the alcohol and the crowd screaming below me. I closed my eyes and moved my hands over my body, feeling the sweat underneath my dress as my fingers grazed my hips and up my waist and along the edges of my chest and I basked in the limelight, "*Knocking me out with those American thighs.*" Then the music started to swell and the drum beat louder as everybody waited, waited, waited for it, "*Let me hear it now, YOU! SHOOK ME ALL NIGHT LONG!*" The place erupted and I was transported back onto the bar in college, to the me I used to be. *I'm still me*, I thought. *I'm still me and*

I've still got it. I've got it but I'm even better—I've still got it and more.

I raised my hands and then all of a sudden felt something fall between my feet. I looked down and saw an oblong beige disc. At first I thought it was a coaster but then realized: it was my chicken cutlet bra! How could it possibly have slipped out? In a swift move I kicked it and prayed no one had noticed.

Luckily, the set ended and we jumped off the bar and ran to the bathroom to douse ourselves with water. I ducked into a stall, peeled off my other cutlet, and stuffed it into my purse, baffled by its twin's malfunction. I joined everyone else at the sinks touching up their lips and realized I had forgotten I still had the fake eyelashes on and my cheeks were still sparkling with glitter. All that time talking to Steven with my Cabana Glama makeup on! God knows what he must have thought.

Tami said she felt her behind buzzing and pulled out her phone. It was a new photo of Chris and Drew and Jeff in the pool, butt naked from behind.

"Ugh, all your disgusting men, skinny-dipping in my pool," Alyson said as we walked back out toward the bar. A funny smile spread across her face and she said to Tami, "You know what would be hilarious? See that guy over there with the striped shirt?" She pointed toward the dartboards at a group that looked like college students. "I dare you to go over there and kiss him. I'll take a picture and send it to Chris."

"Which one?" Tami asked.

"The cute one," Alyson said. "They would freak. You've got to do it."

Without even a pause, Tami walked over with us

stumbling at her heels. She whispered something in the coed's ear, and barely a second later her mouth was on his. At first I saw him freeze up—and then the kiss kept going.

"Holy shit!" I said, and put my hand over my mouth as if that would stop it. I thought I saw his tongue flick once or twice and wondered what it tasted like and if his lips were soft.

Aly snapped the shot. "Got it! This is the best, Tam, the best!" she screamed.

Tami turned her back to the dumbfounded guy and reached for Aly's phone. "Let me see it," she said.

There was no stopping my thoughts from blurting out: "I cannot believe you just did that!"

"Yeah, baby!" Tami replied, still looking down at the picture.

"No, really—you seriously just kissed that guy! A stranger! In a bar!"

"Okay, Sandra Dee, take a chill. Chris'll probably whack off to that picture tonight."

I glanced at Ivy, doubled over in laughter along with Carolann, and took their cue to shrug and laugh it off too, adding yet another sexed-up image of Chris to my collection, one hand on his cell phone, the other stroking himself stiff to a picture of Tami making out with a stranger.

Another round of shots and a round of darts and then the bar and everything in it melted into a blur. "After-party at our place!" I heard Tami announce, and at some point we all piled into the car, window cool against my cheek. Breaking out the six-packs and everyone to the upstairs porch.

"Turn up the music, Jess!"

I wanted to dance, but every cell in my body felt heavy with gravity, anchoring me to the couch. I stared up at the Big Dipper—*Follow the handle, is that the North Star?* I wished it would tip and drip me down a cool glass of water.

"Are you thirsty?" someone asked, and I was confused how someone could have heard me but maybe I had said it out loud.

Finally I could feel the promise of sleep, sweet sleep, luring me down to my bedroom. I stepped into the darkness and barely remember my head hitting the pillow.

CHAPTER THIRTEEN

THE NEXT MORNING I WOKE UP with a pounding headache and my dress from the night before still on.

I peeled myself out of bed and stumbled to the bathroom. Considering the amount of alcohol I'd ingested, beyond the headache I felt surprisingly okay. Definitely bloated, but generally okay. What I needed was about a gallon of water and a good greasy breakfast, and at that moment I could have sworn I caught a whiff of eggs and bacon coming from down the hall. I threw on a pair of shorts and a clean T-shirt and made my way to the kitchen, where I found everyone already up and sitting around the table.

"Morning," Ivy said.

"Must have coffee." My voice sounded scratchy. "My head is killing me." I poured myself a large mugful and the aroma thankfully started to work its magic.

Carolann picked up where she'd left off: "And then when he said, *Darling, the envelope, please.* That was too funny."

"Jessica, when you bet that guy twenty bucks and hit the bull's-eye, I thought I was going to crap my pants," Tami said.

A bull's-eye? Me? The game of darts slowly came

back, something with boys versus girls and an ultimate bet-the-pet challenge. But I didn't even have a pet.

"You did *not*," Alyson said. "How did I miss that?"

"You were too busy bumping and grinding on your middle-school crush, Aly. Brad was so into you last night," Tami said like a teenager, leaning back in her chair.

"He was just wasted."

"He may have been wasted but he was pining after that fit little booty of yours. You can give your trainer friend Antonio another call later to say thank you."

Alyson mouthed, *Fuck you*, and took a long sip of her coffee. "By the end of the night he was actually getting kind of annoying."

"Annoyingly adorable," Tami opined. "Feels pretty fucking good to know we still have it, ladies, doesn't it?"

It had felt pretty good. Although my head now didn't.

I took a piece of still-warm bacon off the skillet and bit into it, feeling the oil seep into my system and start to right it. "What time did we get home?" I asked.

"I don't know, two, maybe three?" Tami answered. "You disappeared a little early."

Three was early? "I was out cold."

"Colin told me that band is playing at Red's again tonight," Carolann said.

"Who's Colin?" I asked.

"You know: you were talking to him and the tall one—what was his name, Steven?—for what seemed like forever last night."

I knew I should have stopped after that second beer. I didn't remember talking to anyone named Colin. "Oh right, I remember him," I lied. "You know that guy Steven's a big-time Broadway producer—it's such a weird coincidence to have met him down here."

"We know, we know, you went on and on about it," Aly said, rolling her eyes.

I had? Yikes. I wondered what else I might not be remembering. "If I could somehow land him as a client, it would be huge for me at work." *Unless my dance on the bar has already put an end to that.*

"From the way you were cozying up, it looked like you'll definitely be working together," Tami said.

I felt myself start to blush. We might have been talking close, but that was because the music was so loud. I brushed it off: "Oh yeah, right, give me a break. We were talking about *work* the whole time."

"Whatever you say," Tami countered, and got up to put her dishes in the sink.

I honestly hadn't thought Steven was interested in me in that way. Maybe we'd both been drunk and a little flirty but it had felt more innocuous work-flirty to me. *It wasn't like I sucked face with a total stranger.* That part of the night I definitely remembered. All of us would re-member it because we had pictures.

Tami continued, "Anyway, we can do better than that lame-o place. I mean, really, last call at one thirty? I vote we drive into Charleston. There's something like sixteen restaurants and bars within a block or two that are sup-posed to stay open until four. The more choices the bet-ter."

"I'm going to need a serious nap if we're planning to stay out until four tonight," Ivy said.

"Well, we don't have to decide right now," Alyson said. "I booked us a cabana at the private beach at the

Sanctuary—it's not far, we can bike there. And I signed us all up for a group tennis lesson, so we have to be back by three."

Ugh, tennis. I liked Ivy's napping idea better.

My wish to remain idle must have been apparent because Carolann said, "Come on, Jessica, go get your suit on. You'll feel better if you sweat it out."

I went back into the bathroom and popped three Extra Strength Tylenols and downed a glass of water. Before we left I called Aaron but he didn't answer at home or on his cell. He was probably on his way to that Gymboree birthday party for Madison's friend. I texted him, *Having fun, heading to the beach now. Call me later,* and threw my phone and a hat and a few magazines into my beach bag.

The bike ride was thankfully flat for the most part, but the morning air was already steamy. I needed more caffeine and a jumbo-sized Gatorade. A juicy hamburger with pickles and melted cheddar and a salty side of fries. And a milkshake. Just thinking about it made my stomach growl and I realized I had forgotten to pack any food. I hoped this private seating area was near a snack bar.

To get to the beach we had to walk on a narrow path through a tangled thicket, wood splintering beneath our feet from decades of exposure to the salty air. One of my flip-flops slipped and I missed a step but I caught a piece of the railing and stopped myself from taking a nosedive into the prickly thorns. Finally we hit sand and I looked out upon a wide expanse of glorious empty beach that made the schlep worth it. A refreshing breeze blew off the water.

"We could have never gotten through the path carrying loads of beach crap," Alyson said, and it was true—I immediately noticed the calmness around us, kid voices and screams clearly absent.

We found the row of green-and-white-striped, cushy upholstered lounges being held for us and complimented Alyson on her great call on making the reservation. Thankfully one of us had the foresight to do some planning for the weekend and I was appreciative, notwithstanding the tennis plan.

I claimed the chair next to Ivy and laid out my towel, smoothing the edges. After spraying on sunscreen, I took out my brand-new issue of *Us* magazine, slowly turning each page to savor the guilty pleasure. I skimmed the ads for new face creams and upcoming reality shows and lingered on the photos of celebrities caught doing what we do—*They pump their own gas. They eat ice cream!* The glossy paper felt good between my fingers, so much more satisfying than scrolling through dizzying images on a computer screen.

Before it all became accessible in an instant, I used to count down the days until my *Young Miss* magazine arrived in my mailbox. And when it finally came I'd run upstairs to my room, shut the door, and flop down on my bed to devour every word, finding out the answers to everything I was too embarrassed to ask my mother or even my friends: *Is it possible to shave off a tan? If he acts like he hates me, does it really mean he likes me?* For years, *YM* was the older sister I never had, my go-to source telling me what to want and what to wear, everything I needed to be in the know.

I looked out past the sand and the water toward the hazy horizon and felt so far away from home, far away and liberated from my usual beach demands. *Find the shovel, the red one, Mommy, and come on, jump over the waves with me and buy me ices now, pleeease.* Since arriving in South Carolina, it had been surprisingly easy—too easy, almost—not to worry or wonder what the kids and Aaron had been up to, aided by the fact that no one had mentioned our children since we got here. It was as if we had an unspoken pact to suspend their existence for the weekend. It worked: for once I felt free to do nothing except sit and veg out and listen to the soft and steady splash with no one to take care of except for me and my lingering hangover.

All of us were unusually quiet, a rare moment in our talky girlfriend world. It was silent between us on the beach, peaceful without conversation. I glanced over at Tami lying still with her eyes closed, sunning her tanned body alongside the rest of us. I still couldn't believe she'd actually kissed that guy. Lying there she looked totally unfazed, unchanged by that kiss, tongue and all. I doubted Aaron would ever forgive me if I kissed someone else, let alone sent him a picture of it. But who knew what made Chris tick? Maybe it was just another game in their sexual repertoire. Maybe they just lived on a different marriage bandwidth. One at warp speed, so different from Aaron and me.

The silence didn't last long.

"What do you have on your toes, Ivy, Very Berry?" Alyson asked.

"No, it's Red Royale."

"Is that the new Essie?"

"No, it's OPI."

"Oh. It looks just like Very Berry. I almost went with

Bermuda Triangle, but decided on Tropical Sunset for a change. It's a little darker."

"I like it. It's got a hint of tangerine that's supposed to be very in this summer," Ivy said.

I looked down at my own toes, painted some pinkish shade of I-had-no-idea-what-color, grabbed off the shelf in the nail place on Ninth Avenue. I had been lucky to squeeze in a quick pedicure to clean up my feet before the trip with barely enough time to dry before running back to the office, let alone research in advance which shades were now popular. But Ivy and Alyson, when it came to decorating the surfaces—their nails and their windows and their flat-bellied bodies—they were pros. It had been fun so far to play drink-up and dress-up for the weekend, but all the girly topics they liked to discuss and debate so much were foreign to me. I had been hoping on this trip we'd have a chance to take our friendship a level or two deeper, but a part of me was beginning to wonder if there *was* a deeper.

Their words rolled with the waves lapping on the shore and my eyes grew tired and heavy. I knew I should probably put on more sunscreen and reminded myself to make my annual dermatologist appointment when I got home. And I needed to send a follow-up e-mail to Steven, something clever and memorable to get to a real pitch meeting. *Dear Steven,* I crafted in my head. Too formal. Maybe ditch the *Dear? Steven: Great to meet you down in South Carolina* . . . Bo-ring. *Remember me, the drunk girl dancing on the bar?* I shifted in my chair and felt my right knee twinge from the bike ride, or it could have been from the dancing, all of that dancing to all of those great old songs, and within a few minutes I slipped into a half-doze nap.

Clouds must have passed above me as shade cut the heat, and I reached for my towel to cover my legs. My lips felt salty and I needed water but didn't want to move, hoping to drift back into my dream. But my thirst won out, and I sat up and reached into my bag for my water bottle, now warm, checked my watch, and saw it was already eleven thirty. Almost an hour had passed, sixty whole minutes not spent doing or giving or making, and instead I had let myself lie, selfish and still, baking in the sun.

A child's laughter broke the air. I hoped I was still dreaming but annoyingly, a boy about three ran into the water in front of us. "Don't throw sand, honey," a mom's voice said, and I felt suddenly cheated, having lost my childfree utopia.

"I might have to go back to work this fall if Peter doesn't get a job soon," Carolann announced.

So much for not talking about home, I thought.

"Didn't you start those classes to get your real estate broker's license?" Tami asked her. "It would be the perfect job for you—you're pushy in that oh-so-nice-about-it way that makes people do what you ask them before they even know they agreed. You'd sell hundreds of fucking houses. Thousands."

Carolann took a moment to respond. "Thank you, Tami—I think. But the classes were boring."

"Anyone can get through one week's worth of classes," Tami said. "Think about the upside once you get it over with. The market's really starting to turn around."

"But you're *sooo* busy as it is with the kids and volunteering for the school," Ivy said.

"Come September both kids will be in school until

three o'clock, Ivy. And as much as I do like volunteering, I might not have a choice." I couldn't see Carolann's
expression beneath her sunglasses but her voice had a
serious tone.

I didn't know if Carolann was still selling clothes for
Maliblu but I sure wasn't going to be the one to bring it
up. "What did you do before you had kids?" I asked instead. She had never mentioned a previous career.

"I was at Good Sam, on the administrative side. Co-
ordinating all the cardiologists' schedules; what a nightmare. Mark my words, Jessica: there is no way I would
ever go back there. So much politics and the hours were
terrible. I need something with more flexibility."

"Like real estate," Tami pushed.

"I heard there's an online course you can take to get
your interior designer's license," Alyson offered.

"What a joke," Tami said. "How do they test you for
that—is this throw pillow a) teal, b) chartreuse, or c) this
pillow is totally hideous and you should throw it the fuck
away?"

"Home design isn't interesting to me," Carolann said.

"Well, what *are* you interested in?" Tami asked.

Carolann let out a hopeless sigh. "It has been so long,
I don't even know."

I could never imagine ending up like Carolann, bereft
of confidence and unable to even articulate my own in-
terests. I loved my work; I loved being in the middle of
Times Square, getting paid for my expertise and feeling
a part of something bigger than myself—it energized and
satisfied me in a way no other part of my life ever could.
I cherished my family time and craved more of it, but
it was scary to think about being stuck at home every

day, giving away pieces of myself to fulfill everyone else's needs until my own desires were left shriveled under the car seat like a dried-up raisin.

"Don't sell yourself short," I told Carolann. "You've got legitimate fundraising experience. Party planning, operations. Organizing a team to raise over twenty-five grand involves a huge set of skills that lots of companies need." I wasn't saying those things to make Carolann feel better; they were all true. But she didn't look convinced.

"Two years in a row now you've proved you're a pro at on-the-bar dancing," Alyson teased. Not the direction I was heading, but at least it made Carolann smile.

Tami joined in: "That's perfect! Flexible hours. A nice fat paycheck. Your boobs are still perky enough to take your shirt off every once in a while." Carolann looked embarrassed but let out a laugh. "Now we just have to come up with your stripper name. What was the name of your first pet and the street you grew up on?"

"I had a cat named Sunshine. And I lived on Woodridge Terrace."

"Sunshine Woodridge," Tami said. "I like the wood part. How about Sunshine Hardwood? That could work. How about your mom-stripper name, Aly? Although you used to make more money than a stripper when you were out selling drugs."

Alyson selling drugs? Then I remembered that she had done it legally, in pharma sales.

"I meant to tell you, I ran into your old work nemesis in the Muddy Cup the other day. Cynthia Kelly. I remember you used to fight her tooth and nail for those hot doctor accounts. She's at Novartis now and said they're hiring. She said you should call her."

Alyson casually picked up the magazine on her lap and started flipping through the pages as if she might find her response inside. Finally she said, "You know, I'm way too busy with my very important job of picking the napkins for Jeff's little two-hundred-person I'm-the-Greatest, Vote-for-Me event at our house next Saturday."

Tami snipped back, "God, Aly, enough already about the freaking napkins. Every time you mention Jeff's campaign it's like, let me go get my tiny violin."

I hadn't ever heard Tami zing Alyson like that before. I waited for Alyson to take a swipe back but she just sat there, silently turning page after page. I couldn't tell if she was fuming or upset, or both.

Tami didn't let it drop. "If you're so miserable being Jeff's honey-do campaign wife, just tell him to fuck off and have someone on his staff do the grunt work. I mean, you don't have to necessarily go back to work to get out of it, but you used to love your old job, out there hustling, kicking Cynthia's ass every quarter. It'd be good for you to get some of that Aly-fire back instead of sitting around seething on the sidelines, watching Jeff."

Alyson slapped the magazine down on the chair. "You honestly think I'm jealous of *Jeff*? Running for these stupid positions that mean absolutely nothing except to fuel his pathetic ego? It makes me sick what a big fat waste of time and money it is, and all of it for what, the Ramapo Council of Village Idiots?"

"Well, at least he's out there trying for *something*."

Ouch. This fight was going way past their usual barbs and I wondered why Tami was bringing this all up with Alyson now? I thought this was all home shit and we were supposed to be away.

"You think you know everything, Tami, but you don't, you don't have a clue!" Alyson yelled, her eyes blazing with rage. "Maybe you'd like to know, maybe you'd *all* like to know: Jeff has basically used up all of our savings and has been pulling out of our 401(k) to fund his little bullshit pipe dream, even with all of these fundraisers I have to host. Maybe *that's* why I'm not walking around singing his fucking praises all the time."

Pulling from their retirement? I thought they had loads of money. All their luxury cars and arcade games and three-speed rotisseries; the personal training sessions and expensive fertility treatments, if they were even still trying—who knew at this point? And now the campaign. It all added up, it added up to miserable, and I wished Tami hadn't pushed Alyson to expose their private financial troubles.

Troubles, relatively speaking. Alyson was lucky to even have a 401(k) to pull from; she was better off than 99.9 percent of the rest of the planet, but I certainly wasn't going to say that. I knew that stressing about money, no matter how much you had or didn't have, was one of the ebbs of marriage everyone goes through at some point, one of those biggies no one warns you about before you begin. I wanted to tell her I knew what it felt like to live through the dreams of your husband, and when they didn't pan out exactly as you hoped—financially or otherwise—that hollow sense of disappointment and loss when you realized that the perfect life you wished for in your fifth-grade diary isn't where you are, or might ever be. But we learn to compromise along the way; we move to the suburbs and we host fundraisers if we have to; we spend and save and take and give and hope the checkbook—and the partnership—ends up balancing in our favor in the end.

But I couldn't say anything even close to these things. People were weird about money. You could talk about stripper names and IUDs and how many times a week you're having sex with your husband, but any real talk about money, no way.

Alyson sat there looking gaunt in her bikini, her face twisted in an infuriated pout, and I suddenly felt sorry for her. She had put herself out there and everyone was silent.

I took a deep breath. "I understand how—"

"NO. YOU. DON'T!" Alyson screamed. "I'm sick of everyone saying they understand, you DON'T understand, NO ONE understands."

"You don't have to bite my head off," I mumbled, and then Tami jumped in.

"I care about you, Aly," she said in a softer voice, as if she realized she had taken things too far. "We all do. And we can help you get through this."

But Alyson didn't seem to appreciate Tami's conciliatory tone. She looked even more angry, her face and neck turning a shade of purple under her sunburn, and she shouted, "If you really cared you'd leave me the fuck alone!" and then took off down the beach.

There was something in the slow sigh as Tami stood up and started after her that made me think this wasn't the first time she'd been here with Alyson. "Save my seat," she called back over her shoulder.

I watched as the two became distant dots on the shore. Tami knew Alyson longer and better than any of us—if anyone could calm Alyson down, it was her. But I still couldn't understand why she had felt the need to set Alyson off in the first place. I hated how she always insti-gated fights and then was the one to fix them, the sadist and the savior. It was one thing to motivate and support your friends to do more and to be more, but Tami knew the election was a sore spot for Alyson. And now we all knew more about why.

The little boy who had been splashing in the waves started wailing, "I don't want to get out now, Mommy, I don't want to!"

"Tami was awfully harsh on Alyson, don't you think?" I said to Ivy and Carolann.

"Close friends can be as vicious as sisters, Jessica," Carolann replied. "I love my sister but she's always tell-ing me just about everything I don't want to hear."

"Alyson has seemed kind of down lately, maybe she did need a Tami intervention," Ivy said. "Although I don't think Alyson going back into sales is the answer. You can be perfectly happy and not work."

"That's true," I said, not wanting to revisit that topic. My head pulsed in a dull, dehydrated ache and I felt the backs of my legs sticking to my chair. I stood up and walked down to the water to cool down and my feet froze as the first wave hit them, but after a few minutes I eased my way in up to my waist and dunked the back of my hair. I loved the beach but rarely swam in the ocean, too worried about pinching crustaceans and jellyfish and the umpteen million other treacherous sea creatures swim-ming underneath.

Yet even after my dip, the pressure in my head per-sisted. "I think I need to go back and lie down in the air-conditioning for an hour to get rid of this headache,"

I said, drying my legs with a towel. "The humidity out here is killing me."

"Are you okay?" Ivy asked, looking concerned.

"Thanks, I'm fine, except for my head. After a nap in the A/C, I'll be good to go." I gathered up my belongings. "Meet you guys back at the house later?"

"Feel better," Ivy said. "We've got a big night ahead of us."

"Don't worry, I'll be good to go," I assured her.

Back in the room, I turned up both the air and the fan on high and lay down on my bed, but the second I closed my eyes my phone vibrated on the nightstand. It was a text from Aaron. *Home from party, lunchtime & getting P&M down for a nap. Have fun.* He was dreaming if he thought he would get both of them to nap at the same time. But for today, that was his problem to deal with, not mine.

I tried to close my eyes again but kept thinking about Tami and Alyson's fight and couldn't fall sleep. I rolled over and stared at the ceiling fan whirling and remembered reading on the plane about the Sanctuary's newly renovated five-star spa. Maybe I could stop by and see if they could fit me in for a massage. A massage could help make my headache go away—and might even let me escape that looming tennis lesson. The more I lay there and thought about it, the more excited I became about a possible hour of pampering, and I finally decided it was worth a shot.

I got up and threw on a sundress. What else? Sunglasses, my wallet. A book. I automatically picked up my phone but paused before putting it in my bag. My fingers wrapped around it like a Venus flytrap. *Put it down,* my vacation voice commanded. *You'll never truly be away*

unless you leave it behind. I pressed down on both buttons to turn it off, all the way off, until the screen went
black. *There.* I left it on the bed, slipped on my flip-flops,
grabbed the keys, and went out into the bright afternoon,
feeling better already.

The reception area was empty and I crossed my fingers it was a serendipitous sign everyone was out enjoying the gorgeous beach day instead of at the spa. "May I
help you?" the lady behind the counter asked in a smooth
Southern lilt.

I smiled sweetly and tried to look especially weary. "I
hope so. I'm away from my toddlers this weekend for the
first time and I would do anything if you could fit me in
for a massage."

"I remember what it's like to have little ones," she
said, eyeing the schedule on her computer. "My babies
are seventeen and twenty now. How old are yours?"

"Almost two and almost four. Two girls—and quite
a handful. And you look amazing—you must have given
birth when you were a toddler yourself."

She smiled and clicked the mouse a few times. "Normally we're booked solid but I do have a last-minute
cancellation for an Abhyanga treatment with Marilyn in
about forty minutes. You can sit in the sauna or have
a spa lunch out on the veranda while you're waiting, if
you'd like. And if you really want to relax, we could add
thirty minutes of Reiki for a total of ninety minutes. How
does that sound, dear?"

I had no idea what Abhy-whatever or Reiki was, but
the thought of spending an hour and a half in a dark
room with someone doting over me sounded like heaven.

After lunching in my white waffle-weave robe and

slippers, I curled up on a comfortable couch in the solarium to wait for my appointment, sipping cucumber water and breathing in the spa air redolent of lavender. What a find this place was. I felt like I had slipped into someone else's life, playing the role of the Southern belle. And boy did it feel wonderfully decadent to be by myself on my own free time with nowhere to be but right there, and no one to be with but me.

Marilyn led me into a treatment room and covered my body with warm blankets. I closed my eyes and tried to focus on the music, a faintly tribal Indian or Asian chant of some sort. She laid her hands on my forehead for nearly a full minute without moving them, then rubbed her hands together and placed her fingertips gently on the tops of my shoulders. It felt nice to have someone's warm hands on my body, but where was the massage part? I hoped it would start soon.

Suddenly a drop of warm liquid hit in the center of my forehead. And then another. "This will start to remove your stagnant energy and stimulate your Prana," Marilyn said in a whisper. Uh-oh, was I in for one of those holistic treatments where they do a lot of hocus-pocus but don't ever give you an actual massage? The hot oil drip continued on my shoulders, my wrists, on each of my open palms, and then I even felt drops above my belly button, which tickled a little. It felt as if my body was being prepared for an embalming. *Goodbye, Aaron,* I thought, picturing myself entombed underneath the resort's floorboards along with the other uptight Northerners they wanted to get rid of.

I sincerely tried to listen to Marilyn's voice to imagine my impurities loosening, but my mind kept drifting back to Aaron and wondering how he was doing, shuttling the girls in the car to and from their activities. And that stupid deer eating up our bushes. I didn't believe in guns but I had a serious death wish for that deer. Why couldn't it snack next door on Jeff and Alyson's shrubs or the ten gazillion acres of trees and forest around us? What was it that made our bushes so goddamn deer-delicious? Just thinking about it made me tense up and Marilyn must have felt it because she reminded me to take deep breaths in through my nose and out through my mouth. "That's good, like that. Now keep breathing."

Maybe I couldn't clear my mind though I could keep breathing—breathing was one thing I could do automatically, in and out, and as she starting rubbing my shoulders I could feel the tension finally start to release. The music of the waves built up and then gently washed over the shoreline, washing over me, and I lost myself for what felt like a minute, maybe two, and then felt a gentle nudge. "Ms. Almasi? I hope you enjoyed the treatment. There's a glass of water on the table for you. When you're ready, you can get dressed and I'll show you back to the locker room."

It was over? I squinted at the clock on the counter behind me and could see that it was true, my ninety minutes had passed. I must have fallen asleep! But as I got dressed and was about to lament the most expensive nap of my life, I realized I felt pretty terrific: not only had my headache completely disappeared, but my muscles felt blissed-out and rejuvenated, as Marilyn had promised. Whatever shamanism she was performing in that room had worked.

Behind the register I saw a display of rings and hair

bands and delicately woven macramé bracelets, and in my post-treatment high decided to buy a purple bracelet for Tami and a green one for Carolann, light blue for Ivy and red for Alyson, little mementos of our trip. The receptionist placed each bracelet in its own color-coordinated silken bag and at the last minute I decided on an ivory one for myself and wore it to go.

Bejewel your spirit, awaken your soul, it said on the receipt, and for the first time in my life an advertising slogan actually spoke to me. With my Prana now in better balance, I drove back to the house feeling fantastic and looking forward to the night ahead.

I opened the front door and was surprised to hear voices upstairs. I walked through Tami's room to get to the porch—her room was a mess, suitcases open on the floor with clothes overflowing—T-shirts and a lilac bra and sweat socks rolled up in a ball next to her dress and sandals from last night. As I got closer to the veranda I could smell the distinct aroma of pot.

"I thought you were playing tennis," I said.

"Shhhh!" Ivy said. They were all standing against the railing looking down, including Alyson and Tami, who I noticed were next to each other. Nothing like smoking a peace pipe to help smooth things over. "Come here, you've got to see this."

I peered down into the swampy brown water next to the house and saw tangled trees and reeds and some rocks along the edges. "What—I don't see anything."

"See that?" Alyson said, pointing to what looked like a rock. "Watch it." I stared at the rock for a minute and nothing happened. Maybe I needed to be stoned to appreciate staring at a rock. But then it dipped slightly below the surface and came up a few inches away. Tami picked a stone up off the porch and threw it at the mound. It landed a couple of feet away.

"What on earth is that?" I asked.

"An alligator," Tami said nonchalantly. "Or is it a crocodile? I can never fucking remember—pointy nose, square nose. One or the other."

The creature submerged under the murky water and for a minute I lost sight of it. Where did it go? It came up once again, closer to the shore—it must have been five feet long. Its middle was protruding as if it had recently eaten a big meal.

"That thing is so huge it looks like it just swallowed a child!" Ivy exclaimed

"Maybe it did," Tami said.

"That is so not even funny. How do they even let alligators in here?"

"Duh, they live here. They're protected, like eagles," Tami answered. She flopped down on the couch and took a long toke from the tail end of the joint between her fingers. The smell was faintly sweet, almost like a piece of burnt pizza sprinkled with oregano that had dropped to the bottom of the toaster, and for a second I thought about asking for a hit, but I'd just spent all that money to cleanse my body, so it seemed like such a waste to now breathe in smoke, even if it was technically organic.

Tami passed the joint to Ivy. She took a turn and then Carolann grabbed the last little stub and inhaled deeply, like a real expert. I hadn't remembered ever seeing Carolann smoke pot before.

"These beasts are protected?" Ivy asked. "We're the ones that need to be protected. It's sooo dangerous. I mean, what if? Can you, like, imagine walking alone at night—one bad step and you're that thing's dinner." Her eyes were red and wide in stoned paranoia.

Death by alligator wasn't a danger I'd ever considered to be a real possibility. I shuddered and sat down next to Tami who was now thumbing through a copy of *Cosmo* sitting on the table.

"*Vaginal Rejuvenation. Is it right for you? Take this quiz to find out.* Oh, this is priceless. *Has your partner's penis ever fallen out during intercourse? Check here if your vagina is as wide as the Lincoln Tunnel.*"

"It does not say that, let me see," Alyson said, grabbing the magazine. I searched the space between them for any remnants of their fight but the air seemed clear through the smoky haze. "*If you leak when you cough, exercise, sneeze, or laugh, insurance may pay for your vaginal tightening.* Is this an ad or an article?"

I had experienced a couple of sneeze pee leaks since giving birth to Madison, especially while doing jumping jacks, and had been panicked my incontinence might mean an early trip to the Depends aisle. *Kegels, Kegels, Kegels,* my ob-gyn had said. She hadn't mentioned anything about surgery.

"Sometimes I laugh so hard the tears are running down my leg." Tami began giggling and it spread like fire and soon I was laughing too.

"That's a good one," Ivy said, wiping her eyes. "I can't imagine someone doing surgery down there, though. It must be awfully painful."

"Well, Ivy, I would assume you would be under anesthesia," Carolann replied, sauntering over to the cooler and taking out a beer.

"I wish they gave you anesthesia when you get a bikini wax," I said.

"You still get waxed?" Tami asked. "I got mine lasered a few years ago and fucking love it. And you know, if you keep waxing as you get older, your lips get saggy."

"I can't believe that's true," I said, hoping it wasn't.

"I don't think waxing's *that* painful—I mean, you get used to it," Ivy said. "I've been thinking about lasering, but it's so permanent. How do you decide what shape?"

"Brazilian's always a good choice," Tami said.

I couldn't imagine how much it would hurt to get lasered, let alone lasered Brazilian. I had once been convinced during a waxing appointment to try a Brazilian. Aaron had never mentioned whether or not he liked my usual bikini wax, and I thought it couldn't hurt to surprise him with something new. I lay on the table with visions of oral sex dancing in my head, and found out it could hurt—it *killed*. My technician spent a searingly long half hour ripping out hair I never knew was apparently carpeting my most private crevices. She had me holding my leg above my head like a contortionist, flipped me into X-rated poses, and proudly displayed strip after strip. *See? I make it all clean now.* I had managed to nod a polite smile, cursing under my breath. After the torture was finally over, she proudly presented the result in the mirror: a neat little runway. The more I looked, the more I actually liked it, and although I left the salon limping, I felt surprisingly empowered by my new secret do.

That night I wore a dark purple negligee and unveiled myself sans panties to Aaron, awaiting my reward—the deep, hard kisses, the karma sutric sex . . . He did give me an emphatic "*Nice!*" when he saw it, but then he closed his eyes and we had our sex as usual. I should have pushed his head down, I should have demanded more— but I wanted the desire to come from him that night, not me. I wanted him to want me more with my new sexy trim, and maybe he did, but he didn't show it. The pain didn't equal the passion after all, and when it grew back super itchy a few weeks later, it sealed my decision never to do it again.

"Is Brazilian still popular?" Ivy said. "I'd hate to get lasered and then find out after I got the wrong thing."

"It's not that big a deal, you just ask the technician," Tami said. "I was actually thinking about getting vajazzled."

"Va-what?" I asked.

"Vajazzled. You haven't heard of it? Remember bedazzled, on your jean jacket? You go all bare and then glue on rhinestones—in the shape of a rose or a word or even the American flag. There's a whole vajazzle website you can order from and I heard there's a place in Ridgewood that can do it for you."

Please tell me you're kidding.

Alyson suddenly stood up and pulled down the front of her bikini bottom, displaying her bare crotch, except for a red rhinestone bow under a faint C-section scar. I was shocked to see her bare vagina, but even more shocked to see it decorated like a present.

"Oh my god, you didn't tell me you did it already! You little fucking sex pot. I love it!" Tami said. "See, isn't it cool? Ivy, you should definitely do it. We should all do it! What do you have down there now?"

"It's not very creative compared to that," Ivy said, and proceeded to unzip her shorts and show us her pubic hair buzzed super short in a neat triangle.

I'd wanted to get more intimate with these friends, but not like this.

"You know, once you get lasered you can wax shapes in to change it up," Tami explained. "Sometimes I go with an X, but I thought it would be fun for the weekend to try something new."

"Let me see," Alyson said.

"Next up in the Vagina Showdown," Tami said in a deep announcer voice, and then pulled down the front of her bikini. Under her butterfly tattoo was a bulls-eye, shorn into her crotch like a Target logo. I could see the bare pink lips of her labia exposed underneath and quickly averted my stare, but not before noticing her lips didn't look saggy at all; maybe it was true what she said about the waxing.

"I love that!" Ivy said. "Who's next? Jessica—what do you have?"

I sat on the couch, silent.

"Oh come on, don't be a party pooper."

I looked around—we were up on a roof out in the open and close to the houses next to us. I could even see people walking on the beach. I now wished I was stoned like they were, or at least buzzed.

"I'll go," Carolann said. Even Carolann had a designer vagina; a strip of hair as thin as my pinky. "Okay, Jessica, it's your turn."

I felt my face get hot, but could tell I had no choice. I quickly lifted up my sundress and pulled down the front of my underwear. The stunned looks on their faces said it all.

"Whoa—native!" Tami said.

"You know, I read somewhere recently that full bush is coming back," Ivy said.

I felt like a total freak but somehow managed to joke, "Who knew I was so trendy?" and everyone laughed. I couldn't help but start to laugh too, so hard I snorted, which made everyone laugh even harder. "I've got to be honest, I had no idea about any of this. It's not like I stand around with the women in my office comparing bikini lines."

Carolann said, "When we get home, Jessica, I'll set you up with my girl at Waxarama. She'll do you right."

Pubic-grooming advice from Carolann—who would have thought.

I couldn't imagine the look on Aaron's face if I came home with a rhinestone vagina. Or what my gynecologist might say. And what if Phoebe saw me getting out of the shower? *What's that, Mommy? Mommy decided to decorate her vajayjay.* That would be some potent material for her future therapist.

Carolann finished her beer and flung the bottle to the side with such carelessness it almost skittered off the porch, and then practically floated over to the cooler to fetch another drink. Stoned she seemed so different, so unlike her usual uptight self. She popped the top off the Corona and in a dreamy voice said, "Peter loves all the different designs I surprise him with on our Take Back Mondays, when we smoke a joint together and watch porn."

Carolann? Porn?

"What kind?" Tami asked. "Peter strikes me as a barely legal kind of guy. Or maybe Japanese rope bondage?"

With a completely straight face Carolann replied, "Well, Tami, Peter usually prefers girl-on-girl. I hardly watch, but after being married eleven years we needed something to spice things up."

I wondered what other racy tidbits stoned Carolann might feel compelled to share. "Why Mondays?" I asked.

"Well, Jessica, once the week gets going we are both so tired, and then the weekends are usually too busy running around taking the kids to hockey and soccer and ballet. Sunday nights I have to get the kids ready for school, make the lunches. Sex is the last thing I'm in the mood for on Sunday night. So we put it on the calendar for Mondays, before the week gets too crazy."

Her sex life seemed as planned and organized as her PTA volunteering schedule. *Although better on the calendar than not at all*, I thought. But the image of Carolann and her husband in front of their TV every Monday night, as regular as football, kind of grossed me out. Sometimes it was better not to know.

"Well, good for you, Carolann. We could all use a little more porn," Tami said.

I felt all eyes on me—my turn to share. "Aaron knows if I'm in the mood based on what I'm wearing—I have red light, yellow light, and green light outfits."

"Like what?" Ivy asked.

"Red light's the old T-shirt, the one that screams, *Don't even think about touching me.* Yellow is a maybe—like a little pair of cute boxers and a tank top. And green's the full-out lingerie. He has to take them off me because they're way too uncomfortable to actually sleep in."

My confession wasn't as scintillating as Monday Night Porn and they sat there, waiting for the punch line that wasn't coming. We hit a brief silence and I realized I still had their bracelets in my bag. "I almost forgot—I have something for you."

They all seemed genuinely touched by the gifts. I reached back into my bag to grab my phone to find out what exactly Japanese rope bondage was and then remembered I'd left it in my room.

"Be right back," I said, and ran downstairs, my mind flooded with sex. Aaron and I had never watched porn together; no sex toys, no anything that remotely resembled kinky during our marriage. Hell, we'd had none of it even before we were married. Were we boring, or unaware? Or both?

I turned on my phone and five messages popped up—3:20 p.m., 3:40, 3:45, 3:47, 3:49. "Call me, I need you, it's important," Aaron said on voice mail, and all I could think of was who fell and hit her head, who god forbid wasn't there when he turned around in the crowded food court at the mall? I couldn't believe that in my one afternoon sans cell phone there had been an emergency. I looked at my watch—5:15, over an hour since his calls. I dialed quickly and the phone rang three times before he picked up. "Is everyone okay?" I asked, breathless.

"Well, not exactly," he said. "Dave came from Scarsdale with the twins to watch the Mets game, and his daughter Alexis, she shit all over Phoebe's room."

"She *what*?"

"She shit. She's freaking five years old and still can't make it to the bathroom. They were in Phoebe's room playing *Dora* or whatever while Dave and I were in the den, and then all of sudden Phoebe came in screaming, *She pooped, she pooped on my pillow!*"

There was nothing Aaron hated more than cleaning up poop, except for maybe vomit. I let out a relieved chuckle. "So what did you do?"

"I ran into the room and Alexis was sitting on the bed with her pants off and poop smeared all over—all over her, all over the pillows, the blanket, the rug. It's *everywhere*. I need help."

Ugh, her brand-new rug. "Isn't Dave still there?"

"He's here, he's got Alexis in the bath now."

I didn't want to know why it might have taken a whole hour to get Alexis in the tub. "Did you put everything in the wash?"

"I threw out the pillow, it was so gross. Can I throw out the blanket too?"

"No, you cannot throw out her blanket. Put it in the wash on 'super white disinfect' and add one-third of a cup of bleach. And the carpet cleaner is under the sink."

I talked him through how to first turn on the washing machine—he'd never used it, not even once until that moment—and then how to wipe up the shit with a wet paper towel and spray the rug with the carpet cleaner and let it sit before scrubbing and vacuuming.

"I seriously cannot do this," he whined. "I am not cleaning any more shit that is not my own kid's shit! Dave, get in here!"

I had tried to keep a straight face to help him through the cleanup, but picturing him on his knees scrubbing with those yellow rubber gloves on, I couldn't hold it in any longer. I burst out laughing. "You're really in deep shit, Aaron!"

He starting laughing too. "It's like a Category 5 shitticane hit Phoebe's room." We laughed big hard belly laughs, like we hadn't laughed together in a long time.

After a minute he caught his breath and said, "I miss you, Jessy-bear."

"You're just saying that because I'm not there to clean up the shit."

"No. I miss you because I *really* miss you."

I let his words hang for a second; they sounded desperate but sincere. "I miss you too," I finally said. I did miss him. It felt good to miss and be missed, and for once, for Aaron to be the one at home appreciating me. And it felt especially good to miss cleaning up the worst mess in our parenting history. "But you have to admit you miss me *a little* because of the shit."

He paused. "Okay, maybe just a little."

I wished Aaron the best of luck with the rest of the cleanup and ran back upstairs to tell everyone. "You will never guess what happened!" I cried, and relayed every gruesome detail with an extra smear on the wall or two for effect.

"A toast to being away!" said Ivy, handing me a cold bottle of Corona Light out of the cooler.

"A toast to husbands cleaning up shit by themselves," I said, happy in so many ways to be away from home.

CHAPTER FOURTEEN

WE NEVER MADE IT TO CHARLESTON for dinner. By the time we showered and got ready it was almost nine, and even Tami had zero motivation to drive forty minutes there and back just for a wider choice of restaurants and a later last call. Instead, we went the easy route and ate at the resort, and by eleven we were back at Red's. People were packed in so tight there was barely room to move, though Carolann found space at an outdoor bar we hadn't even known existed the night before.

"Hey, look, there's Brad and company," Tami said, and there was something in her voice that told me our return to Red's might not have been on a whim. By the light of the tiki torches, I watched Tami and Alyson weave their way over and hug Brad and Sean and the others effusively as if they were long-lost friends. I craned my neck to see if Steven might be with them; it would be great to have one more chance to leave him with a slightly more professional impression. But I didn't see him.

With a hip swish and a hair toss Tami and Alyson walked back with a pitcher of margaritas a few minutes later, no doubt courtesy of their paramours.

"You guys are too much," I said, and as Ivy started

pouring the drinks into plastic cups, I felt someone standing next to me a little too close.

"Well hello, Jessica," Steven said.

"Hi." I felt startled though I should have expected to see him. "Need something to wet your whistle?" *Wet your whistle? Where did that come from?*

"Uh, no thanks, I'm good." He held up a bottle already in his hand and gave me a funny look. That was all I needed—Steven Masterson going back to Boston remembering me as a lush with fake eyelashes and now also a bumbling idiot. "Have you guys been here all night?" he asked. "I hope we didn't miss your encore performance."

"Yeah, well, we only perform here on Friday nights," Tami teased. "But we're available for weddings and bachelor parties. Or maybe our own show, off-Broadway?"

"Consider it done," he replied, looking amused as he took a sip of his beer.

I wasn't sure if I liked Tami cozying up to Steven to plan the details of her Broadway debut. Before she could take her reckless flirting too far, I quickly maneuvered the conversation back into shoptalk in which she couldn't possibly participate. Which producers still hadn't recouped their investment, even with sellouts on the national tour circuit. The rumored hot-and-heavy affair between the married star of *Phantom* and one of the stagehands.

"Are you 100 percent sure he's not gay?" I asked.

"Completely positive. He's definitely straight."

"I don't know," I said, finishing the last of my drink, "I would put money down he's at least bi. One of my creatives said he's seen him more than once after the show at the Ninth Avenue Saloon." *My creatives.* I loved hearing myself say it, as if I owned the place.

"Straight as an arrow. Twenty bucks," Steven insisted.

We shook on it and I thought our touch lasted a nano-second too long. Maybe Tami was right; maybe he was interested in more than just work. I'd been there many times before, a little too late at the bar after a show, right up against the edge of *shouldn't*. Back when I was an intern I'd let myself push it—*Share a cab home?*—eager to experience what more would feel like. But that was a million lifetimes ago, long before Aaron. I had to admit, it did still feel pretty good—it still felt pretty great, actu-ally—to know that as a mom with two kids, I still had the power and allure. Yet I didn't want to sleep with Steven; I wanted to work for him, and I needed to play this one right.

It was twenty minutes past last call and they finally ush-ered the pack of about thirty of us still partying out the door. The warm Southern air held us all together in front of the bar waiting for someone to take the lead to the next venue.

"Anyone up for a smoke?" Tami asked a small group of us within earshot.

Steven immediately said, "I'm in," and started to fol-low Tami as she walked toward the water, then turned to me. "Are you coming?"

I paused before answering, "Right behind you."

Tami led us on a path along with Alyson and Brad and a couple of other random people I didn't recognize, and we huddled in a wooden stairwell sheltered by the dunes, out of sight but still within the din of the after-bar crowd. Tami pulled out a small Ziploc baggie containing several prerolled joints—my Ziploc baggie's usual contents were pretzel nuggets and the occasional goldfish crackers, and I smiled at her duplicitous Ziploc life.

The last time I'd seen a plastic bag with pot in it was sophomore year of college, the day the band UB40 came to campus. On a lark I had signed up to work wardrobe instead of ticket-taking like the rest of my friends, and while they got stuck tending front of house I got to watch the sold-out show from the side of the stage with the roadies, an all-access pass around my neck. After the second encore, I headed back to the dressing room for my job of packing up the wardrobe cases and tried to look busy working and not notice as a couple of band members milled about in what I supposed was their usual postshow hang. The drummer pulled out a plastic bag filled with weed and quickly rolled and lit a fat joint. He sucked in the smoke and nodded to me to take it from his hand. Pretending as if of course I regularly hung out backstage and smoked pot with rock stars, I held the joint to my lips and took a deep breath in. The smoke singed the back of my throat and I immediately coughed it out. "Strong stuff," I managed to say, feeling my face flush; the drummer laughed good-naturedly and said, "Don't ya know it," and took another long, smooth toke. After a few more tries I kept the smoke in for longer, although I'm not sure if I ever really inhaled. But after some time, boy did I feel it—the room pulled in and time moved in circles as my lips and teeth and toes went nicely numb; in between laughs and handfuls of leftover cheese crackers my thoughts drifted in and out and through my brain: *Oh my god, I am getting stoned, really stoned! I am hanging out backstage and getting high with UB40 and today I folded their underwear.*

Tami took out one of the joints and lit it with a match—the familiar smell wafted over us and mixed with the salty air and I couldn't wait to be the next to inhale and feel that mellow tingle again.

I felt the sand crunch beneath my toes as I walked toward the marina, dangling my sandals in one hand and holding a plastic cup with what looked like a very watered-down vodka cranberry in the other. I couldn't even remember how long I'd been holding it, or even where I got it. With every few steps I felt it splash, on my hand, on my foot, each time wondering where it came from and then realizing it was me who was spilling the drink. The bay and the lights in the distance came at me as if through a viewfinder: a blink and a click and in a second they appeared. I lifted the cup to my lips and tasted the sweetness, tart and wet and warm on my tongue, and could feel the alcohol seeping straight through the lining of my cheeks directly into my bloodstream, funneling through my veins, pumping through my ventricles, in and around and back out again, lost and amazed in the slowed seconds of stoned awareness.

"Did you see *Stories I Have Told?*" Steven asked.

His voice brought my gaze back outward, back to realizing I was walking on a beach and I was not alone, that I was walking with a man who was basically a stranger. The air suddenly felt cold and I noticed my shoulders were bare and that I wasn't wearing the sweater with which I had started the night. I looked ahead and didn't see Tami or Alyson or anyone else—just a long line of wet sand and pebbles lit by the light of the moon.

I glanced to my right and noticed Steven had rolled

up his sleeves, and that he had thick strawberry-blond hair on his forearms. *What if he grabs me? What if he grabs me and rapes me and throws my body behind a rock to drown in the rising tide?* I didn't have a key or a stick or anything to defend myself with, just a credit card and a few folded bills tucked in my back right pocket.

It's just the pot, my rational voice reminded me. *Nothing's going to happen, he's a colleague, for god's sake, not a murderer. Just breathe, take a deep breath and the paranoia will pass.*

Of course: the pot. I took a breath and felt my heart slow to a more regular pace. Up ahead I heard Tami's laugh and was relieved; the group wasn't far. I quickened my steps to catch up and tried to remember what it was that Steven said that I was supposed to respond to.

"I loved that show," I eventually said, wondering if my reply came out at the five-minute delay it had felt like in my head. "I didn't know it toured to Boston."

"I saw it in New York. My buddy from college was the director and invited me to opening night."

"No way." I slapped his arm and felt the hard bicep under his shirt. "I was at that opening too." *Small world getting smaller every minute.* How was it possible Steven and I had never crossed paths before? We had so many connections, so many six-degrees between us.

"I have something for you," he said, pulling a small bundle wrapped in tissue out of his pocket.

I looked at him quizzically and began to peel away the layers—*A present? For me?*—wondering what on earth it could be. As I tore away the final piece of tissue my mouth dropped open: it was the other half of my chicken cutlet bra. Even in the dark, I could feel my face turn beet red.

"I was wondering where this m-might have landed," I stammered, and then began to giggle. And then the giggle turned into a full-out laugh. I could barely breathe I was laughing so hard and started babbling, "Thank you, Steven. Thank you so much. Really! These things cost like forty bucks a pop! I am so glad you found this!"

"Don't mention it," he replied, laughing with me.

"Oh, don't worry. I will *never* mention it. As long as *you* promise never to mention it," I said seriously. "I wouldn't be able to look you in the face at the next League conference without totally cracking up."

I glanced up and saw that Tami and Alyson and a line of other people had turned onto one of the last docks of the pier. *Where is Carolann? And Ivy?* It felt like I hadn't seen them for hours, but maybe it had only been a few minutes.

"His boat's down this way!" I heard Brad shout.

The rough sand scratched the bottoms of my bare feet but I couldn't manage to send the signal from my brain to stop and put my sandals back on. We stepped onto the dock and it took an unexpected pitch downward. "Whoa," I said, and almost lost my balance, but Steven took my arm to steady me. At the end of the pier, we reached a long metal ramp leading up to a huge ship, *The Alexandria*, white and boastful and gleaming in the moonlight. *This is fun*, I thought; I had never been on a yacht before.

"Whose boat is this?" I asked, but if he answered, I couldn't hear. As we stepped into the main cabin, a surge of music blasted through the air.

Champagne popped from a bar tended by none other

than Carolann, standing amidst mirrored rows of shiny bottles. Every surface of the boat was smooth and lustrous, glowing in the light of candles everywhere. Attractive strangers milled about, lounging on low couches with martinis in hand and dancing on the deck to the pulsing music. It was as if we'd entered a party in the French Riviera, suddenly friends with a billionaire.

A man in a white linen shirt standing behind Carolann opened a bottle of Patrón, and when a shot came my way I drank it down like nectar.

"Let's do body shots," a woman next to me suggested to no one and everyone, and I watched as the tequila man stared her down with seductive brown eyes and then walked over and slowly licked the side of her neck. He poured the salt and licked it again and, after taking a swig from the bottle, sucked on the lime she'd placed between her lips while his free hand squeezed her ass.

"Who's next?" he asked with a strong foreign accent and I heard Ivy say, "Me!" as she floated over with a cigarette dangling between her fingers. *She is so fucked up,* I thought; I'd never seen her smoke a cigarette. And as I watched, he did her too—he licked her neck but instead of doing the shot out of the bottle, she got down on her knees and lifted her shirt and leaned back and he poured the tequila down her bare stomach. He lapped it up like a tiger and then he moved his head up to her breasts to suck the lime she'd buried between them.

Steven pulled me onto the deck outside, into a crowd swaying to a reggae beat. Flashes of Tami and Alyson on the dance floor, guys pressed against them in front and behind, making a sandwich. I giggled out loud, a Tami-and-Alyson sandwich.

"What's so funny?" Steven asked, passing me a joint—more pot for me, the more the merrier, pass it around. *Whoa, Jessica, let someone else have a toke.* I stumbled to the couches lining the deck and felt a tug on my arm. "Come sit." I fell onto a lap and was startled to feel something harden under me. *Well hello there.* I slid off and sank like butter into the fluffy cushion, light as a feather, stiff as a board, and let the party happen all around me.

I heard a splash and thought for a second someone might have gone overboard but spotted a Jacuzzi across the deck. Shadows of bodies filled the tub, illuminated by blue and green lights below; five, no six or maybe more people, "Everybody in!" coiling around in a tantric circle. Tami slid in topless—*Where did her dress go?*—and I watched as she made out with the man beside her, such a kissing bandit—*Where's the camera now?*—and then she turned to another as the hands of many caressed her chest and her neck and her bare freckled shoulders. Carolann sat on the edge staring in a daze, making tiny splashes with her toes pointed like a ballerina's. Was that Sean or Colin? I was never good with names, but whoever it was whispered in her ear. Carolann smiled and stood and led him up the main staircase, *exit stage left,* like I was watching a play. *Step right up, get your tickets now.*

"Check it out, there's a dolphin!" someone shouted, and I heard myself say, "I want to see it too." I rose from the couch as if pulled by a puppeteer and followed the rush of people up the stairs, one flight, two, but when I got to the top deck there was no one else there. I noticed a door to my left and turned the knob but it was locked and I could hear the unmistakable *Oh yes, oh yes* of people having sex on the other side.

I heard footsteps banging up the stairs behind me and felt frightened, like I wasn't supposed to be there—*You'll be in trouble*—and I ran and ducked down behind a metal pole to hide. I stayed there, frozen for what felt like a long time. So long my right foot fell asleep. I didn't want to move but it felt so uncomfortable, finally I had to stand up and stomp it awake. Just then, I thought I saw a shadow moving on the deck and quickly ducked back down. *Totally paranoid. Goddamned pot.*

I poked the top of my head up and tried to make out the shadow. It was about ten feet away, leaning against the railing; it looked like a woman with long dark hair. Her head was tilted back and then I saw there was more, a man with his head buried between her legs and the woman was groaning with pleasure. His hand squeezed her breast freed from her blouse while his other worked her hard from underneath. She stroked his hair, guiding him, "That's it, right there," circling her hips in a quickening rhythm, and I sat there transfixed, shocked to be watching as he lifted her higher, faster, writhing together right in front of me, and even more shocked at the stir I started to feel in my own underwear.

The light shifted and suddenly I could see more of the woman's face. At first I thought it was a mistake—it couldn't be; it must have been my pot-and-alcohol haze. But her profile was unmistakable and when I caught the sparkle from her crotch in the moonlight, I knew. It was Alyson.

Click click click, the whole night, the whole weekend, the whole year lined up like a freight train in my head. I turned to run and stumbled down the stairs but couldn't figure out where to exit and I flew through a galley and a stateroom and across an empty deck, smack into Steven.

"Are you okay?" he asked. *Was he following me?* He was so close I could smell him—Patrón and soap, so different from Aaron.

"I . . . I . . . I just saw something."

"The dolphin?"

"I wish," I said, feeling suddenly sober. I buried my head in my hands. "This night has gotten totally out of control."

"Tell me about it—Colin just puked his guts out on the dance floor. A few weeks ago, when his wife told him she was leaving him, I had a feeling this vacation might get ugly. But not this ugly."

I didn't know what to say. I didn't know Colin, I didn't know his wife. I sat down on one of the deck chairs. "How long have they been married?"

"About seven years, I think."

"How long have you been married?" I wondered out loud, glancing at his ring.

"Nine years last month."

So why are you here? Why are you out partying instead of home with your wife and why am I standing here alone on this boat with you? I knew I should turn and hightail it out of there, say, *Good night, nice to meet you, let's forget we ever met.* My head felt strangely clear but I still must have been stoned because instead of running away or asking any of those questions, what flew out of my mouth next was, "Are you happily married?"

Oh my god, I thought, *he's going to think I want to fool around!* Those were words said right before a kiss:

Are you happy? No? Well then, let's get busy. But I didn't want to kiss or do anything like that with Steven. I just wanted to tuck myself into a ball and crawl into the hole I'd dug—so what if the boat sank.

But he answered easily: "We are. We met on the set of *Rain Over Easy*, remember that show? She was an understudy and I was cutting my producer chops on Miranda Sinclair. What a handful she was. Miranda, not Becky. The show didn't last a year but Becky and I are still going strong; we're among the lucky ones, I guess. My married friends seem to be dropping like flies. Poor Colin, he had no idea it was coming. How about you? How long have you been married?"

The way he spoke, it was like we were old friends sitting in a coffee shop, not on an orgy party-boat off the shore of Kiawah Island. "Going on ten years," I said. *Nearly a decade. A decade of my life and it's gone by in a blink.* Except lately it felt like we'd been dredging through mud. "It's hard sometimes, don't you think? My husband Aaron, he travels a lot and we moved last year and now have to commute like an hour-plus each way. It's really taking a toll."

"Commuting's a killer. I did that for a year from Providence up to Boston and it was the worst. So draining."

"I know, it's like we're running and running and then we finally fall into bed at night but we're both too exhausted to do much of anything. We've been stuck in this tired, boring funk for a while now and it seems like everyone around us is having a lot more sex than we are. A *lot* more." Had I just said that out loud? To Steven Masterson from Stages in Boston?

But he didn't seem uncomfortable at all. He sat down

on a lounge chair across from me and said, "Well, first of all, it's a guarantee most people are overreporting. And every couple's different. A lot for one couple might be a drought for another. Have you talked to him about it?"

"Not really. I want to. I still love him. And beneath it all I believe he loves me. But part of me is scared if we start that conversation, he's going to tell me something I don't want to hear, like maybe he's bored with me. Or even worse, that he doesn't want me anymore."

Never had I shared such intimate marital details with anyone, not even Liza—I'd never admitted those words and thoughts even to myself before.

"Look, I don't know your husband. But guys are pretty simple creatures. Most of the time if you tell them what you want, they'll respond. *Hunt. Fetch. Have more sex with me.*"

"But I want him to say that to *me*."

"So tell him."

It seemed so obvious, spoken on the deck of that yacht with the muffled sounds of the party still going on below us. Obvious and right. I felt so grateful for Steven's advice and relieved he wasn't one of those creeps just trying to get lucky. And I somehow knew that when Aaron and I did open up about our fears and wants and needs in and out of the bedroom, it would start to be good between us again. It might be even better.

"Thanks for listening, Steven," I said quietly, instantly jolted into the self-conscious realization that I was in the midst of a sexual therapy session with someone I wanted to work with. "This isn't like me, to blab about personal stuff like this." I felt my face blush. "I hope you don't think I go around discussing this kind of thing with all my clients. I mean, client prospects." *Shit, I shouldn't have said that. I shouldn't have said any of what I'd just said.*

"Please, it's fine. Sometimes it's easier to talk it out with someone on the outside. And you should absolutely call me next week to discuss a few projects we have coming up."

A splash and a *"Woo-hoo!"* sounded from the deck below. The throbbing beat of the next techno dance song echoed through us and out over the water, into the night.

A screen door slammed and I was startled awake by Tami's voice: *"Daylight come and we have to go home."*

"Enough already with the song, Tam," Alyson said, sounding annoyed.

"Ah, there's the sleeping beauty. We were wondering where you disappeared to."

I opened my eyes and for a second had no idea where I was—windows, curtains, table—none of it looked familiar. I stared down at my body splayed on the couch and consciousness hit me like a boulder. My right ankle throbbed and my throat felt like someone had braided my tonsils with wool. I squinted at my watch: 7:27 a.m.

Ivy and Carolann walked in, giggling. "Or we could go out for breakfast," Ivy said, kicking off her heels. "A Grand Slam at Denny's would taste really good right now."

"I can't believe you'd still be hungry after your grand slam last night," Alyson teased.

"Ha ha," Ivy said. She strolled into the kitchen and stared into the refrigerator. "I guess we should probably use up the eggs and the rest of the Bisquick before we leave. What time's our flight, like around one?"

"One forty-five, Ivy," Carolann answered, plopping down on the love seat across from me. I noticed the buttons on her blouse were one askew. "It's about an hour drive to the airport—and we need to leave enough time to get gas and return the rental car. I cannot even believe we have to go home this afternoon. Next year we have to stay another day."

"Another day at *least*," Ivy said. She closed the fridge and filled up the coffee carafe with water. "On second thought, what I really need more than food right now is a hot shower. My hair totally reeks like fish. How on earth did you guys convince me to go swimming at four o'clock in the morning?"

"That was Xavier's idea," Carolann said. "Or was that Milo you ended up with, Ivy? For the life of me, I could not tell them apart."

"To be honest, I'm not even sure. They were identical with those incredible brown eyes and both soooo hot. Whichever one he was kept calling me *bonita* and *sexy*, over and over," Ivy said dreamily.

I had hoped once daylight came I'd wake up to find what had happened on that boat to be the hallucinations of a totally stoned mind. But the more I heard them speak, the more I knew it had all been very real.

"Carolann, that reminds me, you never finished telling us about your soirée in the upper-deck bathroom," Tami said.

"Wait a second, the one with the outdoor shower?" Alyson said. "Brad and I were in there too. The view of the stars was incredible. Like a planetarium. And the tiling was exquisite; it must have been straight from Italy. It made me think we should build an outdoor shower. I think there's space, next to our pool house. I'll bet I could find those tiles online."

A mosaic reminder of her wild night—in her own backyard?

Tami sat down on the couch at my feet, crossing her legs. She took a rubber band off her wrist and tied her hair back in a loose bun as long blond tendrils fell onto her sunburned cheeks. "So, Jess, let's hear the skinny about Steven. Or hopefully it wasn't so skinny."

I desperately needed a glass of water before I could break it to her that there was no skinny, that Steven had dropped me off in a cab hours ago and all we had exchanged were work e-mail addresses, not bodily fluids. I tried to clear my throat. "Nothing happened," I said in a hoarse whisper.

Tami grinned like a Cheshire over the rim of her steaming coffee cup. "Come on now, chica, we need some scoop. So we can give out the awards, like Most Improved. Carolann, I think you win that hands-down this year. And for Best Ass. Steven's definitely in the running for that prize. Most Likely To Hunt You Down on Facebook Even Though You Told Him Not To? That one might actually be a tie, between Ivy's Venezuelan dude and Aly's Brad, don't you think?"

"Plus, you're the last one for our poll: Circumcised or Not?" Alyson added. "Ivy's twin had a definite hoody. Brad, no; Tami's short little Romeo, no." Tami shot Aly a look. "Carolann—you said Colin's wasn't, right? Gotta love those Irish guys. So now we need yours. I have five bucks Steven's hot dog was kosher style, but Tami begs to differ. So am I right or am I right?"

"I didn't see his penis," I mumbled, feeling ridiculous to have even said so.

Tami rolled her eyes. "Look, Jessica, there's nothing wrong with admitting how pretty fucking awesome it feels to experience a little pleasure for once. God knows, you needed it. We all do. Once a year, a little sun, a little fun, a little something to help you recharge. It's just sex; it's a physical release for your body that makes you feel good. Like yoga."

"Maybe hot-box yoga," Alyson clarified.

Carolann chimed in, "When we got back from South Beach last year, Peter thought I was so into him because I was relaxed and rested from lying out on the beach and going to the spa. If he only knew."

Now *I* knew, thank you very much. Now I'd be going home knowing everyone's secrets, including their pubic coiffures.

Tami nodded. "Shit yeah, Carolann. The more sex you have, the more you want it. We all know it's impossible to keep it red hot your entire married life. *Everyone* needs some outside stimulation, and if they say they don't, they're full of shit. Husbands are useful for a lot of things, but by definition, they can't give you what we all need: novelty."

"That is so true," Ivy nodded. She squeezed herself on the couch between Tami and me. "And you know you don't have to worry, Jess, once we get on the plane, the record's sealed—it's totally separate from h-o-m-e."

I wasn't so naive to think people didn't cheat—I knew it happened a lot more than I ever wanted to admit. But I didn't think it happened like this, in a Team Mom cheating competition. With penis prizes afterward.

Maybe in their world it was just sex, a quick catch-and-release and in a few hours they'd be heading *h-o-m-e*

happy with their orgiastic souvenirs. If that was their ultimate goal of the trip, from what I'd seen, they definitely
got their money's worth.

And, bonus, it was all a donation to the school.

The four of them sat there looking tan and satisfied,
albeit a bit tired, waiting for me to add another juicy
dollop to their morning-after salacious sundae, assum-
ing my night with Steven ended the same way—that I
was with them, *really* with them on this weekend's ride.
Maybe I had been on board for a little sun and a little fun
and maybe I had taken my flirting well past the point of
where I ever would have taken it if I was home and sober,
but actually having sex with strangers was not what I
thought I had signed up for.

I wasn't sure how to convince them that I hadn't slept
with Steven, but before I could start to try, I needed a
supersized dose of caffeine.

"Can I have some coffee?" I asked, and my voice
cracked again. Tami sighed and walked into the kitchen.

I felt Alyson's eyes boring into me and when I caught
her stare, I could have sworn I saw an edge of worry
start to appear on her forehead, a faint crease above her
eyebrow I'd never noticed before. Did she know I had
seen her up close on the deck of the yacht last night with
whatever-his-uncircumcised-name-was? Or maybe she
was just zoning out after pulling an all-nighter. She took
out her iPhone and flicked her finger across the screen.
"Ivy, you are going to love this one." She laughed and
passed the phone over.

"*Ay, caramba*, I do *not* remember that," Ivy cringed,
and gave the phone back to Alyson.

Alyson flipped through a few more pictures. "Here's

a classic one of you," she said, and handed the phone to me.

There I was, eyes half-closed in those terrible positions with Steven's hands on me and mine on him, on his ass, his arm, his crotch, laying across a pile of strangers with my shirt hiked up. I knew what I did and I didn't do last night but anyone looking at those pictures would assume I had participated. I didn't technically cheat, not physically, but I was more out of control than I'd ever been in my life, and seeing those pictures made me regret how far I'd let myself go. I regretted all the drinking and, ugh, the smoking that left my throat scorched.

Tami handed me the cup of coffee and the burnt smell made my stomach turn. Then Alyson grabbed the phone out of my hand and I could see her worry line turn wicked. "Yep, these are priceless," she said, and I fully understood: she had pictures. If she suspected I was the only one who didn't cheat, if I broke the pact I didn't even know I was making—god only knew what my punishment might be this time for not quite fitting in. In jest, or even worse, in a moment of anger, in a click, she could send those images right to Aaron or anyone else's inbox. Or post them online. My marriage, my reputation, my career could be ruined, just like that.

I had to get home to Aaron, I had to tell him that nothing happened. And I knew I had no choice: I had to play along with the morning-after tell-all and act as if nothing was askew. Record sealed or not, with those photos I couldn't risk Alyson or Tami or anyone else thinking I hadn't been all-in.

So I sipped my coffee and pretended the best I could, *Yep, that was some party,* as I crumbled inside. There was no way I was going to lie and say out loud that I cheated on Aaron, but I didn't say that I did and I didn't say that I didn't. In fact, I didn't say much of anything: my voice was so spent, it was easy to pretend I'd come down with an acute case of morning-after-pot-smoking-laryngitis. "Oh my god, my voice is totally gone!" I think they bought it, I hoped they did, and I kept telling myself I had to keep it up until we got home, until I could talk to Aaron and explain.

Alyson kept passing her phone around the room to grimaces and grins, mighty as a queen, high with her power.

Don't press send, I silently begged her. *Whatever happens, don't press send.*

CHAPTER FIFTEEN

BUT I COULDN'T TELL AARON, not right away. When I got home I was surprised to find our nanny Samina in the kitchen feeding Phoebe and Madison dinner.

The girls toppled me with tight missed-you hugs, which turned out to be even more delicious than I had imagined.

"Where's Daddy?" I asked.

Samina explained that Aaron had left two hours earlier to catch a plane to California.

"But he wasn't supposed to leave until tomorrow morning," I said. I knew it was the week of his annual Silicon Valley start-up conference, three days jammed with back-to-back business-development meetings, panels, and networking events. It wasn't that strange that he needed to fly out early, but he could have called and told me. Or at a minimum, sent me a text.

I tried his cell and it went straight to voice mail. He was probably in the air, and would be for the next five-plus hours.

I tried to hide my disappointment with a smile for Phoebe and Madison. They *oohed* when I took their swirly lollipops and Palmetto tree snow globes out of my bag, and my heart started to melt as they showered me with welcome home cards decorated with stickers and glitter and tiny pieces of tissue-paper confetti, spelling out my name in big, capital letters: *MOM*. I almost hit the floor when I found a card Aaron had made for me too.

Tucked inside I found the best surprise.

It was a homemade photo book—printed-out pictures of Buttercup, my childhood teddy bear. I remembered how nervous I had been, revealing to Aaron early in our relationship that yes, I was one of those people who still had a stuffed animal. But his reaction was the opposite; in fact, he told me about his own, Mr. Boots the monkey, and wished his mother hadn't carelessly thrown him away. He looked at me with those hazel blues and told me I was his Jessy-bear, and the nickname stuck, taking my love to a place I'd never imagined it could go.

Buttercup usually sat on a shelf in Phoebe's room, a special guest at tea parties and for good-night snuggles when I told the girls stories about my childhood. A past-and-present piece of who I was and dreamed I would be, now keeping watch over my real-life future. I flipped through the pages of pictures and my eyes filled with tears as I saw that Aaron had taken Buttercup over the weekend to visit all of my favorite places while I was away. There she was, propped on the counter next to the muffins at the Muddy Cup; snug in Madison's lap in the playground swing. At my favorite stand in the farmers' market—*How did he know?*—the one all the way in the back with the best strawberries and blueberries, hands down. Page after page, place after place, there was Buttercup, right there with them as a surrogate me.

And in the last picture, at the end of her long day

Buttercup rested on my pillow, with a note scribbled in Aaron's handwriting underneath. How sorry he was that he had to run out early. Telling me how much he missed me; how much he missed us, together.

I love you, Jessy-bear.

He had spent the weekend dreaming up this book and making these cards and taking care of our daughters while I was poisoning my body and mind in Kiawah and Gomorrah. Searching for the affection and love I thought I was missing when it was right there at home, waiting for me. And always would be.

Each speck of glitter reflected my guilt tenfold. *But you didn't technically do anything wrong,* I reminded myself.

I got the kids down to sleep way too late and lay in bed, replaying the speech I had rehearsed the whole way home explaining to Aaron that nothing had happened, despite what it might look like in Alyson's pictures—and he'd take me into his arms and say, *Of course, I understand.* But then I started to panic. What if telling him put a crack in our foundation instead of bringing us closer? Or what if he didn't believe me? That would be a disaster way worse than never saying anything at all.

Still, it wouldn't be as bad as him seeing those pictures first.

I heard the patter of feet coming down the hall and turned to Phoebe's silhouette next to me.

"I can't sleep, Mommy."

"Jump in," I said, too exhausted to walk her back to her room. She curled comfortably in the center of our bed, and I had the feeling she'd probably spent the past two nights in that same spot.

Within minutes she was out cold but I wasn't even close; the disjointed images of the weekend kept flashing on the backs of my eyelids in a tortuous private slide-show. I went into our bathroom and searched the medicine cabinet for something to make me sleepy and wished I hadn't flushed the rest of those hospital Xanax. I didn't even have a Tylenol PM in the house.

Maybe a bath? I turned to admire our beautifully restored claw-foot tub. *It's like art we can bathe in*! I remembered telling Aaron when we bought the house. But we'd never once used it.

I let the water fill the tub and slid into the hot bubbles, noticing the back tilted a little too upright to fully recline comfortably. I looked around the bathroom from my new tub-height perspective and noticed the light from outside threw an eerie gray shadow across the white tile wall, like a soiled ghost waiting to jump in.

I never liked this cavernous bathroom. I wanted to love it, the porcelain we spent months choosing and those towel warmers we just had to have, but never turned on. All the special features of the house we'd been so excited about before we moved in—the bonus attic storage space and the formal dining room I had pictured us throwing elaborate dinner parties in sat bare and unfinished, a repository for unwanted toys. Our neighbors certainly seemed to love filling their houses with more than enough stuff—and when new wore off and the parties ended, they went out and found other ways to keep the boredom at bay, a constant stream of drinks and thrills and pills and once-a-year binges in pursuit of the shiny and new as if they were still teenagers, upping the ante to new highs to make them feel alive.

And I'd convinced myself I needed it all too.

All those nights out at the bar at Varka well past midnight—*Come on, Jessica, have another*—swept up in their gimlets and makeup and boot cuts that in those moments made me feel attractive and connected and a lot less lonely. But I always woke up the next morning feeling bloated and parched. I should have realized well before our trip that what turned them on never made me feel as good as I thought it would. I should have listened to that voice telling me all along that I didn't fit in, but I had been so weak and needy that I let them drag me out and into the belly of their discontent.

Now I'd landed where I thought I wanted: smack dab in the middle of their inner circle. I hated the pressure of keeping their secrets and managing my own lies about what I did and didn't do, yet another layer of deceit hanging over my head. I hated feeling complicit. I hated imagining the chitchat and fake smiles at school pickup and dinners out with husbands, the birthday parties and the backyard gatherings, trying to pretend nothing was different when now I knew so much.

We were tethered in so many ways, I couldn't say *See ya* and poof, just like that, find myself with new friends who were more like the me I wanted to be. It was going to be complicated, trying to figure out a new paradigm. There were strings, there were carpools, there were end-of-the-school-year picnics. Phoebe and Emmy played together nearly every day; Alyson lived right next door.

I could be busy with work, send the nanny for pickups. Begin to extricate myself in that gradual way that friendships start to wane. Opt out of those couples' nights—*Sorry, the sitter isn't free.* I knew sidelining myself would mean I'd be alone a lot more often, at least for a while. But maybe if I took a turn inward and let them all pass by, I'd discover it was possible to find lasting pleasures in loving what I already had.

Toweling off, I looked down at my bathing suit tan lines—and my huge, coarse bush. I stared at myself in the mirror: it did look kind of grizzly. Until yesterday, I'd never given it a second thought. *That was only yesterday*. How crazy, it felt like weeks ago. There was no way I was going to get lasered or, god forbid, vajazzled—and I certainly wasn't ever going to set foot in Waxarama—but, I had to admit, it probably would look better with a little trim.

I searched through the bathroom drawer but couldn't find the cuticle scissors. They weren't in the medicine cabinet either. Huh.

I put on my robe and went down to the kitchen in search of the scissors, riffling through the junk drawer, through the scrap paper and broken crayons and a few errant wine corks. But I couldn't even find a pair of the kids' craft scissors. I stood there racking my brain on where to look next and was about to just let it go when the light through the window above the sink illuminated my kitchen utility chicken shears hanging on the wall.

I stepped into the downstairs guest bathroom and put my leg up on the toilet seat, noticing the wallpaper was already starting to peel behind the sink. How was that possible? We'd just put it up a few months ago. I sighed, adding another task to our never-ending fix-it list, and focused instead on my little grooming project. With each snip, big chunks of hair fell into the toilet, and I was psyched—it was so much more efficient than those cuticle scissors would have been.

I stood up on Madison's step stool to get a look at my work in the mirror. It *did* look better trimmed down. But the right side was a little denser than the left. I went back to the toilet, pulling the hairs up between my fingers on each side like a stylist, to make sure they were even, going a little deeper to cut the ones closer in on the sides, and then all of a sudden . . . OW. I looked down and saw blood trickling down my leg. *Oh my god, I cut my vagina lip! With the chicken shears!*

I quickly grabbed gobs of toilet paper to put pressure on the cut, but it wouldn't stop bleeding. A hundred panics flew through my head. What if I passed out on the bathroom floor in a pool of blood? Or what if I actually needed stitches? And oh my god, it was the chicken shears—I could have salmonella! Could I drive myself to the hospital, get there and back without anyone knowing?

I held a wad of toilet paper on the cut and slowly made my way back up the stairs, careful not to bleed on the carpet. I closed our bathroom door and cautiously checked the cut—it wasn't as bad as I thought, just a nick, and had almost stopped bleeding. I put on clean underwear and a T-shirt and was about to get back into bed when I heard my phone vibrate on the nightstand.

Just landed.

I dialed and Aaron picked up. "Hey, you're still up."

"Can't sleep. I wish you were here."

"Me too. What a nightmare. We sat for almost two hours on the runway."

"Ugh, the worst. It's too bad you had to leave today."

"I know. I got a last-minute call asking me to be here for a dinner tonight, a dinner that I'm now late for—it figures. Were you proud of me, getting the nanny to come and cover without bothering you on your trip? Hang on a sec . . . Going to the Rosewood," I heard him tell the taxi driver.

And as much as I wanted to have our heart-to-heart right then, I knew it wasn't the right time. Not on the phone, rushing out of the airport. *It can wait a couple of days*, I told myself. I just prayed Alyson had put her trip photos in the vault along with the rest of the weekend as promised, or better yet, used some good judgment and deleted them altogether.

I told Aaron how much I loved the Buttercup book and the cards and that I couldn't wait to see him in a few days. We said good night and before I knew it, my eyes were opening to the predawn light leaking through the edges of our bedroom window, thanks to our Blinds to Go blackout shades proving incapable of performing their one required function. I couldn't fall back asleep so I showered and got dressed for work, and while waiting for Samina to arrive I searched online and was relieved to find you cannot get salmonella if you cut yourself with chicken shears.

Then I checked my inbox and saw Ivy had already sent the first après-weekend e-mail: *BEST TRIP EVER! Good luck with re-entry everyone. I am COMPLETELY rejuvenated and ready to pack the lunches (ugh).*

Tami wrote back: *Hope your first Monday night back tonight is FUCKING marvelous Carolann, ha ha.*

I felt like I needed to add a reply to the chain. I typed, *Still no voice! I need a vacation to recoup from our vacation.* At least the second part was true. But as I was about to click send, I thought, *What am I doing?* What was the point of engaging in the e-mail blabber if I wanted to take a step aside? I erased my response and figured I'd just run into them during the week.

But I didn't see anyone. I landed right back into a hectic work week preparing the "win" campaign creative for Marco's show, which had been nominated for three long-shot Tony Awards: Best Musical, Best Original Score, and Best Supporting Actress. If any of them hit, we had to be ready to change out every piece of advertising immediately—and if we got really lucky and that award turned out to be Best Musical, we'd be buying up loads of extra media and plastering the accolades all over the place. And I might also be looking forward to an extra bonus come year-end.

It took me until Wednesday afternoon to find a free minute and to get up my nerve to follow up with Steven Masterson. He took my call right away, and now we had a pitch meeting on the calendar in two weeks up in Boston. Sybil was thrilled.

Aaron reported he was having a stellar week at his conference; his first panel about the future of data mining had gone over huge and he had two more panels to go. In fact, it was going so well, he now had to stay until Saturday for a special postconference, invite-only "Innovators of the Future" meeting.

Not telling him about the trip was eating away at me but I couldn't discuss it over the phone. Only three more days, I could manage for three days—but I wasn't sure if I could make it through three more nights. Every night since Aaron's departure, Phoebe had come into our room complaining she couldn't sleep. I wanted to be strong and send her marching right back to her own bed, but with

Aaron out of town it was just easier to let her sleep with me, even though she kicked and flailed and kept me up half the night.

Our mornings were brutal, and getting worse each day. By the end of the week, Phoebe clung to my leg screaming, "I don't want to go to school, Mommy, don't make me!"

Don't *make* me? "Only two more weeks of school left," I reassured her. She was obviously overtired and I felt guilty having disrupted her usual sleep schedule. But the way she was carrying on, it seemed like there must be something else.

I asked her if she was sad about the end of school coming so soon, and she shook her head no.

"Do you feel like you're getting sick?" I put my hand on her forehead: cool. "Is someone not being nice to you?" *Is Samina locking you in the closet when I leave for work?*

Finally she said, "Emmy took my purple headband and won't give it back."

That's what was making her so hysterical? I knew her purple ribbon headband with the rhinestone bow was her favorite, but really? "Did you let her borrow it?"

"She took it in school and won't give it back. She won't give it back!"

"It's okay, sweetie, it's okay." I hugged her close. "I hear you and I will talk to her mommy and get it back, okay? Maybe Emmy got it confused with her own purple headband," I tried, and that seemed to calm Phoebe down, at least enough to get us out the door.

I e-mailed Alyson on my way to work to confirm our weekly ballet carpool for Saturday morning and added,

PS: Have you seen Phoebe's purple headband around? She might have left it at your house.

Alyson wrote back with no mention of the headband, just that she'd be taking Emmy to ballet that week, she was dropping her off at her mother's house afterward so Emmy would be out of the way for Jeff's Saturday-night fundraiser party. *That actually works out better*, I thought; now I could go straight from ballet to pick up Lupita and Samuel for our trip to the Museum of Natural History planned for Saturday afternoon.

I was going to write back to ask if our usual Friday coffee at the diner was on but stopped: even if it was, I couldn't imagine sitting there talking, or trying not to talk, about last weekend.

I decided not going to the Friday coffee would be the first official step of my disengagement. It would be easy; I'd just say I was on deadline and had a conference call. And instead of going to the gym or catching up on e-mails during my new free Friday-morning window, I would spend that time playing with Madison. She was almost two—two already!—and before any more time zoomed by I wanted to play with her, really play; I wanted to turn off the computer and turn up the music and shake the maracas to the "Monster Boogie." I wanted to build giant Lego castles and take an art class together. Madison was always getting the short shrift of mommy alone time—second child, along for the ride—and I knew if I didn't make the time now, in a minute she'd be a teenager and wouldn't want to hang out with me.

A whopping twenty-megabyte e-mail landed in my inbox and disrupted my reverie. *Trip Photos!* was the subject, and I was the only person listed in the *To:* line.

From: Alyson. Holy shit. Maybe she *did* know I was covering up the fact that I didn't actually fool around with Steven; maybe she realized I was a potential risk of spilling their weekend's secrets. *And if you ever open your mouth, here's what I have on you?*

It took an excruciatingly long time for the images to appear—the files were huge. I held my breath as they came up one by one: our smiling faces, the five of us arm in arm with drinks in hand, the glittery eye shadow and low-cut tops, and a few shots devolving into some of our late-night drunken moments. My heart hurt from the wait for those biggies to hit, the ones I had seen on her phone. But then the last photo appeared and it was just Tami, with her straw beach hat over her face, sleeping on the plane.

Maybe I had it wrong, maybe this was Alyson's roundabout way of saying, *This is our story, this is what we're sharing, and the rest is now put away for good.*

I told myself not to worry about it. Instead of replying with a question mark or calling her, I simply pressed delete.

I was about to leave to take Phoebe to dance on Saturday morning when Aaron called. He was catching the seven a.m. flight and would be home by five. Finally.

"So Alyson just called me," he said.

Maybe she had dialed his number by mistake about a change in the carpool? "We're walking out the door—does Emmy need a ride to ballet?" I asked.

"What? I don't think so. I wasn't even going to pick up but I saw Alyson's caller ID and thought maybe there was an emergency. But she said she was calling me because she's worried about you. That you haven't been yourself lately."

The wrecking ball had hit: *Alyson called Aaron.* Directly. Suddenly I thought maybe she had told him everything—about the trip, about Steven, the pictures—or worse, had already sent them. *Aaron could be looking at those pictures right now.* I knew I should have explained everything right when I got home, even if it was on the phone. Now it was over and he would never trust me again.

"I haven't been myself lately? That's bizarre. She's the one who's been going off the deep end," I said, trying to keep my heart in my throat and quickly come up with a mea culpa that wouldn't sound defensive.

But thankfully I didn't have to.

Aaron said, "The whole conversation was laughable. I told her you were just fine, and that I wasn't going to waste my time getting in the middle of some girl bullshit. That if she had something to say to you, she should be a grown-up and call you herself."

"Was that it?" I asked, holding my breath.

"There was one more thing—she told me not to mention she called. I thought, *Oh yeah, that's what I'm going to do, keep it a secret.* What an idiot. I hung up and called you right away."

"Like you weren't going to tell me," I said, feeling a huge surge of relief that Aaron had halted Alyson's encroachment just like that. What a bitch. Sending me threatening e-mails, trying to taint Aaron with suspicion and doubt. But Aaron was on my side; he was my husband. *In times of happiness, in times of trouble.* In times when the psycho next-door neighbor rears her malicious head.

I told Aaron I needed to talk to him about the Kiawah trip when he got home. "Suffice it to say, I won't be going on another weekend away with this group anytime soon."

"And I'll catch you up on my week out here," he said. "All good stuff. Love you."

"Fly safe. Love you too," I replied, and started counting the hours until he landed.

Fifteen minutes later I found myself back in my usual Saturday-morning ballet-watching bench spot. No sign of Alyson, Carolann, Tami, or their daughters yet. I hadn't seen even one of the moms all week and suddenly I felt butterflies, wondering when they would show. I still couldn't believe the nerve of Alyson. I didn't know exactly what I was going to say to her, but one thing was for sure: there was no way I was letting this latest stunt of hers go.

Strains of choppy piano music wafted through the air and I tried to keep Madison occupied with her two My Little Ponies as Phoebe and her classmates held hands to form a circle and started their warm-ups—"Stretch up to the sky and down to touch your toes."

I looked around at the smattering of other moms who had been sitting with me in that waiting room nearly every Saturday morning for a full school year, their not-quite-familiar faces, siloed in their digital comas, staring down at their cell phones. Not exactly the most warm and welcoming bunch. Eventually I'd have to start putting myself out there again, smile, *Hi, which one's your daughter*? Volunteer at the school book fair, sign up to be a class parent. My stomach tightened, just thinking about it. But I'd have to get more involved if I wanted to find some new friends. More good eggs like Lupita, who I was excited to spend the afternoon with on our overdue trip to the museum. Who else might be out there . . . maybe the other Jessica? I'd had a nice conversation with her stuffing envelopes at the last auction meeting. Michelle Upton was also a possibility, if we could ever find time to connect. Whenever I ran into her at the school between pickups and drop-offs, she always had a warm smile for me.

Just then, Alyson appeared at the entrance to the waiting room. Her hair was pulled back in one of her usual tight ponytails, and her makeup was perfect, her lips finished with a shine. I noticed she still had remnants of peeling sunburn on her nose and cheeks, but the fluorescent light made her skin look blotchy and pale.

Her eyes darted around looking for a place to sit, and when her gaze caught mine, I gave her a curt wave. She nodded and then sat on a bench on the other side of the room. My section was pretty full but still, to not come over and say hello—there was no doubt in my mind she knew that I knew about her call to Aaron.

I glanced over at her sitting among the others, sporting her usual stoic stare, lips slightly pursed as she flipped through her e-mails. If she felt at all uncomfortable, I couldn't tell; I never could tell with Alyson. She had perfected the bitch veneer, that cold, hard exoskeleton from head to toe, shielding her from the pain and bumps and bruises the rest of us suffered through and seemed to wear on our faces and in our demeanors. Maybe somewhere deep inside her was a hidden reserve of kindness and compassion, but her constant stream of nastiness really made me wonder.

I decided to focus instead on Phoebe and the girls practicing for their upcoming recital, weaving their sweet spring tableau of insects and flowers. Phoebe was in the ant group, on their backs with their arms and legs moving up and down, in and out, up and down in unison, and I appreciated the instructor's nod to Busby Berkeley, one of my favorite old-time choreographers. Then one by one, each ant stood and picked up a colorful tissue-paper bouquet and sashayed over to the line of butterflies holding their hands high, creating a tunnel for the ants to dance through. Phoebe took her turn, tiptoeing through the tunnel in her pale pink slippers, and then all of a sudden I saw Alyson's daughter Emmy bend her elbow and bonk Phoebe on the head with her butterfly wing.

Maybe Emmy's elbow had slipped; maybe it was an accident. But she had a self-satisfied look on her face that made me think it wasn't.

Phoebe made her second turn through the butterfly tunnel and Emmy took another swipe at Phoebe's back. The little fucker.

And, I noticed, she was wearing Phoebe's headband.

I sprang up to the glass and pounded my fist, "You have *got* to be kidding me!" but the other mothers barely glanced up from their e-mails and texting, and the ones who did just stared at me blankly. Behind my back, I could feel Alyson smirk.

I spun around and looked straight at her. No one was going to hurt my kid. "What the hell was that?" I demanded.

"I don't know what you're talking about," Alyson said.

"You know exactly what—Emmy whacking on Phoebe in there. And taking her headband?"

"Phoebe *gave* Emmy that headband. You sound seriously paranoid, Jessica—are you going crazy or something?"

All the moms in the waiting room were staring at me. Even Madison was looking up with a confused expression on her little face. But I knew there was no way I'd imagined what Emmy had just done to Phoebe. It had happened, even if no one else backed me up.

"I know what I saw," I replied, enunciating each word to let the double meaning of seeing her on the deck of that yacht take a moment to sink in. "And I know all about your secret little reach-out to Aaron this morning. Did you really think he wouldn't tell me? Your schemes might work on other people, but they're not going to work on me. And now seeing Emmy in there, following in your footsteps—actually, it's just sad. And it's not okay."

Alyson glared. "I wasn't going to say anything, but Phoebe has been bullying Emmy for months now. Calling her names, pulling her hair."

Phoebe? Alyson was full of shit. "That's a lie and you know it."

"I am not allowing Emmy to play with Phoebe anymore."

"There is no way I'd *ever* let Phoebe play with your daughter again after what she did to her just now, that's for sure." I turned and saw Phoebe standing alone next to the piano, looking as if she was about to cry. I wasn't going to let her stay in that room with the next cruel generation of little bitch emissaries just getting started with their vicious ways. Living next door to them, growing up alongside them—the thought of it suddenly made me feel sick.

And for once I had no problem saying exactly what I was thinking: "Go fuck yourself, Alyson."

The waiting room fell silent and all heads turned to Alyson, who stood there with a look of utter shock, as if in her entire life no one had ever crossed her in such a way. She opened her lips but all that came out was a feeble squeak.

I calmly opened the studio door and got Phoebe and Madison the hell out of there.

On the drive into the city, I told Lupita what had happened in ballet. The PG version, since the kids were there in the backseat.

"I am glad that I have a boy," she said. "No offense, of course. It's just that girls can be so mean."

"Especially when they learn from their mothers."

When Lupita asked about my weekend in Kiawah, I didn't get into the details. As tempted as I was to bash Alyson, I felt like if I gossiped about her and everyone else's exploits, I'd just be perpetuating the nastiness I wanted to be rid of. Today and from now on, I planned to focus on the good, be in the present with people I wanted to be with.

Lupita said, "I have some exciting news."

I felt bad having hijacked our whole conversation with my *girl bullshit drama*, as Aaron had called it. "Tell me, tell me."

"It's about my meeting with the descendant of Aaron Burr." Lupita described how the previous Friday morning, she had traveled to the small brick house on a street near an elementary school in Ho-Ho-Kus to pursue one of the last research leads on her professor's exhaustive list. A woman who looked well into her seventies welcomed Lupita inside; they sat and chatted for a long while about the woman's husband, who had died of cancer just a few months before. Lupita gently reminded her of the reason for her visit, and the woman stepped into another room and returned with a brown shoe box. She told Lupita, "My husband always said I should take these to *Antiques Roadshow*, but I never had the chance."

When Lupita opened the box, she couldn't believe her eyes. She asked if she could excuse herself for a moment to make a phone call, and twenty minutes later her professor's car screeched into the driveway. He sat at the dining room table and took deep, slow breaths as he carefully studied the pile of tattered letters written in faded quill ink. When he was finished, he looked up at Lupita with tears in his eyes and whispered, "Thank you."

For in that house in Ho-Ho-Kus, Lupita had uncovered a treasure trove of letters between Burr and Hamilton, letters which were thought to have gone down on a ship with Burr's daughter, Theodosia. The letters proved incontrovertibly what Lupita's professor had thought all along—that Hamilton and Burr *did* share a connection through Suffern. And that connection was none other than Hamilton's mistress, Maria Reynolds.

Historians knew that Maria had hired Burr as her divorce attorney. But the letters confirmed Burr and Maria did much more than process her divorce papers together. They met many times in the Suffern cottage on Provost Drive, owned by Burr's wife's family, as Burr wrote to Hamilton, gloating about their intimate liaisons.

Lupita explained, "It was one thing for Burr to slander Hamilton in the press, to question his ethics and his character and whether or not he was fit to govern our country. But it was another for Burr to steal the woman Hamilton loved and rub it in his face. That was why Hamilton went after Burr with such force in the *New York Evening Post,* printing the strong words that instigated their duel. The letters in that shoe box proved that Burr and Hamilton's duel was not to settle their political differences. It was much more personal. They fought their duel on that fateful day over Maria."

"But—this changes history!" I shouted, trying to keep my hands steady on the steering wheel.

Lupita smiled. "Technically, it does not *change* history. But I suppose the world will now see this chapter with a whole new understanding." Her voice trembled with excitement. "My professor and I pulled all-nighters this past week and submitted the paper to a number of national journals. He said he has friends who might be able to expedite the authentication and review process, but now we just have to sit back and wait."

"This is beyond huge! We have to go out and celebrate."

"Today we will be celebrating *dinosaur* huge," she laughed, and Samuel yelled out, "*Rwrarrr . . .* dinosaurs!"

We got lucky and found a parking spot on a side street a few blocks from the Museum of Natural History. On our stroll to the Central Park West entrance, we passed the New York Historical Society on the corner of 77th Street. "Your mom is going to be in there," I told Samuel. He looked up at me quizzically but I knew he would soon understand just how well-known his mother would become.

As we swung through the museum's revolving doors and into the ornate rotunda, I felt like I had just been there even though it had been almost a whole year. Samuel, Phoebe, and Madison craned their necks upward at the immense dinosaur skeleton towering above us.

"That's the biggest dinosaur I have ever seen!" Samuel exclaimed.

"Wait until you see the fourth floor," I said.

We walked past the admissions line packed twenty people deep and breezed right up to the members-only desk. I couldn't believe I had even thought twice about sending in our membership renewal. *We need to use it more often. Once a month; from now on we're coming at least once a month*, I promised myself.

We took the elevator straight up to the fourth floor and came face-to-face with the menacing teeth of a T. rex in the first gallery. "Whoa!" Phoebe said, and ran over to the display, while Madison made a beeline up the ramp behind the brontosaurus. Lupita stayed with Samuel and Phoebe while I scurried after Madison, speeding by the triceratops and some of the specimens I'd forgotten about, like the dinosaur with a bill like a duck's. The kids were drawn like magnets to the touch screens positioned throughout the galleries, and I had to admit it was cool to see the bones come to animated life. But the computer graphics couldn't compare to the looks on the kids' faces when we reached a sign that read, *Touch me!* and they were allowed to feel a real dinosaur arm bone and an 11,000-year-old mastodon molar.

"It's bigger than my whole head!" Phoebe marveled.

"Mine too," Madison said in her cute high-pitched voice. "It's too bigger than my head."

We slid into the last available bench spots in the theater to watch a movie about the dinosaur family tree, squeezed shoulder-to-shoulder in the middle row between a family who said they were visiting from Australia and an older couple from St. Louis. I glanced around at the crowd of strangers who had come together in this theater from across the globe and down the block, women holding babies and tourists with backpacks covered in patches and toddlers running in front of the screen with too much energy to sit through to the end of the film. It wasn't quiet, like a regular movie; the room hummed and clicked and sneezed. And I loved feeling crowded in the middle of it all. I missed being a regular in that theater. And I felt a physical pang—I really missed living in the city.

Phoebe and Madison both sat on my lap, barely able to fit anymore. I kissed the tops of their heads and watched them watch the screen, eyes wide. They were getting so big, so fast. *Too fast,* I thought, and I wished they'd fit right there on my lap for the next million years.

But the movie ended and the lights went up and we heard the announcement that the museum was going to close in an hour. We had originally planned to catch the space show in the planetarium but there just wasn't going to be enough time.

"One more stop before we go," I said.

We went back down to the first floor and took a picture of the kids sitting in the giant clamshell in the Hall of Biodiversity. A few steps to our right, we peered through a doorway and when Madison caught sight of that ninety-four-foot blue whale suspended from the ceiling, she stopped in her tracks and said, "Wow, Mommy."

"Wow," I echoed. It took my breath away every time. I held Phoebe's and Madison's hands and Lupita held Samuel's, and we walked down the stairs to stand beneath it. Blue waves and glimmers of light washed across the ceiling and the tranquil sounds of the ocean enveloped us, and we all looked up in awe at the whale's immense beauty.

Parents were stopping their kids from running around, scolding them—*Hurry up, it's time to go, the museum's closing soon.* But we stayed right up until the end and let them spin and dance under that enormous wonder of the sea.

Outside the museum we bought hot dogs and pretzels and water and parked ourselves on an empty bench under the shade of some trees. I tore off a piece of hot pretzel and tasted such a perfect bite, crunchy on the outside and warm on the inside, with just a hint of salt.

Aaron's text popped up: he'd just landed. In a few minutes we'd need to get back in the car so we could be home when he arrived.

A young couple studying a guidebook walked up and the woman said, "Pardon? Do you know, where is . . . Strawberry Fields?"

"Of course," I smiled. I hadn't been asked that question in a long, long time. "Walk down about six blocks and make a left into the park, right across from the building where Lennon lived, the Dakota. You can't miss it."

They thanked me and as I watched them walk away, I was amazed that of all the people on the street, they had asked *me* for directions. "I don't even live here anymore," I thought out loud.

"But you look like you know where you are going," Lupita said, and I realized it was true.

* * *

I heard Aaron open the front door and drop his bags in the hallway.

"I am so glad you're home!" I kissed him hello; he smelled like airplane. "Jump in the shower, we're going out to dinner."

"Dinner? We have Jeff's fundraiser tonight. And we're already late."

"We're not going to that fundraiser," I said. "Wait until I tell you about the fight Alyson and I had today in ballet, you would not believe the—"

"I literally just spoke to Jeff on the way home and promised him I'd be there to introduce his new technology platform. He has a speech written for me and everything. Plus, we spent five hundred dollars on a table."

"Forget the money, Aaron. I cannot be in the same room with Alyson. Seriously, it would be way too uncomfortable."

"We can leave right after the speech; I promise. Or you can stay home and then we can go to dinner after, but I have to show up." He glanced at his watch. "Fifteen minutes ago."

I couldn't let Aaron go to the party by himself. I didn't have to speak to Alyson but I absolutely had to make sure she didn't get near my husband. Who knew what she might pull to get back at me for telling her to fuck off today?

"Half hour tops," I conceded.

No matter what, I had to stick to Aaron's side all night.

People were packed shoulder-to-shoulder in the foyer of Jeff and Alyson's house. So many faces I hadn't seen before, and many I hadn't seen in a long time. I spotted Michelle deep in the crowd near the stairwell standing next to her husband, Randy—I remembered he was the head of the zoning board, of course Jeff would want him there for his political nod. For sure I wanted to make our way over to say hi to them. I recognized the mayor of Suffern walking in, and behind him, the state senator. An impressive crowd.

Thankfully, Alyson wasn't there to greet us at the door.

A banner hung on the wall above the place-card table—*157 days to go until Election Day, November 4!*—the same large marble table that always featured at its center a huge fresh flower arrangement, even on non-party days. I leaned in to smell one of the beautiful white blossoms—was it a gardenia or maybe a peony?—and was surprised to discover it had no perceptible scent. "These aren't real," I said.

"What?" Aaron asked over the din.

"Nothing." And I looked around and realized—the plants above the bookcases, on the side tables, all of the greenery adorning their house that I had so admired—it was all made of plastic. Alyson didn't have a green thumb; she had an account at Home Goods.

"Hellooo, stranger, where have you been?" I heard Ivy ask. She scootched in next to me and squeezed my arm. "Hey, Aaron, good to see you."

Aaron nodded. "Hi, Ivy. Drew."

Ivy found their place card. "Table two. You guys?"

"Table fourteen." *Back of the bus.* I was half-surprised to have found our card at all.

I couldn't help but notice how low Ivy's dress was

cut, dipping right into her cleavage, the same spot where that stranger's head had been buried doing body shots between her boobs.

I cleared my throat and tried to tuck that memory back, way back, so it wouldn't leak out. *Keep it light, keep it simple.* "So, everything good?" I asked her.

"C'mon, dude, let's hit the bar," Drew said to Aaron. "Jeff told me there's Jäger bombs to be had."

Ivy rolled her eyes. "Jäger bombs, really? What are you guys, fourteen?"

Aaron protested: "Actually, I have to go find Jeff." But Drew grabbed his arm and Ivy and I followed them into the living room.

Aaron declined the Jäger bomb, thank god, and opted for a beer. He passed me a glass of wine and I watched as Drew expertly dropped the shot of Jäger into a cup of Red Bull and downed it. He licked his lips. "Now that's the way to start a party!" A thin line of saliva dripped from his chin and he wiped it with the back of his hand.

Aaron grimaced and then excused himself. "Jeff has a speech I have to look over," he explained, and I waved goodbye and tagged along behind him. We searched for Jeff in the library and I was about to suggest circling back to the foyer when I felt a tap on my shoulder. "Hey there, chica," Tami said, glass of champagne in hand, *kiss, kiss.* Not her first, I could smell from her breath.

I craned my neck to see if Aaron was still in front of me, but he had disappeared into the crowd. *Shit.*

Tami took my wrist and led us toward the kitchen. "Come, I need a refill."

"Did you see which way Aaron was heading? I forgot to tell him to—"

We both stopped as we heard a loud pleasured grunt from the far end of the hall. "Ooooh . . . someone's getting busy!" Tami said gleefully, and tiptoed toward the bathroom.

She mouthed, *Love this!* and put her ear against the door. Then she slowly turned the knob and thrust it open with her hip—and there was Alyson up on the vanity with her legs wrapped around Tami's husband, Chris.

Tami exploded, "Are you fucking kidding me?"

At first I thought maybe it was just another game in the Tami and Chris playbook—*hide and seek and screw the BFF*. But I could see shock and hurt in Tami's eyes, even though just a short week ago she'd been doing the same—although at least it was with a stranger, not her closest friend's husband.

Chris quickly hiked up his pants while Alyson slid off the counter and casually pulled down her dress. She turned to check her lipstick in the mirror, looking not the least bit fazed.

Tami screamed, "You two-bit backstabbing whore! After all I've done to help you out of every fucked-up mess in your life, Aly, this is how you thank me?"

Alyson replied calmly, "I believe we're even now."

Tami stared at her and then a look of recognition came over her face. "If you are actually demented enough to still be mad about me fucking your freaking prom date the summer after we graduated from high school—almost twenty years ago—you are one sick fuck."

"For your information, I have proof you and Dwayne fooled around *before* that summer. And *you* calling *me* a whore? Don't make me laugh."

Tami's blood boiled over and seemingly out of every

pore. "I might not be a Mennonite but I would NEVER do this. Never! There are limits, Aly. But you wouldn't know anything about limits, would you? Fucking everything that ever so much as waved a dick at you. Blowing Mr. Brockman in the pottery room after school. Gangbanging all the counselors on that Scared Straight wilderness trip. Shacking up in those pathetic motels by the hour on Route 17 with a string of horny contractors looking for an easy lay. You think you're such hot shit but you're just starved for attention. And now you're just a washed-up thirty-five-year-old whore."

"You only *wished* Mr. Brockman looked at you the way he looked at me!" Alyson countered, then turned and started down the hall.

"Me? You've been literally tearing your fucking hair out ever since I had another baby. The one thing you want so bad and can't have, poor you," Tami said sarcastically.

That stopped Alyson in her tracks. She spun around but didn't say anything.

I didn't want to defend Alyson. I certainly didn't want to step into Tami's line of fire. But I couldn't stop myself from interjecting, "Miscarriages can be really tough."

Tami rolled her eyes. "Don't tell me she's been spewing that miscarriage sob story again. Not only is she a slut, she's a liar, and has been since she learned how to say, *Fuck me*. You should know—maybe you ALL would like to know," Tami said to the small crowd that had gathered. "The reason Emmy doesn't have a little brother or sister is because Jeff won't sleep with her and hasn't for the past two—or what is it now, Aly—almost three years?"

I was never good about guessing what people did

or didn't do in their bedrooms; to hear Alyson and Jeff weren't sleeping together came as a surprise, not a bombshell. Yet what I could not believe was that anyone would stoop so low as to lie about having a miscarriage. I thought back to that day in Alyson's kitchen . . . I'd disclosed one of my most private secrets to help ease her phony suffering?

Alyson just shrugged and slipped into the crowd.

Tami turned to Chris. "And you—all the cunts in the universe and you had to stick your dick in hers? You're a DEAD MAN."

Chris took off and Tami tore right after him. I decided it was well past the time to find Aaron and take our exit.

Most of the guests had made their way outside near the pool, where round tables had been set up on the lawn. Up on the top tier of their deck next to their grill island stood an outdoor inflatable movie screen playing a slide-show of Jeff at different community events: Jeff smiling at the Rotary Club breakfast; Jeff setting up the stands at the Saturday-morning farmers' market; Alyson and Emmy and Jeff picking apples at The Orchards, smiling in the picture I recognized from their holiday card last year.

Jeff's campaign manager stepped up to the podium, straightened his tie, tested the microphone, "One, two," and then cleared his throat. "Okay, people, take your seats, we're about to start."

I found Aaron sitting at our table chatting with a couple I didn't recognize. I gave them a polite smile and whispered to Aaron, "We should go."

"Jeff said the tech piece is right after the appetizers."

I debated whether to sit down or try to convince Aaron to leave as the montage continued: Jeff and Chris with Drew and Peter drinking beers at Sutter's Mill after a basketball game; Jeff cutting the ribbon with a state official at the opening of a renovated playground. I noticed a photo of Aaron and Jeff in the pool holding Emmy and Phoebe high above their heads and I suddenly felt sad thinking about how long ago that seemed.

A picture faded in of me, Tami, Carolann, Ivy, and Alyson—the five of us, arm in arm on the deck at Red's in Kiawah last week.

Holy shit, Alyson inserted one of the trip pictures. An innocuous one, but still—if she was mad enough, it was possible . . . In fact, that might have been her plan all along, to put those incriminating pictures up on the screen in front of the husbands. In front of everyone.

Jeff appeared on the deck with Alyson at his side. I noticed she had changed into a red dress so tight you could see her hip bones.

I tugged on Aaron's arm. "Come on, let's leave now; I can explain," I urged.

The pictures kept rolling. Alyson and Jeff smiling cheek-to-cheek on the dance floor at the school auction; Emmy on Jeff's shoulders at the Suffern Memorial Day Parade, waving an American flag.

Then a picture flashed up on the screen that made the crowd gasp. But it wasn't a picture from our trip.

It was two half-naked men on a bed. The first man I immediately recognized as Jeff's campaign manager in a black leather body harness. The second man's face was partially obscured; he was kneeling with his lips around the campaign manager's impressively long penis. But even though his eyes were closed I could tell from the profile it was Jeff, wearing a pair of lace bikini briefs that looked a lot like Alyson's La Perlas.

"Whoa, Nelly," Aaron said.

The campaign manager looked stunned at first. Then he turned to Jeff and punched him in the face. Jeff teetered but didn't fall, and then hit him right back. The two flailed at each other and fell into a jumbled heap and rolled into the movie screen, which deflated only halfway, so as their wrestling match continued, everyone could still see the jumbo image of Jeff's mouth wrapped around that enormous penis.

Alyson stood with her hands on her cheeks, attempting to look horrified. But I could see her lips trying not to curl upward and I knew: Alyson was the one who had put that picture in the slideshow. She was the one who had sabotaged Jeff.

That was certainly one way to get out of hosting fundraisers.

I turned to Aaron. "Ready to get out of here?"

"Without a doubt," he replied, springing to his feet.

The melee on the deck blocked access to our usual backyard path, so we walked down their driveway and out into the cul-de-sac along with other astonished partygoers. It was barely eight, too early to go home. So we sat on the edge of the curb, watching the exodus of cars heading down the street.

And I told Aaron everything.

The cell phone photos and Tami's dared kiss. The bar and the bra and Steven. He listened, asking questions every so often and laughing at the ridiculousness along with me. Turns out he had never heard of vajazzle, either. And he liked my bikini area as is, no grooming necessary, let alone with chicken shears.

He shook his head as I described seeing Tami and Carolann and Ivy and Alyson on the boat.

"And I swear, I didn't do anything. Except totally embarrass myself, drunk and stoned in front of a potential new client."

Aaron was silent now.

"You believe me, don't you?" My words hung in the air.

"Of course I do. We all have nights where we get out of hand," he said with a sheepish smile.

"Speaking of out of hand, I didn't even tell you what happened tonight with Chris and Alyson." And Tami had missed the whole blow-up in the backyard; she was going to be pissed. "Maybe this is the kind of thing that goes on here all the time and we just didn't see it. Or didn't want to."

"Who the hell knows what these people do; they're a bunch of morons. All those couples' nights when you made me go to Marcello's and that awful Mediterranean place down on Route 59? The conversations were as blah as the food. I couldn't care less whether or not the Yankees make the playoffs or how much horsepower your new truck has. I always thought this group was *bo*-ring."

"Even Jeff?" I smiled.

"I have to admit, Jeff just got a lot more interesting."

"You don't have to worry about those couples' nights anymore, at least not with those people. We'll just have to make more of an effort to go out and find some new friends. Maybe Michelle and Randy—I meant to introduce you tonight—we could make plans with them."

The cars streamed away, tail lights following in the dark.

"Maybe we shouldn't have done this," Aaron said quietly. "I mean, I love the house, I do. But I feel like I'm never here to enjoy it. Even when I'm in town, the girls are always sleeping by the time I get home. Commuting really sucks."

"I know. It's a lot harder than I thought it would be."

Aaron kicked the loose gravel with his toe. "I miss my girls. I miss you."

It felt good to hear those words. I rested my head on his shoulder. "I miss you too. It's been a long week without you."

"Last weekend was endless when you were away. You have no idea how hard it is to take care of these girls."

Seriously? I turned to rip him in retort, though as I opened my mouth I saw he had a boyish grin on his face. I punched his arm. "Ow!" he said, and smiled. He knew just how to get me. He knew me better than anyone, and I felt a hint of our old closeness again.

"Listen, I need to talk to you about this work thing that's been heating up with a start-up in Palo Alto. They had me come out to meet their CEO before the conference and their clean tech technology is mind-blowing. Jess, it's incredible—they figured out a way to transform the natural power in water systems into energy, and their model is totally scalable. And fully funded, with some seriously huge backers."

Uh-oh, start-up fever again. Even in the dim light I could see the excited gleam in his eyes. "What exactly is clean tech?"

"It's part of the whole green movement—finding ways

to make renewable energy. Clean electricity that leaves a smaller environmental footprint."

I liked the sound of it, *renewable energy*. And I also liked the sound of *fully funded*.

"Last night they made me an offer to be their new COO. It would be a definite departure from digital for me, but it could be an exciting move, taking on something totally new in a growing field."

"Didn't you just say it's based in Palo Alto?" For a split second, I actually hoped he would say it was.

"Their main office is, but they're opening a New York office, in Brooklyn."

I paused. "We could just sell the house and move there," I said, kidding but not.

"Come on, Jess. Brooklyn? Really?"

Yes, I thought. *Brooklyn. Really.* Suddenly I could see how Brooklyn made all the sense in the world. "So many start-ups and thought leaders, so many of the people making things happen are out in Brooklyn now. People we want to be around and hang out with—who we want Phoebe and Madison to grow up with." *And it's in the city.* My pulse started to quicken, just thinking about it. Except when I imagined saying goodbye to Lupita. She was the one friend I didn't want to let go.

Aaron stood and took my hands to help me up, and our fingers stayed interlocked as we walked up our driveway.

Our house did look like a birthday cake up on the hill, with its white shingles and creamy trim. A sweet confection, so tempting. And the first bites, delicious. But mouthful after mouthful, day after day, it was way too much—all that flour and sugar leaves you sick to your stomach and empty inside. And hungry for more.

I was ready to be hungry. For less.

As we reached our front door Aaron said, "Maybe Dave's daughter shitting all over Phoebe's room was a sign."

I laughed. "I thought you did a pretty good job cleaning it up, considering."

Aaron reached for a strand of hair that had fallen on my cheek and tucked it behind my ear. It was an absent-minded gesture, something he had done the first week we'd met, standing on the corner of Bleecker Street after our second date, deciding what our next stop of the night should be. That first, delicate intimacy had caught me by surprise and I took it as a sign, a good sign, that he could very well be a keeper. And to think that on that night so many years ago, I had been right.

"So Brooklyn, huh?" Aaron said, and my heart leapt as I heard the possibility in his voice.

"Park Slope. DUMBO. Carroll Gardens. Williamsburg." I closed my eyes, imagining us very happy wherever we landed.

"Anywhere but Williamsburg. My grandfather would roll over in his grave if we moved to Williamsburg."

He turned to me and we kissed, soft and tentative at first, connecting us back and moving us forward into our future, together. He whispered, "Are you feeling better? I mean, down there?"

"Much better now."

"Should we go upstairs and take a look to make sure?"

"Yes," I said. "Definitely yes."

CHAPTER SIXTEEN

MADISON HELPED ME SPREAD OUR QUILT on the soft grass. "Can I have a Rice Krispie Treat now, Mommy?" she asked. "Please?"

It was hard to say no to that *please*. She was talking a mile a minute now, like a switch flipped to *On* when she hit her second birthday last month.

"Not yet, sweetie, after dinner, before the fireworks," I said, and started to unload our insulated picnic bag full of fresh pasta salads and roasted veggies and a home-made banana loaf and what looked like a delicious marinated grilled chicken Caesar from the farmers' market stand a few blocks away. "Can you run over to Daddy and Phoebe and tell them it's time to eat?"

I watched as Madison skipped freely across the park's freshly mowed lawn to Aaron and Phoebe throwing a Frisbee with Lupita and Samuel.

This could be our park, I thought, *if we end up in the loft on Front Street.* I loved the DUMBO neighborhood— *Down Under the Manhattan Bridge Overpass,* we had to explain to Phoebe, not the flying elephant, much to her dismay. Not only was Brooklyn Bridge Park lovely, with its running paths and playgrounds and beautiful vistas, but I also loved the feeling of the cobblestone streets leading down to the water and the old renovated warehouses.

Aaron and I had both liked so many of the apartments we'd seen in Brooklyn that day, some in brand-new, modern glass buildings, but our favorites were the ones in the prewar spaces. There was even a duplex in a brownstone near the Promenade in Brooklyn Heights. It needed a little work, but I didn't mind. We already had a bunch of possibilities, within walking distance of the subway and zoned in areas with up-and-coming public schools.

I knew no matter which neighborhood we chose, this time, I'd be smarter. Take the time to get to know people and not just jump in. Be careful and not get too close too fast; I'd let things happen naturally, the way true friendships are meant to grow. Of course, it was possible I could get lucky—it didn't happen often, but sometimes the person next to you on the swings at the playground turned out to be a gem.

Samuel jumped and caught the Frisbee and as he raised his arms in a cheer, Lupita kissed the top of his head. He threw the disc to Phoebe, a little too high. It grazed her fingertips, just out of reach. She ran to where it landed on the grass and picked it up. "I got it, Daddy!"

"Throw it back to me," Samuel said.

We were not only celebrating our nation's birthday with good friends, we were also celebrating Lupita's recent news.

The Hamilton-Burr paper had been accepted as the cover article for the fall issue of the *American Historical Review,* one of the oldest and most prestigious academic publications in the country. And when word of her discovery of the letters was strategically leaked on the Internet by one of her professor's friends, the offers started to flood Lupita's inbox. Berkley, Michigan, Duke, Arizona State, Johns Hopkins, and other top schools from coast to coast, all trying to entice her to continue her studies there.

Lupita had just told us she'd made her decision. After the holiday, she would accept a scholarship from New York University to finish her undergraduate degree and begin graduate work. NYU had presented Lupita with a package she couldn't pass up: in addition to subsidizing nearly all of her tuition, the history department would also accept some of the grad credits she had earned in Mexico.

I couldn't have been more thrilled for her. And while I'd tried to stay objective during the process, I had selfishly been crossing my fingers she would pick NYU—located in the heart of Greenwich Village, and Brooklyn was just a few short subway stops away. Now both of us, together with our families, would be looking forward to a fresh start this fall in New York City.

I wondered where the Suffernites were congregating today. I knew one thing for sure: they weren't in Alyson and Jeff's backyard. For the past month, it had been mostly quiet next door; I'd heard Jeff was spending the summer out on Fire Island, and that Alyson had decided she and Emmy would stay with her parents for a while. Tami and Chris were working it out with a little outside help from a marriage counselor. And Ivy had texted me a few days ago with the news that Carolann had started a summer class at Ramapo College toward a certificate in special events management. *Good for her,* I'd thought when I read the text.

Plus, Ivy had some exciting news of her own: she was pregnant—just eight weeks, *so keep it low*. If I was doing the math right, I knew it was quite possible that child would have an excellent chance of entering the world with a *qué bonita* set of deep brown eyes.

That would be enough local Suffern scuttlebutt to last a while, along with god knows what rumors about why we left. Or maybe our names were already forgotten, almost as if we had never been there in the first place. It didn't bother me either way; soon we'd be gone. Our house already had two interested buyers: couples from the city with young kids looking for more space. With the housing market in Suffern on an upswing, we were even poised to come out with a small profit on the flip.

It wasn't a last goodbye, though, since we'd already promised Michelle and Randy to come back and visit. We had finally made plans with them for a family-friendly hike up the mountain trail in Kakiat Park and, to my surprise, we all made it to the top, helped along by handfuls of trail mix and singing about a hundred rounds of "The Ants Go Marching." As we stood there, admiring the peaceful Ramapo Valley stretching green and wide below us, I caught a glimpse of what our lives might have been like if fate had moved us in next door to Michelle and Randy instead of Alyson and Jeff—a totally different suburban trajectory, one with yogurt-covered raisins and sing-alongs and sharing real laughs with down-to-earth friends. In that Suffern parallel, we might have found our place.

We finished our dinner as the sky started to darken into summer evening, and I took out the sweatshirts I had brought for the girls even though the air was still warm. The park was starting to fill up with other families and couples gathering to watch the fireworks, and I was glad we had arrived early.

"Ready for the carousel?" Aaron asked, and the kids

jumped up. "I can take them if you two want some time to relax," he said to me and Lupita.

"I would like to try a ride," Lupita said.

"Let's all go," I echoed, and we walked together toward the river's edge, to the hand-painted horses, lovingly restored to their original splendor, circling to the music within a stunning glass pavilion. Through the clear panes we could see the panorama stretching wide behind it, the Brooklyn Bridge on one side and the Manhattan Bridge on the other, and across the river the sun about to dip behind the glorious Manhattan skyline.

As we stepped on, I thought about how I'd been spinning in circles for so long, like so many mothers, trying to live a life that was supposed to be best for my kids without losing the essential bits of myself. Listening to everyone else's opinions about the "right" way to nurture a family. Everyone's except for mine.

But through the dips and leaps, sometimes things open up. Today I could start to see the pieces of what Aaron and I had wanted coming together—now in Brooklyn, who knew? Maybe it wasn't everything we thought we needed, but it was enough for our family. Even if that meant living without Aaron's double sink.

My heart went out to all those other women still out there twirling, whether in the city or the suburbs, desperate to find the perfect place to land. Dreams tucked away in the back of their closets, counting the days until their toddlers graduated from high school for their present to begin.

They had no idea what they were missing.

Acknowledgments

I want to thank Kaylie Jones, who is one of the smartest, bravest, and most talented people I have ever met. She is a true advocate for writers and the craft of writing, and because she believed in me, this book is in your hands today.

I am especially grateful to Johnny Temple and everyone at Akashic including Johanna, Aaron, Susannah, and Ibrahim; Lynn Nesbit, for connecting me with my agent extraordinaire Stefanie Lieberman; and my fabulous publicist Kathleen Zrelak, with thanks to Lynn Goldberg for her introduction and support. I couldn't ask for a more passionate, responsive, and good-looking team of literary gurus to help birth this baby. I thank (and blame) Kevin Fox for saying yes, you can write a novel; and Jennifer Belle for her classes and workshops with Renee Geel, Emily Axelrod, Elin Ewald, and Michael Sears. A heartfelt thanks to readers Laurie Loewenstein, Dawn Zera, Marni Pedorella, Tamar Newberger, Chip Cordelli, Jose Parron, Julia Ryan, Heidi Packer Eskenazi, Julie Jacobs, Gary Adelman, Adam Bernstein, and Tomm Miller for being incredibly generous with their time, honesty, and insights.

Thank you to my friends, colleagues, and family who never stopped asking (aka nudging), *How's the book going?* Special shout-out to Craig H. Long for unlocking the Suffern Village Museum for me; and to Lisa Cohen, A.J. Jacobs, Claire Gilman, Jennifer Romanello, Jennifer Unter, Lisa and Matt Shatz, David Bergman, Kimberly Berman Cohn, Jaimie Bolnick-Yannalfo, Caren Sinclair Kay, Rachel Rimland, Stacey Brooks, my parents, and Abby Endres and the always amazing team at LIFT, for their above-and-beyond support.

And to David, Avery, and Carson—thank you for enjoying takeout dinners as much as (if not more than) my cooking, and for making me feel every day like the luckiest person on the planet.